Blitzball

Blitzball

BARTON
LUDWIG

www.heartlabpress.com

"Nothing is so painful to the human mind as a great and sudden change." – Marry Shelley, *Frankenstein*

WECLOME TO
REICHFIELD

PROLOGUE

"Thomas," I yell. "Thomas," I whisper into the walkie-talkie. He has gone radio silent, and for good reason. The draugar are on the loose. They'll stick their long nails into his head and eat his Aryan brains.

We've just moved to Reichfield, a small town in Pennsylvania. I know Thomas's house because it's exactly like my house. All the houses are the same, uniform. I tiptoe barefoot down the linoleum floor and up the brown carpeted stairs to the second floor. There's a crash. Draugar?

I stop and hold my breath in front of a portrait of Thomas and his dad in a small aircraft, a Fieseler Storch. Thomas sits in the pilot seat in a tan leather bomber, pushing the control yoke full forward. His dad, a regal man in his fifties with salt and pepper hair, has his arm on Thomas's shoulder. Shortly after the picture snapped, Thomas would have pulled on the control wheel and the plane would have jumped to airborne.

I listen. Silence. I move farther up the stairs past a picture of Thomas's pilot permit. On the landing, I turn to the right and creep past a family picture of them hiking on the Danube on a bright cheerful day.

"Thomas," I whisper. "Thomas, where are you?" I put my ear against the large wooden door of his dad's study. I hear something inside. A creak. Maybe they've got him? He needs my help. Summoning all the courage I can, I push open the door of the study.

It's Thomas's dad. His head tilts upwards, looking straight up at the ceiling. Draugar. The draugar have gotten him, infected him. They'll devour his flesh. They'll drive him insane. He's in some sort of trance. He doesn't notice me standing there.

"Thomas, code red. Code red," I yell into the walkie-talkie.

Alarmed, Thomas's dad pushes the chair back and sits up. His shirt is loosened. A pair of small trousers lie on the floor. Then a boy pops his head up from underneath the desk; a boy who has my short brown hair, my oval eyes and a similar plaid shirt. A boy, I realize, shock overpowering the terror that consumed me just a moment ago, who kind of looks like me.

CHAPTER 1

9 yrs. later

North Prep's uncivilized fans are even more rowdy today than usual. Today, they brought a chicken and dressed it in a red and black jersey to look like one of our players. They chant something in Spanish and laugh. I watch as the chicken runs around in circles, chased by our referee. They are trying to demoralize us, as if we could be any more demoralized. We haven't won a game yet this season or even last. Our referee finally catches up to the chicken and leaps on it, attempting to restrain it. He lets out a cry as the chicken pecks at his hands. Quickly he drops it and the chicken runs around some more.

Volkhardt Werner, a seventeen-year-old short kid with premature balding, is the only one who doesn't appear completely discouraged. It's difficult to believe we're the same age. He looks like he's forty. Werner glances at a sketchpad that has drawings of a ball's trajectory going into the net and what looks to be possible angles of impact. I'm guessing he's assessing probability.

Coach Helene, a gruff and overbearing woman who closely resembles the ugliest of pit bulls, pulls us over. She looks directly into Thomas's eyes, as if they have some sort of soul connection. As if everything is residing on his skill. Those DI-X infused steroids crushed into Thomas's macaroni as a kid definitely paid off. Coach Helene smiles at the reflection of herself in Thomas's gelled, copper hair. He's her prodigy.

"Thomas, you got this. Just let 'em chase us. Don't be in a rush to score. Be patient and pass the ball around."

"Huh?" Karl lets out a chuckle, causing his chin fat to shake like jelly.

Coach Helene puts her hands on her hips. "Something funny, Karl?"

Karl's face fat swallows his smile. "It's just we never score so-"

"Well as you know, this game will be different, Karl," Helene responds in a tone that says, I'd like to think so but I know that's akin to believing in the Tooth Fairy.

Little do they know that this game will in fact be quite different, thanks to us. I chuckle when I think of North Prep's star player, Kero Reyes in the hospital. Thomas and I made a mixture of ketchup, something called Sri Racha and a self-made botulism toxin. Then we put it on his burger when he wasn't looking. Jon Mengela, who we refer to just as Mengela, helped us engineer it. He did it all in his makeshift sedan mobile lab. Thanks to our magnificent trio, Kero will be out for months.

I spot my older sister Pauline in a short skirt. She jumps. "Addie, Addie-" She waves to me with excitement.

I cringe. I glance back to see her just standing there and staring at me with bedazzled eyes. Okay, I get that she thinks I'm awesome and all, but why does she have to be here every single game? Couldn't she keep busy with applying to university or something? She shouldn't even be here. Instead, she should have graduated two years ago with her class like a normal person. It's not like she wasn't on honor roll but no, she had to stay for "enrichment." Who even does that? For some reason, her face looks redder than normal. Inflamed, almost. Especially when she looks directly at me. I hope she's not coming down with something. The last thing I want is to get sick, especially with soccer season underway.

Today her bleached-to-death platinum blond hair looks even more straw-like than usual. I know she bleaches it as I once saw a package in the trash. She denied it of course. She claimed that it was designed only to bring out one's "natural Aryan color."

"So, if I used it to dye Anne's hair, what you're saying is that it wouldn't turn blond because she's a brunette?" I asked.

My younger sister Anne has the most beastlike head of brown frizz that I've ever seen.

"So it wouldn't change?" I asked.

"Correct." Pauline nodded.

Somehow I doubt that. I opened my mouth.

"Don't Addie," Mother had said, shaking her head, with her thin mouth turning downward.

On the side of the field, Ava takes a selfie with her phone. Like Pauline, she wears a shorter than short jean skirt which leaves her legs completely bare. Over her t-shirt, she wears our teams red, black and white soccer jacket that hits right below her skirt. Everything about Ava says "look at me". From her perfectly styled blond waves to her long scarlet nails, I can only imagine that everything in her life is about getting our attention. "Look at me." Her friend snaps a photo of them. "Look at me." Her friend snaps another photo. "Look at me." Uh-oh, Ava isn't watching what she's doing and bangs right into Pauline. Pauline grabs her arm. *Oh no, do we have an injury?* Although the thought makes me happy, I feel myself gagging. Just the thought of blood makes me want to vomit.

Distract yourself, Addie. Coach is saying something. I tune back in.

Coach looks at Mengela. "Guys, let's wear them out in the first half. Then we can win by taking the game right to their defense. Got it?"

There are nods. Thomas takes a quick sip from his red and black water bottle.

"Got it? Got it?" Helene waves her fists in excitement. She must intend to look powerful and strong. Instead, with her blobby sweatpants, she reminds me of the picture we looked at today in science of a green blob-like amoeba. Under a microscope it looks big but in real life it's tiny and just causes diarrhea.

We got it Helene you Arsch. Hate. I feel hatred. I don't hate her because she's a woman. I hate her because she has chin hair that she refuses to pluck. It's asymmetrical. It sets her face off balance. To balance it, I would have to draw a hair right above her forehead, but I can't. I can't. I can't.

"Addie?" Helene looks at me. She probably senses that my mind is somewhere else and it is. It's her fault. Balance your dummkopf face.

"You ready?" Helene says in a nurturing tone that makes me feel as if I'm five. She puts her arm on my shoulder, a gesture that makes me wonder if I somehow forgot my dick in the locker room. She makes me feel like that in art as well. At least here on the field, she treats me as if I'm somewhat capable of kicking a ball around. I look away to see our referee, covered in scratches, holding the chicken.

I look back to Helene. She smiles. "Play hard."

"Küss mein arsch." I smile back.

"Thanks Addie."

It's quite fortunate that Helene is from New Hampshire and doesn't understand German. Otherwise she would have realized that I said, "kiss my ass". Thomas overhears.

He smiles. "Küss mein arsch," he says, imitating me.

We run out onto the field along with North Prep and take our places on the perfectly cut grass. The stadium erupts with cheers. It's completely packed. The weather has been good for early fall, so the roof is open. New students who come to our school are surprised when they walk out of the crumbling Reichfield High Collegiate building that looks like it's stuck in the '70s to this modern work of high-tech craftsmanship. All the money we get from the municipal goes into our field.

On the days that Reichfield has a game, the nightlife in town is dead. Everyone in Upper Reichfield is here except Steinfeld, the Jew. Soccer's our town's main form of entertainment. This is especially true after the drive-in theater was burned down by a group of Lower Reichfield hooligans. If you're not into soccer, you might as well say that you are a homosexual Martian living on the moon. Steinfeld comes close to that. When everyone was voting whether we should get new jerseys this year or use the money for something else, Steinfeld made it known that he was neutral. He refused to take a side. As a result, the money ended up going to put up a brass school flagpole instead. The green flag on the pole has the slogan, "Jedem das Seine," which means "Justice for Everyone." I look down at my faded jersey, resentment flaring in my chest. We look mismatched, like foreigners on our own land. They amp up the field and they couldn't do that for our jerseys as well?

The game begins. We're playing a 4-4-2 formation with Thomas and myself in the two attacking positions. Usually I'm on defense as Mengela's a stronger offense player on average. However, today he's playing defense as he burned his leg with chemicals and now it hurts so he can't run much. North Prep's in a 4-5-1 position with a new player as their sole attacker. Player 18. That would have been Kero Reyes. He's obviously not Kero Reyes as he's smaller in build. Also, Kero Reyes never wears a helmet. To top it off, the new player looks a bit flabby, with man boobs. It was probably the best they could do with such short notice. Obviously.

We kick start the game. With no Kero Reyes to bear down on us, we're actually passing the ball around quite well. Suddenly, our left winger is played in by the central midfielder. He finds himself whipped in a dangerous cross but the center back is able to head it clear. Things are going well. I'm sure Coach thinks so too. We're going to win, I can feel it.

Swiftly, Thomas sends a long ball in. The midfielders contest it. A player in the midfield gets control of the ball. He passes it to Thomas.

Thomas's muscular lean legs and most undoubtedly steroid-strengthened hamstrings enable him to run faster than anyone on North Prep. Thomas is in shooting distance. He fires a shot at the goal. The goalkeeper of North Prep dives to stop it. The ball shoots past him into the net. Our whole team cheers. Thomas scored the first goal. We're now leading by a goal. I know I should be happy but part of me feels resentful. It should have been me.

"Genius," Coach Helene yells. "We can do this guys, don't lose your cool."

Lose our cool? Cool is something Coach Helene knows nothing about.

The game continues. North Prep kicks off. We pass the ball smoothly, building our attack from the defense to the other half. After about a half an hour of kicking the ball back and forth, things are going pretty well. We're still in the lead. Yet, for some reason North Prep is still strong even without their star player. What gives?

In this half, North Prep begins to come alive. Why aren't they demoralized? They should be. This isn't right. A complete one-two pass by Player 18 leaves the defense of our team completely open. Player 18 has complete control of the ball. He comes face-to-face with Werner at our goal. Player 18 easily puts one past him. They've drawn level with us. No. Werner takes it to heart. All those diagrams couldn't prevent the ball from going into the net.

Curiosity overrides anger and frustration. *Player 18, who are you? You're not as bad as I hoped. Where did they find you? Where were you hiding in that scheisse neighborhood of Lower Reichfield that you call your home?*

The game continues and we're unable to keep up with the firepower of North Prep. I watch as Player 18 does tricks that cause the few members of the crowd from their side to go wild. The coarse North Prep fans flash us some ass. I feel nauseous.

How is this possible? Twice Player 18 hits the crossbar having fired from outside the 18-yard box. A furrow forms on Coach Helene's forehead. Her mouth locks in a perpetual frown, double the size of her regular one. She actually looks better like this as it hides her chin hair. Helene barks instructions but nothing we try works. That's no surprise. She's not exactly a strategist. Who gets an art teacher to coach soccer anyway? If it weren't for North Prep stealing practically all of our government funding, perhaps we'd have a better coach. If I were in control, I'd have spent more of our budget on paying for a good coach rather than amping up our stadium. But no, Reichfield chose the field over paying another salary.

I see an opening. I rush toward the ball. Now's my chance. I'm going to outshine Thomas. I get the ball and head toward the opposing goal. Reichfield cheers. Now's my chance. I'm running. Out of nowhere, Player 18 appears behind me. He emerges out of my blind spot as if by black magic. He steals the ball away with ease. Maybe along with black magic, they have an invisibility spell as well. Lowlies and their voodoo shit.

Player 18 dribbles the first and then the second and then the third before doing a quick one-two with his teammate to put him right in front of the goal. He's in another one-on-one situation. This time instead of putting the ball past the goalkeeper, Player 18 does a leg over the ball trick which sends the keeper diving in the wrong direction. Player 18 sends the ball easily into an empty net to the admiration of his coach, team and the

North Prep fans. They cheer and start singing their Spanish chant, that has one line that sounds like Chinese, which all of their Asian players laugh at.

The whistle blows for half time. *Scheisse.* Player 18 might even be better than Kero Reyes. This can't be.

"Okay," says Helene, flailing her arms widely in the air. She reeks of B.O. and earthy deodorant. I think perhaps her earthy deodorant smells worse than her B.O. Why is she sweating? It's not like she's the one out there getting pummeled.

"Gather round," Helene barks.

We all gather around. I hold my breath, trying not to breathe in her stench.

"We're going to change the formation. We're going to cushion the increasing pressure that North Prep has been mounting on their defense."

"No," I say quietly. Helene turns toward me. Oh-no. Got a whiff of her stench.

"Excuse me, Addie?"

"No," I say louder. "There's no way we'll ever win if we change the formation to 4-3-3. We're losing. To go all out at such an early stage will expose us to more pressure."

"Really?" says Coach Helene with disdain. "What is it you, Addie, a player who's never even scored one goal, even though you've had plenty of opportunity, feels we should do?"

"Playing three midfielders against five will totally wreck us." I gulp. "I feel we should maintain the formation and try to contain them with four midfielders." I force myself to stand up straighter and look more confident.

I breathe in, my voice growing stronger. "Then, if we don't score, we can make substitutions and change the formation afterwards. They'll be feeling confident and more relaxed. We can capitalize on that and try to get a draw, at the very least."

I smile. I made my point. Perhaps the team will side with me.

"Okay," she says in a way that makes me think that maybe she's considering my strategy. Then, she smiles. "Well, that's why I'm coach, Addie, and you're out there on the field. Now go, go, go."

"But Coach." I clench my fists. I hate this woman. Make up your mind you fotze. Do you want to be a coach or an art teacher? Coach or art? You schizophrenic granola piece of poo.

"Das pisst mich an," I say to Thomas. He nods, understandingly. Thomas sees my logic. He knows that what I suggest is miles ahead of anything Helen could ever hope to think up. Thomas recognizes greatness.

The game picks up with North Prep dominating the attack from the midfield. Sure enough, I was right and my whole team can see it. Our three midfielders are unable to handle their five midfielders. As North Prep mounts pressure against us, I can feel the frustration of my fellow players rising. Thomas grows red in the face. Whenever he gets angry, he turns beet-red and his freckles become even more prominent. Fury mounts in his eyes as he approaches Player 18.

Suddenly, Thomas lunges on Player 18's backside, tackling him. A whistle. The referee pulls out a straight red card. It's not like we can even contest that. Off on the side, I watch as Thomas swears and bangs his fist against his knees.

Don't worry Thomas. I'll get my turn. And finally, I do. Mengela shoots the ball in my direction. Running with the ball, I pass it to Heinrich, who I sometimes mistake as Karl or Karl's brother only because of the extra pounds. He actually runs pretty fast for a clinically obese guy and he's not panting at all. It's like he defies the laws of fat science, or rather fat biology. They have their voodoo magic and shit and we have fatty-turned-roadrunner. I've often wondered if Mengela did any experiments on that fleshy beast.

I run close to Heinrich, expecting a return pass. *Come on Heinrich, buddy. Pass it back.* To my amazement, Heinrich that wichser doesn't. His double chin shakes as his head twists from side to side. What are you doing Heinrich? Heinrich runs with the ball. What are you doing, you globby fat goat? Heinrich shakes his head. *Ugh. Scheisse.*

Sure enough, a defender from North Prep dispossesses him of the ball and sends a long shot deep into the other end. Player 18 receives the ball with his chest and then controls it down with his right foot. He then sprints straight toward our goal. From twenty yards, he fires a long shot. The ball shoots right past Werner into the top right corner of the net. The crowd from North Prep cheers.

I smile but I'm not smiling out of happiness. I smile to contain my rage because if I don't smile, I will explode. My fists clench. My jaw tightens. I glare at Heinrich, that fat globby schnauzer.

"Die zicke. Why didn't you just pass the ball?" I yell.

North Prep celebrates. I fume. I close my eyes and imagine with one swift movement, pulling the grass off the soccer field like a magician pulls off a tablecloth, causing North Prep players to scatter into space. Who is Player 18 and why is he better than Kero Reyes? Player 18 removes his helmet. Long brown waves flow out. Wait. Those weren't man boobs, those were real boobs. Player 18 is a girl. It's now apparent to all of us at Reichfield, that we really do suck. We were beaten by a girl. How is this possible?

CHAPTER 2

"It's illegal. It's boys against boys," Thomas yells.

We watch as Helene goes to the referee to argue just that. Moments later she comes back, shaking her head.

"It's a no-go," Helene says, "they're saying we have to let her play or it's discrimination or something."

"Snails," Thomas fumes. "Boys. It's the freaking rules."

"Well, yes but we can't discriminate against her biology or the state will shut us down."

I know she's right. I think of the time we complained about their gay player. We almost faced a lawsuit which, according to our Reichfield lawyers, might have gone to the supreme court. Even if we did manage to get Player 18 removed, it would look bad on us, as if we were somehow threatened by a girl.

"No doubt she used voodoo." Thomas's nostrils flare.

Our team is demoralized. We watch as North Prep does a run-through of their cheer and their uncivilized fans flash their asses once again. I look around at my team. Coach Helene shrugs. *Fick dich ins Knie, Helene. I told you so. Voll der Depp.* I don't even have to say it, the other players know I was right. There is so much self-pity on our side and I can't stand it. If people had just listened to me, we wouldn't be in this mess. I can't be here. I need to get away from these losers. I'm not one of them. They'll just drag me down into their spiral of self-pity.

Then it occurs to me that now's my chance to do some reconnaissance. Maybe I can find out Player 18's secret. For Samson it was his hair. No doubt she's using some spell to make her superhuman. No doubt she used her witchcraft or voodoo to beat us. Shady tactics. Those Latinos have their ways. If I take her by surprise, she won't be prepared. She won't have her potions ready. We're supposed to be the superhuman race. Thomas has his steroids and she most undoubtedly has some satanic magic up her sleeve.

North Prep players dance about like lunatics. They chant, "Shaylee, Shaylee, Shaylee, Shaylee." I'm guessing that's her name. There she is in her "Player 18" jersey. She takes a sip from her water bottle, so calm it's maddening. I head to the bleachers and sneak underneath. I start walking toward her. I'm going to follow her and find out her secret and then destroy whatever is giving her this strength. Then I'll bring her down once and for all. It will be she who falls, she who slips in the mud. She will be the one who's embarrassed beyond belief.

From underneath the bleachers, I watch as North Prep celebrates in a circle chanting their school chant with their stupid mascot, an enormous kid wearing a rat head. He's not even wearing a full costume. Only a rat head, with a sweat stained gray sweatshirt and jeans. Why a rat? I don't get it. Oh wait. Now I remember. It was some sort of squirrel, but we ripped off its squirrel tail which was just pinned to this dude's jeans, like pin the tail on the donkey. I guess they just never replaced it.

As I approach, I suddenly wonder, how will I follow her? It's not like I have a car. They have a bus that they all came on which will transport them back. It's not like Thomas brings his car to school and Mengela's sedan is in the shop.

Scheisse. Come on, think Addie.

I look at the rat who is celebrating with them. He steps away. Maybe he's going to take a leak? How convenient. He walks in the direction of the outhouse for the lowlies that we never clean because who cares really? They're just lowlies. I follow him.

He gets halfway to the outhouse but instead of waiting, he unzips his pants and starts peeing on our swing set. Am I really going to do this? Well ... why not? What have I got to lose? I've already been kicked to the ground, metaphorically speaking. My manhood taken from me. We've lost beyond belief.

Okay, I've done this before. A triangular neck squeeze. Something I picked up from a war movie. I can do this. Wait. I stop myself. It was on Helene's rabid dog who had lunged at my throat, not an ape. I had put that beast into a temporary slumber for its own good. This dude's gigantic. Will this even work? I remember once after Helene's dog incident, I tried it on Thomas. However, his muscles were too large and he said, "Oh sweet, you're hugging me." Maybe I have to think of something else ... but then again, this dude's a mascot, not a player. He may be gigantic but he was made a mascot for some reason. Maybe he's a giant wuss. Maybe his IQ is -12. Helene's doberman is probably smarter. It's worth a try. What have I got to lose? I can't wait any longer.

Now! Go now, Addie! Do it now!

I run and I jump on his back. I put my arm around his neck, grab my other bicep, and place my hand behind his head in a chokehold.

"Help," he croaks, thrashing like an alligator. I hold tight and squeeze. The thrashes turn into squirms. And then he falls. His rat head hits the swing and then *thump,* he's on the ground, lying in the puddle of his own urine. I let out a little laugh and a smile forms on my face. *Wow, it worked.* He's knocked out cold. At least something went well today. I remove his rat mascot head and yank off his oversized jeans. As I hurry away, I realize that I'm wearing my soccer jersey. They'll definitely notice. I run back and pull off his dirty sweat stained gray t-shirt.

The bus is about to leave. I have to get there in time. This outfit really doesn't fit me. The head smells like urine. Disgusting. At least it didn't get inside. The pants are a bit too long and they are falling off, but who cares? Who really notices him anyway? He's like a speck of dust in the background which is ironic as he's gigantic. He's supposed to stand out, yet somehow he's invisible.

As I run to the parking lot and jump over bushes, my pants temporarily falling down (I pull them back up), a thought occurs to me. *What will I say to her?* I reach the parking lot and see their bus pulling out.

Scheisse! I run to it.

"Halt mal!!" I yell and then I realize I'm yelling in German. I switch to English. "Stop!"

They can't leave without their mascot, can they?

I run behind it, out of breath. The bus stops. I take a deep breath. I walk up the bus stairs, time slowing down, my mouth suddenly dry. Will anyone notice that my pants are too long or that I'm slightly shorter? As I enter the bus, there's a giant cheer.

Guess not.

* * *

I walk through the bus and players knock me back and forth, pushing me to and fro like a pinball, cheering, delirious from their ill-gotten victory. I see Shaylee at the end. There are no seats beside her. I don't know why I imagined there would be a seat. What was I thinking? In the seat behind her, there's a gigantic black dude. Beside her is a tough looking Mexican next to a muscular girl in a short skirt. In front of her is a skinny Asian. Him I could take.

"I'd like to sit here," I say to the Asian in a threatening voice.

He laughs. "Yeah, right."

"I'd like to sit here," I repeat.

He looks down and looks up at me. He clenches his fist. "For realz? You're a fucking mascot. I was out there on the field, what the fuck did you do? Wear some stupid suit? Dance the Kumbaya?"

He stands up and I see this skinny Asian is literally six foot five. His skinny build and short torso were extremely deceiving.

"Take off your fucking mask. In my culture, we don't hide behind our fucking masks," he sneers.

Scheisse. Not what I was expecting. I don't know what I was thinking. Maybe I was on a high or something from knocking out that dude so easily. Perhaps I thought I was Aryan Galactic Warrior or something. Now reality is setting in. I imagine the scene that will follow. He'll pull off my mask and everyone will stand up and surround me and beat me to death. I'll die at seventeen.

Shaylee leans over the seat. "Let him sit here. We just won, okay?"

He turns to face her, "Nobody talks to me like that."

He walks toward me and backs me into the other seat. I feel myself begin to hyperventilate. It's claustrophobic in this stupid head. I'm sweating. Maybe it would be a relief to lose the mask? That is, before they beat me to death.

Shaylee leaps up and stands between us. She holds Skinny Asian Dude back. "Listen, he probably has heat stroke or something. You've been out on the field. He's been wearing that." She motions to the rat head. "Give him a break."

Skinny Asian Dude looks at me, holding my gaze "Fine, take it," he sneers. Then, surprisingly, he backs off. I watch as Skinny Asian Dude pushes his way to the front of the bus. He grabs an empty seat. "Ridiculous!" I hear him yell but then he joins in on the chant they're singing.

I sit down. "Thanks," I say to Shaylee.

As I sit beside her, I realize that what I considered the "hard stuff", ie. getting on the bus, wasn't so hard as actually talking to a girl, even if she's an "it."

"You were awesome out there." Uh oh. That sounded angry. I repeat it again with more enthusiasm.

"Thanks," she responds. "You know you could take off the head?"

For a second, I forget I'm still wearing the rat head. It all seems so surreal being in this unknown, unfamiliar environment. I suddenly feel empowered. My sister Anne always makes me feel as if I can't do anything myself. Mother acts as if Anne knows everything and can do no wrong because she's in Mensa. "It's hard competing with such a star, isn't it?" Father had said about Anne, shortly before he died. Everything is always "Anne this" and "Anne that". On top of that, every time I'm going somewhere, Anne has to know exactly where I'm going. Sometimes I try to be vague and say, "Out". Then Mother comes over and Anne persists, making me admit where I'm going which is usually just out to see Thomas or something. Once I admit this, I feel defeated. I often just try to sneak out to avoid the interrogation. That way I don't have to tell anyone where I'm going. But now, I've managed to pull off the craziest stunt, all on my own. And they'd have no clue I was here. No freaking clue. They'd never be able to guess. I smile.

"Aren't you hot?" Shaylee asks.

"Yes," I answer. Then, I remember I can't remove the mascot head. "I mean no. I'm fine."

She looks at me, confused. "It's weird, your voice sounds higher."

Scheisse! Maybe it does. When that mascot dude yelled, "Help," it sounded much deeper. He could be a tenor if he wasn't a mascot. *Pay attention to detail, Addie!*

"Was kicked in the balls," I say. *Good cover, Addie.*

"Excuse me?" she says with a confused smile.

"Reichfield."

"Those idiots? I'm surprised they could manage that."

"Huh." I let out a slight laugh. I clench my fists. "You did well out there but don't you think it's wrong what you're doing?"

"Excuse me?"

"It's boys against boys and you're well not …"

Shaylee smirks. "Should have let that guy rip off your mascot head."

"I'm sorry I just don't see how it's fair …"

"Fair?" Shaylee laughs. "Fair? Aren't you our fucking mascot? And don't get me started on fair … Reichfield …" She looks out the window and a wave of sadness rushes over her face.

"Listen, I only meant— "

"Anyway, it's stupid. These gender norms. Male, female … it shouldn't be about that. No, that's limiting. It should be about who plays the best, not whether you pee standing up … I don't believe in labels, especially labels that are suffocating. Fuck that."

"Nonconformist."

I turn around and see a girl with half her hair shaved sitting in the seat across from us. She's wearing an oversized black shirt over baggy plaid shorts. I recognize her as one of their uncivilized fans.

"Yvonne gets it." Shaylee beams as she squeezes the girl's thigh.

"Well how could I not? People are stupid. They try to define me too but I don't let them. I am who I am and I can be gender neutral without aligning myself with either male or female … " Yvonne smiles.

Shaylee sits up on her seat. "Even though I can't fully understand what you must go through, Yvonne, with the ignorance out there, as I'm not trans nor am I gender neutral nor gender fluid … people try to define us as too young, too old, too beautiful, too ugly, too skinny, too fat, too feminine, too masculine, too dumb, too ambitious. They want to define us as that gives them power. They cast you into some role with preconceived notions of what it means to be that role, that category. They want to push you down with their meaningless labels. You know what? It bothers them that I won't let them. I rise up. They think they can control my destiny with words and terms but I control my path. I won't let any limiting label stand in the way of me achieving what I want." Shaylee looks at me. "They can't discriminate even if I'm biologically female. They had to let me play especially, especially after what they did."

Yvonne puts her hand on Shaylee's hand affectionately. "How's Kero doing anyway?" Yvonne asks.

"Recovering …" Shaylee says, her eyes dropping and her lips turning downward. "They don't know if he'll ever play again."

"Must be great to win and all." I change the subject, remembering that we were the ones that did the poisoning. I wouldn't want her to see any glee in my body language. They stop talking and look at me with extreme expressions of disgust.

"To win? Must be great?" I repeat, suddenly unsure of myself. Shaylee's nostrils flare and Yvonne looks like she's going to jump off the seat and tackle me. I feel both their anger growing like a volcano getting ready to erupt. "I mean, that's something that Kero would want right? To win? I wouldn't really know because ..." I gulp. "... I'm a mascot. Must be great."

Shaylee relaxes and I sense all anger evaporating. She lets out a little laugh. "Not really. It's too easy."

"What do you mean?"

"Where have you been? Don't you pay attention? They kind of suck. Me. I like a challenge."

Inside my mascot mask, I feel a vein bulge in my forehead. My muscles tense up. "Oh, come on. They're not that bad," I add with a tone a little too sharp.

"You on their side or something?" Shaylee half smiles.

I let out a nervous laugh. "Ha. No. I just don't think they're that bad. They're worthy of at least some respect."

"Are you kidding me? The dirty moves they make? Their dirty referee? No respect there. If they didn't suck beyond belief, I'm sure that referee would actually be able to make it look like they won but because they're so freaking bad, his corruption can only go so far, you know?"

I feel like punching something. I hold it inside.

"What do you think of 27, Player 27? Don't you think he's at least worthy of your competition?"

"Who? That skinny kid? Ugh. No."

My legs fly up and I kick the seat in front of me. Fortunately, it's at a time where we go over some bump in the road. Shaylee gives me a confused look.

"Reflex," I say.

Skinny kid? I'm not that skinny. I may not be like steroid-pumping Thomas, but I'm certainly not a string bean.

The dude in front of me whose seat I kicked, looks behind. He stands up. Uh oh. If I thought Asian dude was scary, this guy is scary beyond belief. Like Werner, he doesn't even look like he's in high school. However, instead of middle aged, he looks like a 30-year-old wrestler. Suddenly, I feel a giant fist collide with my mascot mask. I fall back on Shaylee.

I come to. *Where am I? Ah. I'm on a bus. That's right. Their bus.* I look around. The bus has stopped. It's empty. Everyone is gone. *Shaylee! I must find Shaylee.* I run off the bus.

* * *

I look left and right and then I see them in the distance. I run behind them down the dirt road. Underneath the mask, a pool of sweat drips down my face and my forehead throbs. You think they'd make the mascot head like a helmet, able to withstand a punch. We get to a large unkempt field, overgrown with grass. There's nobody but us about.

"Dude, why is the mascot following us?" I hear one of them ask.

It suddenly occurs to me how odd it must look to have someone wearing a rat's head and just a normal sweatshirt walking behind you. I would duck behind a bush but there's nothing really to duck behind. I'm glad I'm wearing the head because I probably have a black eye. *Scheisse! Why didn't I think of a better plan?* I need a cover. I stop and pretend I'm taking a leak. That seems to suffice.

In the distance, out of the corner of my eye, I see them cross the field. Then they disappear between a few buildings. *Scheisse.* I run really fast and trip ... and run ... and trip ... and run. These jeans are way too big. I fall down and get back up. I pull my pants back up. Man, I'm taking a beating. I'm sweating so much, I'm drenched. And then I fall again. My body hits the dirt. *Ouch.* I look around. Oh no, maybe I lost them. I get back up and approach the spot where they left the field. There's an alleyway in between two buildings. I walk through the alley. Above, there's a green light bulb. It buzzes. The whole place smells like a mixture of urine and rat poison. I get to the end and there are two paths.

One path leads to a driveway that curves and the other path that goes left has cobblestones and looks more friendly. Perhaps it could lead to a residential area. I figure they're probably heading home so I take that path. I follow it to the end. There are stairs going down. I walk down the stairs. At the bottom is a gate, and I open it.

I'm now in a courtyard that's filled with trash and old pieces of rusted furniture. There are apartments lining both sides. Red, blue and white North Prep Soccer flags drape from a few balconies. They are about the only things that look clean. Can't believe people live in such filth. Cats everywhere. I spot a small black woman hanging her laundry and then I hear the sound of a gunshot. I jump and I realize it's just a motorcycle starting. I make my way carefully across to an archway. I walk through. Now, I'm on a street, if you could call it that. It's full of a dozen potholes and there's grass growing out of the pavement. *This must be Lower Reichfield.*

There are houses on either side of the street and one house smack in the center of the street. The house is completely decked in North Prep soccer paraphernalia with red, blue and white lights hanging everywhere. The windows are covered with giant signs that read in metallic blue lettering, "Go North Prep Go" combined with something in Spanish. On the small lawn stands a plastic snowman in North Prep colors, kicking a soccer ball. Weird. In Reichfield, our houses have signs and flags but we're normal and this is a new level of crazy. I walk around the house. I look back and stare at the broken-down housing complex that surrounded that courtyard. Maybe they went inside. How would I even find them? Then I hear their victory song in the distance.

I run down the road, past a kid who steps back. It occurs to me that this kid is probably used to seeing masked men who rob banks here all the time. No surprise there. He is from Lower Reichfield. That type of thing must happen every day. Perhaps everyone wears costumes like me.

Perhaps it's their clothing staple as they're all thieves. No, it's not so weird that some dude in a rat head is walking through here. Not at all. This thing must be commonplace.

The sound of the North Prep victory chant drifts through the air. It's getting louder. I'm getting closer. I walk up the road. Every house has a North Prep soccer flag on their lawn. I'm not used to seeing so many North Prep flags. If they knew I was from Reichfield, I could be killed. I follow the tune of their victory chant and I come to a house. A house I recognize. Why? Suddenly I feel a punch to the side of my face. My legs give way and I hit the ground.

CHAPTER 3

I come to, the world blurry and spinning slowly. My surroundings resolve into focus, and I spot the rat mascot head lying on the floor. A massive foot steps on it, and a fist collides with my cheek. I try to move. The chair shifts. I look down, blinking hard, and notice that I'm tied up with what looks to be rope mixed with someone's sweatshirt. I look up at a hairy man in a black ripped tank top. I'd feel panic, but I can barely keep my head up.

"What did you do to our mascot?" he bellows.

I notice the words "Puerto Rico" and a black and red dragon tattooed on his forearm, so I'm guessing he's probably from there. Blood drips down from my nose into my mouth. It tastes salty, like my father's herring.

"I am your mascot," I mutter.

"What did you say? What did you say?" The Puerto Rican's eyes widen and he crinkles his nose. He bounces about like a boxer. He lifts his fist again. I tense up and close my eyes, preparing for impact.

"Hector." Shaylee pulls the Puerto Rican away. I listen to them argue in the corner.

"Is he a narc? Shit, Shay!"

Looking out of my bruised eye, I glance around the room. The place is filthy with dust everywhere and painting supplies scattered about. There's an old orange couch, dented and covered with what looks like claw marks. Perhaps some cat was using it as her scratching post. In the corner is an unfinished canvas of what looks to be a poor imitation of *The Basket of Apples* by Cezanne, and a mess of opened paint cans and brushes.

"If he's a narc, we have to do something." Hector glances in my direction.

"I recognize him," Shaylee says, unable to take her eyes off me.

"What are you talking about?"

"He sucks but he's no narc."

"Well, who is he then?"

"He's just some kid from the other team."

"Whose dad could be a narc," Hector hisses.

There's silence. I can feel their eyes staring at me.

"What are you saying?" Shaylee yells.

I flinch in my chair. I squirm as much as I possibly can, hoping no one will notice, twisting my hands this way and that to loosen the restraints.

"Listen to me. Listen to me," Hector pulls Shaylee outside. I wish I could hear what they were saying. I breathe in and out, trying to calm myself down. Yes. I manage to break an arm free—but the other one won't budge. In the meanwhile, I'll keep my newly liberated arm wrapped inside the sweater, seemingly still bound.

While I focus on freeing myself with the smallest movements I can make, I realize I don't hear voices anymore. I think they've gone for a walk. After making sure the coast is clear, I shift my chair across the room to the canvas.

An hour goes by and they still haven't returned. My sister must be worried, wondering where I am. I imagine the look on Pauline's face when they tell her the news that her brother has been killed. For some reason, it makes me laugh. I don't know why, but I feel giggles rising up like bubbles inside me.

Quite some time has passed, I'm guessing. Suddenly, the rusted door swings open and snaps strongly back on its spring.

"What the?" Hector looks from Shaylee to me.

A paintbrush in my hand, I glance at them. "If you're going to kill me, the least I ask for is some credit. Your previous work was atrocious."

They glance from me to the canvas, which is now nearly a complete portrait of Cezanne's masterpiece.

*   *   *

"He has mad skillz, I get it." Hector takes a chug of his beer. He peers at the nearly finished Cezanne. "But can we trust him?"

"Can we trust you, loco?" Shaylee looks at me.

Hector gets up and paces. "He's from Reichfield Proper, why would he help us? We should just stick to our original plan."

"Do you actually make money with those?" I glance over at the paintings sitting in the trash. "Looks like a third grader did them."

"Why did Emilio have to go get shot?" Shaylee runs her hands through her hair.

"You think he asked for it? No, he was dealing with something that you messed up. If you hadn't—" Hector shakes his head.

Shaylee stands up, her eyes blazing. "Don't blame me. I didn't know he'd do what he did … How was I supposed to know he'd take it personally? The guy just hit on me that's all."

They stop arguing and both look at me.

"I don't like this one bit. Let's stick to our plan." Hector comes toward me with a knife. Shaylee pulls him away.

"Listen, I screwed up. Okay? It was me. I'll take responsibility for loco. If he rats on us, we can find him. We can find his family. Hector, we need the cash. They stole the painting and let me remind you we have a limited window to sell the fake ones. If we don't deliver, it might be us ending up like Emilio."

Hector glares at her. He shakes his head.

Shaylee reaches her hand out, pulling Hector's chin toward her. "Listen to me. We can rough him up. We can destroy his life. He's not going to rat." He glances at the rat head. She pulls his chin back. "Ignore that. He can bring in the dough. Let me supervise. I can do this. Let me make up for what I did."

Hector breathes in. "Okay."

Shaylee smiles.

"Buf if he screws up." Hector's eyes bulge.

Shaylee looks at me. "If he screws up, I'll put a bullet through his pimply head myself."

I look up. "Pimply?!"

Okay, a year ago I may have had a breakout spell but I so managed to nip that in the bud.

CHAPTER 4

In a beat up pastel trailer from the '70s, I'm guessing her wheels and her home, Shaylee drives me along a suburban road. A fluorescent light shines from the back and some weeds poke out from the back seat. It smells kind of funky, like a mixture of a skunk and Coach Helene's B.O.

It's dark and probably late. How worried Pauline and Mother must be. They've probably sent out a search party. For some reason this fact makes me smile. Serves them right for giving me extra chores.

I think more about the job offer. I hadn't fully decided how I was going to take Shaylee down and this fits into my plan perfectly. I'll work reconnaissance as a double agent. By getting close to Shaylee, I'll understand what's important to her. I'll learn her desires, fears and ambitions and then, well, I'll exploit them to the best of my ability. Perhaps I'll even chance on her doing one of her voodoo spells and be able to destroy one of her dolls. Of course, I'll do more than destroy her power. In order to take your enemy down in a way which causes the greatest amount of pain, one has to learn what makes them tick. What makes you tick, Shaylee?

Shaylee turns on some Spanish dance music, which I hate to admit is actually pretty good. If I didn't have a black eye and if my ribs didn't ache when I moved, I might be tempted to, "jolly up," as Thomas so often puts it. For some reason I'm extremely hungry. I hope Pauline has left me some of Anne's meatloaf in the oven. I imagine eating it with sweet ketchup.

"So you're on your shitty soccer team?"

"No," I answer.

"Boy, don't lie to me, I seen you."

"Then why did you ask? To clarify, I'm on the great Reichfield soccer team, not the shitty soccer team."

"Seems pretty shitty to me. Have you ever even won a game?"

"Uh, I'm sure we have—"

"Against us?"

"Well … no but that's because you guys use your satanic magic to influence the results."

"Satanic magic, huh? Well let me turn you into a pumpkin right now."

She waves her hands in the air as if casting a spell, "Poof."

I tense up and close my eyes, bracing for impact.

Shaylee swerves the car, almost hitting a truck. She pulls over to the side of the rode. She laughs hysterically.

My muscles are stiff as a board. Gradually, I open my eyes to her mouth, wide in laughter. I can see all her pearly white teeth.

"Wait." She laughs. "Wait, is that what they tell you? That we use voodoo magic and make some voodoo doll of you scrawny players?" She looks at me. She stops laughing. She breathes in to keep herself from laughing more. "Boy, there ain't no voodoo. You guys just suck."

"Oh really? Then what's that?" I say pointing to her windshield.

"What?" She pulls down a brown haired doll in silver starred pants. "Oh you mean Mauricio? Got that at some concert."

Shaylee turns off the music. "Okay listen, you're in soccer so here's the plan, after soccer practice, you come to us when we say so. I give you this phone."

She hands me a device that has no buttons. I look at it and put it to my ear, unsure of how to use it. I look for the button to turn it on.

"I thought you said 'phone'?"

"Yes," she says.

"On," I say, thinking it's voice activated. "Turn on." I speak into it.

She grabs the phone.

"Boy, what phone you be using?"

I pull out my phone. It has buttons like most normal phones. She laughs.

"Are you from the '90s or something? All hipster 'n shit? Hipster with your tech too?" She laughs.

"That's top German tech, I'll have you know," I protest.

"I'm sure it is," she says with an extremely strong hint of sarcasm.

She turns on the phone for me and I see. Buttons light up on the screen. I'm amazed that lowlies have this type of technology. We're the Germans. It's us who should have this type of tech, not them. I suddenly feel angry. I look at Mauricio. I don't care what she says. That guy in those glitzy pants is for sure some satanic doll.

I take the phone. "Listen, I have a job, you know? I may not be able to get out of work all the time."

"Yeah, not my problem."

"My dad died and my mom is depressed and sick. She barely leaves the house. My brother Edison died too, so I have to work," I add.

Shaylee looks at me skeptically. "I'm sorry, what did your brother die of?"

"Measles," I respond.

She smiles in disbelief. "Measles?"

"Yeah," I repeat.

"Boy, if you're going to lie, at least say he died of cancer or something. No one died of measles since the 1800s."

"I'm telling the truth. You think I want to work some shit job in a customs office?"

Shaylee crosses her arms and looks at me skeptically.

"You think I want to sort mail all day like a carbon copy of my dad?"

Shaylee tilts her chin up and looks down at me.

"Okay, fine. I'll find a way."

"You better," she adds.

We pull up a few doors away from my house. Shaylee's beat up trailer must be so noticeable but then again it's nighttime and most people are asleep.

"Look at this fucking mansion," she shouts.

I look up at our duplex and snort, "Hardly."

Shaylee turns off the motor. "It's gigantic."

"This is nothing."

"Nothing? This is Beverly Hills."

"I take it you haven't seen Humphrey Bogart's abode?"

"Humphrey Bogart? Should we go rob his place?"

"Uh ... sure."

"Okay, you'll show us where that is too."

"Sure thing, when we go to California."

She looks at me, expressionless.

"Wait ... How could you not know Humphrey Bogart? Ever heard of the silver screen?"

"Silver?" Shaylee looks at me, confused.

"He's an actor."

I open the car door. Light from her car falls on our Reichfield High soccer flag on our lawn.

She glares at the sign. "We have a deal, remember? You show up or ..." She opens the front door. She gets out. She kicks the sign and then stomps on it again and again. "Deal?" she says looking at me. She stomps on it again for maximum impact.

I nod.

She gets back into her car. "Good." She slams the door. Her tires screech as she speeds away, probably waking up Thomas from his beauty rest.

I reach down to the sign and pick it up. I stick it back in the ground and try to stand it back up. It slightly leans forward. I try to fix it. It leans again. I notice it has a footprint on it. Okay. No fixing it tonight. I leave it. I make my way around the bushes and walk toward my front door.

As I approach the entrance, it suddenly occurs to me that there is no search party. The lights aren't even on. I open the door and look around. Everything is silent. I walk inside expecting Mother to be up and about but she is not. *Phew.* A floorboard creaks and I hear someone stir. Then I notice that she is asleep in front of the TV with a bottle of dad's brandy. On the fernseher, plays the theme song for, "The Carlin Mcmenzel," show. That puppet with it's shiny head and that chinless ventriloquist with his hand up it's ass always gives me the creeps. I walk to the TV and turn it off.

I tiptoe to the back stairs. Thinking I'm in the clear, I quickly race upstairs.

"Hi."

I jump.

It's Pauline. She's standing on one stair. She's wearing a purple dotted nightgown and her hair is pinned up in a messy bun.

"I could destroy you, are you aware?" She sounds like Anne, my other sister who just looks for ways to get me in trouble and if she doesn't catch me doing something, she'll invent it out of thin air.

"De-stroy," Pauline says, now two inches from my face.

I gulp.

"I … I … It was an accident."

"Accident? Are two people in love an accident?"

It's then that I notice that even though Pauline's wearing a nightgown, for some reason she's wearing bright red lipstick. She never wears lipstick. Mom doesn't allow it. Of course, Anne gets away with lipstick because she's Anne even though she's eight years younger than Pauline.

"Love?" Pauline says while looking into my eyes, with tears in hers, possibly from allergies, I'm guessing. "You're not supposed to fall in love before me, you know?" She strokes my cheek.

"What?" I back away.

She looks at me more closely. "Something wrong with your eye?"

I catch a glimpse of myself in a reflection on the giant vase. My hair's a mess and my eye is pretty bruised.

I gulp. "Love?"

"Love," she repeats as she looks at me. "Ava? In that car I heard pull up? You were … making out?"

"What?" My voice cracks.

"You were making out," she repeats. "With tongue?"

Tongue. Ava. No. Gross. But then it occurs to me that this is a great cover.

I nod. She looks pained. Her eyes become teary. Now she's glassy-eyed like a pirate.

"I'll just be going to sleep now," I stammer. I make my way upstairs with my body turned toward her. I get past her and turn back around.

"Love," she says melodramatically with a burst of desperation in her voice. I turn back to see her reapplying a thick red coat of lipstick.

CHAPTER 5

Of all the days I came late for practice, today I'm especially glad that I did. When I arrived, I found Werner laying on the field while Helene stood watch. He was on his back with his legs sprawled wide apart. Thomas and Mengela were on opposite sides of him. A skipping rope was attached to each of Werner's ankles and Thomas and Mengela were pulling at the ropes, forcing Werner to do the splits in the air. Werner screamed a high-pitched scream. It reminded me of the way Thomas had screamed after waxing off his chest hair for a bodybuilding meetup. Apparently, it wasn't only Werner who had gotten such torture. Everyone had lined up and Helene had selected boys at random. Thomas had almost been chosen but then Helene's gaze had shifted to Heinrich.

As we run around the track, I watch as Heinrich limps in front of us. Apparently, Helene believes that such torture will help us to better kick the ball. I look behind me. With ten of our strongest players limping, I seriously doubt that. This wasn't the first time she tortured us. One time she locked me in a room with her doberman and her chihuahua. I had to get out unscathed. It was to teach me how to be fearless. Fortunately, I was able to grab her doberman and put a chokehold on him. The same choke that I used on the mascot. I learned the chokehold from some war show about a battle fought at Verdun. A German soldier had performed it on a French attacker who had snuck up on him during the night. With it, I was able to put the doberman to sleep. However, little did I know that the chihuahua was the more vicious one. It nearly bit my jugular. Helene opened the door just in time. I was traumatized after that incident as just the thought of hurting an animal gives me chest palpitations. It would be one thing if such tortures actually helped us to win, but no. If it isn't torture enough that we're humiliated each game, we have to be tortured by Helene for no good reason.

"What don't I hear?" Helene barks.

"Crumpets and tea, crumpets and tea, we are the boys of RHC," we chant. Helene forces us to chant this. Apparently, she chanted a similar chant at her all-girls boarding school in Whales. I'd of course prefer to chant something more German about might and victory rather than teatime. Every time she makes us chant this awful song, it makes me hate Helene even more than I already do, if that is even possible.

I step off the track onto the grass and walk up to Helene. "Excuse me Coach, I need to leave early today. Have an appointment," I huff.

Helene turns to face me. "Appointment, huh? Your sister Pauline didn't tell me anything about an appointment when I saw her last. And what the hell happened to your face?" Helene motions to my eye.

"Love," I say.

Her face transforms into a confused expression. I realize that this answer does not suffice in this situation. What worked for my sister doesn't appear to work on Helene.

"Love?"

Suddenly Helene's face turns into a smile. Why the hell is she smiling? Did I make her laugh? She's looking at something. I turn around and see Ava standing there waving.

"Okay. Just this once, I'll let you off the hook, okay?" She glances at Ava. "But tell her this time, not to be too rough on you, okay? Water works too, you know, and doesn't cause any scarring."

"Ok-ay."

What is Helene on? No time to care. I got out of practice. This will leave me time to get to work so that I can complete my hours earlier. Then, if I leave work early I'll be able to finish the Cezanne before lights out. I rush off the field.

I think I hear the sound of running footsteps behind me. Platform shoes. I speed up. Did Helene change her mind? I glance over my shoulder. Ava trips over her platform. Most people would stop to help out a girl who's just fallen but I have a tight schedule. I continue walking.

"Ow, ow, ow."

I glance behind me. Ava's limping. She must have twisted her ankle.

"Hey," she says, out of breath, finally catching up to me.

"Hey," I reply, barely paying any attention to her. Girls and their drama.

"Can you stop for a second?"

"No." I continue walking.

She limps beside me. "I ... I wanna ... ummm ... we should totally hang out."

I glance at her, she has dirt on the side of her face and mud on her thin silky blond hair, probably from the fall. In the backdrop, I catch a glimpse of Helene and Thomas. They're looking at me. Oh. I think they expect me to be friendly.

"Yeah, sure," I say with a fake smile. "Let's do that sometime."

"Sometime, right ..." she says. "When?"

"Walk with me," I say, well aware that each step causes her considerable pain. "So we should totally hang out. I'm so into you."

She limps beside me. We're still not out of vision.

"Can you walk faster?" I say, annoyed.

"Hey." I stop, a thought occurring to me. I can use this situation to my advantage. "Do you have a car?"

* * *

Ava drops me off outside of work. I frown at the sight of the boxy, concrete mail processing building. I always feel a certain juxtaposition. The mail is going somewhere and I'm staying here. Well, at least today I got a ride.

"Thanks," I say. Ava touches her hair and faces me. I flash a smile at her. It's somewhat nice to have a girl into you, even if she's now a cripple. I glance at her swollen ankle.

"So we'll hang out, right?" she asks.

I nod. "Of course."

She smiles with elation. This is probably the best day of her life.

"Can you be back here at seven?" I inquire.

"Ugh. How about I just wait? I can do some homework."

Wow, she's really into me. "Sure, why don't you do that?"

I get out of her green sedan. I walk along the path to the building, then turn back as an idea pops into my mind—or rather, growls from my stomach.

I lean over the car window and flash another smile. "You know what you can do …"

*　*　*

I come out of work to find that Ava followed through. I open my burger and gobble everything down. She doesn't touch anything.

"You're not eating?" I say.

She stares at me with starry eyes. "I like to watch."

I continue eating, finishing the last burger bite.

"All done," I say with a smile. I glance in the mirror. There's ketchup on my mouth. "Do you have a napkin?" I inquire.

"All I have is this." She hands me her scarf.

"You sure?" I ask.

She nods.

I get Ava to drop me off as close to the border of Lower Reichfield as I can get without drawing too much suspicion. There's only forest here and a gas station.

"Why here?" she asks.

I look around the gas station. A man stands with his schnauzer by a gas pump. Above the gas pump is an advertisement with a reindeer. Funny, the holiday season is months away.

"I'm hunting deer." I quickly jump out of her car. Wait. Hunting deer? No, I'd never shoot an animal. "Well, not hunting them per se, we use stun-guns and relocate them for their own wellbeing." She looks at me, confused. I quickly add, "It's part of volunteering, you know the volunteer hours we need? But in addition, they pay me a bit, helps somewhat. We really need the money with my dad gone and all."

That answer seems to suffice. "Was really great spending time with you." She looks at me longingly, holding eye contact.

"Same here." I flash her a smile. "And don't forget to fill up on gas."

Having a girlfriend is great.

*   *   *

"All done," I say with a smile, looking at the finished Cezanne. A blank canvas is placed in front of me. "What's this?" I turn to face Hector.

"Another one."

"Okay, what should I paint? Monet's *Water Lillies*, Klimt's *Dur Kuss*, Menzel's *Bartiger Mannerkopf*?"

"Paint that." He points to the finished Cezanne.

"I don't understand." I shake my head in confusion.

"Paint that!" he bellows.

"I don't understand your English."

Hector digs his nails into his palms. His head looks like a volcano near the point of eruption. He swats the air, letting out one serious grumble.

Shaylee puts down her iced coffee and comes over. "What's wrong?"

Hector throws his hands up in the air. "He does not understand English. I tell him to paint that. He says, 'No, I don't understand.'"

Shaylee leans over. "What's the problem, loco?"

"No problem." I stare at the blank canvas. She puts the brush in my hand. It falls to the floor.

"You're picking that up." Her eyebrows lower and her nostrils flare.

"Give me something else."

"Listen." A frustrated smile forms on her face. "You're painting that. We need two copies. We're selling to two different buyers, got it?"

I let out a sigh. "Afterwards, you'll give me something else?"

Her smile widens, but her eyes remain cold. "Of course." Could there be any more sarcasm in her voice?

CHAPTER 6

At the next game, we lose again. I had almost scored a goal. Almost, but then, Shaylee was there and for some reason, I lost my focus. Afterward, Thomas corners me by the lockers.

"What was that?" he demands.

"What?" I say.

"You know what. I saw you. You could have taken her but you let her win."

"I don't know what you're talking about."

"Really, well... you know ... I think you're soft."

I pin Thomas against the locker with my arm against his neck. "Shut up."

"Maybe you have a soft spot for the mule."

I punch him in his steroid built iron abs which hurts my hand more than it hurts him.

"What did you say?" I look him straight in the eyes.

He throws me off of him. "Ava. You've barely got to second base with her. And now you let the freaking flip win?"

We're both silent.

"I want—"

Thomas puts his finger to my mouth. "Shhh ..."

"What?!" I yell.

"Cut the gas!" Thomas tilts his head. He listens.

"What? Why?" I look around.

"Cut the freaking gas," he whispers intently.

And then I hear a curious sound.

Thomas pulls me by the shirt and we walk around the lockers to the bathroom area. Underneath one of the bathroom stalls, I see someone's pants down.

Thomas throws his weight against the stall, busting it open. Inside is a boy from the team whose name I don't know with his dick in his hand.

Thomas grimaces. "Frederick." Thomas glances at me and then back at Frederick. "Well look at this little fream. He's wanking off to us, you know? Freaking cake-eater." Thomas pulls me away, out of the locker room.

Frederick runs after us. "Please don't report me," he wails.

"Report him?" I ask Thomas. "Who would we even report him to?"

Thomas shrugs. "Don't know what he's on. He's crazy."

I don't think too much about the incident until the next day.

When I arrive on the school grounds, all the students are standing outside, looking up at something. I join them, craning my head upwards, thinking they're watching a giant blimp, but then I spot what they're really staring at.

Frederick hangs from our school flagpole.

Thomas moseys up to me. "Shame," he says while shaking his head. He takes a sip of his chocolate milk.

I look up at Frederick's blue face, which almost matches the blue of the sky if it weren't for a slightly different hue. "Who did this?"

Thomas shrugs his shoulders. Suddenly, he looks anxious. Frantically he reaches into his pocket and rummages through it. Then he pulls out his lactose digestive pills.

"Thought I forgot these. Phew Addie, I mean Phew."

I look at Thomas suspiciously. "Did you report him?" Upon speaking those words, I'm aware at how ridiculous it sounds. Who would Thomas report him to? As if masturbation was a crime ...

"Uh, no. I'm guessing he hanged himself, hello? There was some note or something. Said Frederick was upset at our team losing again. Couldn't handle it ... you know?"

We look up at dangling Frederick. A pigeon lands on his sunken head.

"Right, as if someone would bump him," I say, a little laugh escaping my mouth.

"Yeah for masturbation?" Thomas imitates a gun shooting. "Pew."

This sends me into a fit of giggles and Thomas too. Disturbed students turn around to look at us. It's then that I realize that it's not exactly the most appropriate thing to do, to laugh at a crime scene.

Paramedics push through. I can't suppress my laughter. Oh no. I have to leave. They might determine this a crime, though I highly doubt it. However, if they did, my laughter would for sure make me a suspect.

An ambulance worker puts her hand on my shoulder, "I'm sorry, were you related? You know, if you're interested in grief counseling ..." Then I remember, fortunately for me, at times, my laughter sounds a lot like crying. This makes me laugh more. I'm turning bright red.

Thomas covers his mouth with his hand. Unlike me, his laughter sounds exactly like laughter. The nurse gives him a dirty look. He can't get away with it like I can.

I try to suppress my laughter all morning, but I just can't. That ambulance worker really thought I was torn up by the death of Frederick. My only interaction was seeing him with his dick in his hand and now he's dead. If I were to give a eulogy, it would be like this:

"Frederick. He was a great masturbator. Liked the sound of my voice. This got him hard. And now ... he's dead."

My stomach hurts so much now from the laugh attack that I think I might actually cry which would be good if the police came again. Then when they ask me questions, I could feign some sort of empathy. I know it's normal to be upset but I'm really way more upset about my own situation.

Sitting in art with Helene, all I can think about is how I have to go farther with Ava and I really don't want to. For some reason, the thought of kissing her even though she's hot makes me want to throw up. I don't know why. Thomas says that she's "one smokin' hot dame." If she's so smokin' hot, what's wrong with me?

Am I like Frederick? Will I end up like him? The smile fades from my face. What if that were me? What if I were the one hanging from the pole instead? What if someone really did off him because he was a homo?

Ava, Ava. Think of Ava. I glance at her breasts, trying to muster up sexual feelings. *Nope.* Then a thought of Shaylee, coated with sweat and dirt after a soccer game, pops into my mind. Suddenly, I'm hard.

"Ahem." I jump to look up at Helene. Her chin hair looms over me like Frederick hanging from the pole. Unlike Frederick, I find it even more disturbing because today it's twice as long. It must have doubled in size in a week. "Working hard?" she inquires in a tone that says, "I know what you're up to."

I wonder for a second if she has laser vision and can see under the table. It's then that I realize she's referring to my mixed media project which only has a tissue stuck to a bristol board and some jelly beans in the corner. I'm really not trying because what's the point, when I do try, she says it's shit, so why not create shit? She likes shit. I'll create shit. I plop another jelly bean down in the center. I look up and smile at her. My boner's not for you, Helene. As if anyone would have a hard-on for you.

CHAPTER 7

Ava kisses me all over and this is supposed to feel good. However, I feel like I'm getting a fish pedicure, something I saw the other day when I passed a shop in Lower Reichfield. We're under the bleachers and I got out of soccer practice, once again, for a girl. Having sex according to Helene is supposed to make me a better soccer player so she allows for it. I reach my hand underneath Ava's blouse.

"Why are you closing your eyes?" She looks up at me.

"Pleasure," I answer.

"Ok-ay." She smiles with a half smile. The space between her eyebrows wrinkles.

She sits up. "You don't know what you're doing, do you?"

"What? No. Of course I do," I say.

She lies back down and I continue, my hand moving across and then down her side. What am I feeling? Wait, is that the grass?

She sits up, a smile forming on her face. "You don't. Oh my gosh." She laughs. Ava's laughing at me. I feel my cheeks getting hot. "Am I your first?" she asks, smiling.

"No," I say while looking away. "Of course not." I kiss her some more.

"We can stop," she says, "if you want ..."

"No. I want." I grab the back of her neck and kiss her again, this time trying to muster up some more passion.

"Why do you have your hand in my pocket?"

"Is that weird?" I ask.

"No ... I'm just confused as to why ... umm ... you don't have your hand somewhere else?"

Right.

* * *

After the ordeal, Ava dropped me off again and I was able to finish some more works of art. It's a relief to know my day wasn't a complete waste. As I approach my house, Thomas runs out of his.

"You owe me one," he shouts, "I covered for you."

"How so?"

"Ava asked me why you work two jobs," Thomas says lowering his voice. "I told her that you guys need the money as your dad left a lot of debt, which we know isn't really true. Even though he drank, he put money aside for you, enough to get by with one afterschool job."

"Oh."

"You want to tell me why you're lying to her?"

"I just needed space." I shake my head, looking away. I tug at my collar. "She's just so claustrophobic."

"Applesauce," Thomas exclaims, his eyes bulging and hair on end. "How could you want to be away from that dame for one second?"

"Listen, she just wants so much of my time," I protest, defensively. "Everything just feels so clingy." I grimace, looking at Thomas, hoping to get my point across without looking gay. "Listen, she's hot and all but we have absolutely nothing. Nothing. In common. We have nothing to talk about."

"With that dazzlin' muffin and those amazing gams that stretch for miles, you want to talk? Are you serious?"

I feel Thomas examining me, scrutinizing me. His eye twitches.

My muscles tighten. "I want to do more than that of course—"

"Good. I sure hope so," Thomas adds, backing away from me. He turns around and runs toward his house.

"Thomas," I yell.

He turns back. I can't have him thinking I'm gay. An idea occurs to me, something that Landra from "I Love Landra," would say "stops two gaps with one bush."

"Remember that thing you used last summer on that girl you really liked?"

"Oh yeah, that roofie."

"Yeah, got any of that?"

Thomas's face softens. "Why man, Ava's totally into you? You don't want to waste that darb."

"Yeah, I mean, I know she is, just in case—"

"In case what? That doll's totally into you and I mean totally. Full throttle."

"Well … Uh … let's say she changes her mind like girls do. You know, what if we're making out, and she gets me all hot and then she's like, 'Sorry.'"

"Dude, you worry too much."

"Come on Thomas, you know how girls are."

Thomas stops. He thinks to himself. "Okay, I'll see if my dad has some tucked away with his golf clubs and hemorrhoid cream."

"Great."

"Dinner," I hear Thomas's father yell. Thomas walks toward his front door. I walk toward mine.

"Thomas," I say.

He turns around. "What?"

I smile. "I'm really glad we're friends."

"Don't mention it." He nods.

CHAPTER 8

Thomas followed through. Everything is going as planned with Hector leaving early as usual, probably to go rob stores or break shit. As I finish the last brush strokes on the Cezanne, I watch Shaylee type away on her phone and giggle. Beside her is a bottle of beer that's either real beer or root beer. I don't know as it's in Spanish.

I feel the outline of the Rohypnol in my pocket. It grosses me out majorly to think that my first sexual experience will be with a lowly, but then I remind myself it's better than being laughed at in school for doing something wrong.

With Shaylee unconscious, I'd be able to explore the female form without scrutiny. I'll be able to understand it better. It's like an experiment. Experiments are first done on rats and then on people. I realize it will take more than one experience to become a master. It's very good that Thomas gave me more than one Rohypnol. One of them I taped in a plastic bag to the back of my locker for safekeeping. If anyone looks, the darkness will conceal it. The other one, I hid in my sock drawer in an old ibuprofen container.

Wait. What if I'm supposed to give her all three the first time? He didn't say. It's not like there are instructions on these things. Guess I'll find out if it works. What's life without a little risk?

She comes over. "Your phone's beeping."

"I didn't even notice, must have a voicemail or two," I answer nervously.

"Well, it's been doing that for half an hour. It's really annoying." Shaylee gives me a weird look. "You ghosting someone?"

"Ghosting?"

"Right, you're from 1812, when people still leave voicemail. It means ignoring. You ignoring someone?"

"Yes." It's probably Ava now that I think of it. She's even called me more than Pauline this week.

Shaylee leans close to me to examine my canvas. Now's my chance. I gulp. *Scheisse, she didn't bring her beer.* I was relying on her bringing her beer for this to work. I peer over at it, sitting on the table.

"Well, you're almost done," she says.

I look at her, an eyebrow raised. "I am done."

"Yeah?" She looks at the painting, her eyes narrowing. "Well, the other one looked better."

"It looks exactly the same," I exclaim.

She glances at it again. "Okay. Maybe it does."

"Maybe? It looks exactly, exactly, the same."

A call comes in on her phone. She picks up. "Oh my gosh, Yvonne, babe, there's something I have to tell you."

She looks back at me. "I'm going to take this outside. You continue working."

I glare at her. "I'm finished."

"Well then, paint something else." She runs outside. The door swings shut.

I push my chair away and stand up, military style. Turning like a robot, I tiptoe toward her beer. As I'm approaching it, a floorboard creaks.

Suddenly, my head hurts, like it's about to crack open. I remember something, see it like it's happening right now. A flash. The floorboard creaking. Here. Tables. Tubes. A stretcher. A machine. A white light. A man looking at me. He's wearing a face mask.

"You're going to be okay," he says looking over me.

On the stretcher, I look toward the side at my reflection in a glass cabinet filled with tiny bottles. I'm nine years old. My head darts around. There's a boy who looks exactly like me lying on the couch. There's blood on the floor with a pair of boy's shorts. He's not moving.

There's another man in the room. With a face I can't see. He's wearing a tweed suit. He raises his hand. He's holding a gun. Bam. He shoots the boy who looks like me in the head.

I come back to reality. I fall to the floor, grabbing my head. There's a ringing sound in my ears.

Shaylee comes back in and finds me on the floor. "What the hell. Are you an epileptic or something?" She helps me up and lets me recover for a bit on the couch.

* * *

We leave the house.

I glance around, looking at all the North Prep soccer signs on every lawn. I stop. "Where's your car?"

She looks at me. "That was a one time thing." She walks away.

I follow her. Every house has some sort of North Prep soccer paraphernalia on it. One sign on a tree has a graphic of two soccer players kicking a ball with "Soccer player parking only: violators will be kicked," written under it.

She stops and looks back at me. "Uh ... what are you doing?"

"Walking with you."

"Your place is the other way."

"Yeah, so?" I stammer. I look at an emaciated cat who makes it way hesitantly across the street.

"You're not walking with me."

"Come on. I could get beat up here at this time. Here."

"Fuck if I care." She reaches into her bag and pulls out her headphones. She stops. "The only way you're walking with me is if you do exactly as I do, deal?"

I look at a few verbrecher ruffians on the other side of the street who are eyeing me, probably sizing me up. The mascot mask that I wore the first time and the cap I wore yesterday made me feel a lot safer. Why did I forget the cap at home? I'm pretty sure everybody here realizes that I don't belong. I'm a mugging waiting to happen.

I glance at the ruffians, trying not to make eye contact. "Deal."

We walk for a while. I'm so pissed off at myself. What happened in there? All I had to do was drug her beer but instead, instead no I had to collapse in a fit on the floor like some arschgeige. This is not how it's supposed to go. I catch up to Shaylee who's in front of me.

"What are you listening to?" I ask.

Shaylee takes her earphone out and puts it into my ear. *Gross.* I don't usually share, especially not with a lowly but I ignore my disgust as the aggressive beat of the music gives me confidence; the confidence I need walking through such a slum. I totally get why she listens to it. I feel like punching someone in the face. A ruffian passes me. I make the mistake of looking the verbrecher in the eye. Like a wild animal, he looks like he's ready to pounce. I quickly look away.

*   *   *

We stop at what must be the east border of Lower Reichfield and Reichfield Proper. Many people think of Reichfield Proper as being completely separate but parts of Reichfield Proper sandwich Lower Reichfield. On the Reichfield Proper side, I see a development going up.

It's a luxurious condominium with pictures of happy people. On the fence, I see an ad for our soccer team with a life size picture of Thomas's dad, the city planner, holding up our red, black and white flag. There's no way he looks like that, even with botox. It makes him look twenty years younger. For sure, it's totally airbrushed and no doubt they whitened his yellow, coffee-stained teeth. It reads, "Our Kids. Our Pride."

"This town is so shit." Shaylee laughs.

For once, I agree with her. "Tell me about it. I just want to get the hell outta here."

"Good luck," she says while fumbling through her bag.

"Okay?" I don't quite get her sarcasm.

"You think you can just leave?" she says with a slight laugh.

"Well, it's America. It's a free country."

She lets out a snort. "You said, 'free.'"

"Well, it's true. You're free."

"For one, we are not free." She fumbles through her bag some more.

"Excuse me?"

She looks at me. "I had this cousin once. He wanted to be some actor. Had dreams of moving to LA and hitting it big. We got postcards from him and stuff."

"So, he left?"

"No. The postcards weren't written by him."

"What?"

"He's dyslexic."

"Maybe he asked one of his friends to write—"

"Yeah, not likely. Also, when we tried calling him, his phone had been disconnected."

"Ok-ay. What do you think happened?"

Shaylee draws her finger across her neck.

"You think they killed him? That's insane."

"Insane, really?"

"I mean, sure actors can be annoying from what I heard. My friend Thomas used to want to be an actor and he'd talk in this theatrical voice all the time. Thankfully he gave that up. But anyway, killed? Sorry, I'm not buying it."

"Right. So where do you think we are right now?" Shaylee asks.

"Ugh, hello we're in Philly?"

Shaylee shakes her head.

"Okay, we're on the moon."

Shaylee looks me in the eyes with intense seriousness. "We're nowhere."

"Well sure, it's a shit town, so we're nowhere … I can agree with that."

"No, we're literally nowhere. Off the grid. When we were fleeing Chile, I remember hiding coming across the border, right?"

"Okay?"

"But it wasn't the border. It was different. Unofficial almost. There was a big wooden wall and men with guns. It looked like no checkpoint I've ever seen."

"I think you're exaggerating. I mean, you were a kid. Kids are imaginative."

"It had an eagle on it. Not for America."

"You're saying we're not in America?" My mouth forms a slow smile. "That we're not in Philly? Do you know how crazy that sounds?"

"Think. Have you ever even left this town?"

"Well, no."

"Has anyone you've known ever left this town?"

"My older brother. He left when I was a kid. He had a fight with my dad and stormed out. So—"

"Ever heard from him again?"

I shake my head. "But that doesn't mean anything. He could have—."

"Don't you think it's weird he never contacted you or anyone? You're his brother."

I frown. "It's not like we were close ... Okay, I'll humor you even though you sound completely insane. If we're not in America, where do you think we are then?"

"I don't know, my cousin and I came up with a theory. That we're in some buffer zone."

"A buffer zone?"

"Top secret almost, between South America and North America. That's why no one leaves. The people who try to are never heard from again. You see what I'm saying?"

"So you're saying I can never leave?"

Shaylee nods.

I laugh, because there's no other way to respond. "That's crazy."

"There are ways of getting out, how else do you think we get these paintings out? But it's so far up the chain that even Hector doesn't know exactly how they do it."

"A buffer zone?" I say, bewildered.

"So basically, you're stuck like me."

I know there's no way what she's saying could be true however, she really believes it. Her conviction is unshakeable to the point that I wonder if there could be a sliver of possibility that it could be true. Suddenly, I feel even more trapped than ever. Claustrophobic almost, as if great invisible walls are closing in around me.

Addie, she's crazy. I try to reassure myself. She's likely messing with me as girls do. Anne sometimes messes with me to annoy me about stupid stuff. Or … maybe Shaylee's just one of those people who believe in alien conspiracies or something.

Shaylee takes out three tubes of paint. She hands me a paintbrush. I take it reluctantly, making sure not to touch her, as if insanity were contagious. She picks up a piece of wood and squirts a bit of each paint on it. She walks toward the picture of Thomas's dad. She begins to paint what looks like a wheelbarrow.

"What are you doing?"

"You said you'd copy me."

"Well uh, yeah, but what if someone sees us?"

She laughs. "Are you kidding me? Look around. Nobody is here. Nobody is going to know."

"Paint it on that one," she says, pointing to an identical poster a few spaces down.

I walk to the poster. I copy her and paint a wheelbarrow. I walk back.

"Done."

"You're not finished," she says, dipping her paintbrush in more paint. She walks up to the poster and continues painting.

"Did you know in the Congo, there is actually a virus that can give you this condition?"

"Virus?"

"My father's friend who helped us escape Chile, told us about it."

She dips her paintbrush in brown paint.

"Okay..."

She dips her paintbrush in green paint. With the brown paint left over on the brush, the green turns a shade of greenish-brown.

"He was a doctor. I guess he was trying to make us forget our fear, doing that thing doctors do before they give you a needle."

I suddenly have a flash of being nine years old and getting needles, many of them, for some reason. Was I sick? I'm lost in thought and Shaylee is painting. She finishes. She stands back from her painting. I gape. It's of Thomas's dad wheeling a giant flaccid dick in a wheelbarrow.

"So you copy me—" She motions to the other poster.

"No," I protest.

"You have to."

"No. Unlike you, I don't think it's fun to draw dicks on things."

"Well what would you draw instead, Mr. Intellectual?"

"Thomas's dad is not that bad," I lie, "I'd give him a bouquet of flowers."

She laughs. "For what? Being a crummy city planner of some shit town with a shitty soccer team?"

She won't relent. I dip my paint in the green paint. I walk to the poster. Instead, I draw fangs on Thomas's dad and multiple green birthmarks up his arm.

"There," I say.

She looks at the poster. "If you hated him, what would you draw?"

"Oh come on, I drew fangs," I say. I feel a knot in my stomach. For some reason drawing on Thomas's dad makes me feel even more scared than it would on any other person.

"If you hated him." She crosses her arms and stares at me, her brows raised in expectation.

I can see I'm not going to get away with the minimal. I don't hate the guy. I barely know the guy. His dad has done so much for Reichfield as a city planner. It's because of him that we have our state of the art soccer field. It's because of him that we have civilized streets to walk on and safe neighborhoods where we don't have to worry about stray bullets killing us. It's because of him that the cesspool of lowlies stay on one side and we reside safely on the other.

She puts her hands on her hips. "You're drawing a dick if you can't think of something else."

I take the wooden palette from Shaylee. I dip my paintbrush in paint. She watches me. I paint and paint and paint, each brushstroke building on the last, and then I step back.

She looks from me to the painting, her full lips curled in approval. "Nice."

I'm actually pleased with it myself even if the message is not one I agree with at all. I just figured I needed to paint something that she would like or I'd have to sink to the lowly level of drawing a penis. Thomas's dad is now carrying a bag of money with holes. The holes leak out coins and lowlies. The lowlies hang on to the coins for dear life. This is one of those times that I didn't have control of my message but it doesn't bother me that much. If lowlies are stupid and inferior, they deserve to be crushed and have everything taken from them. The strong survive and the weak perish.

* * *

I toss and turn in my bed. I see the kid who looks like me being shot again. I see it over and over again, one hundred times. I see the man in the surgical mask but I can only see his hands, his body, and not his face. I can't make out who he is but his stature looks familiar. Perhaps I've seen him before somewhere. But where? Then I see the kid that looks like me popping up from underneath Thomas's dad's desk. It definitely isn't the same kid. The one in Thomas's dad's study only resembled me while the one with the doctor or surgeon was identical to me. The more I dream of kids that look like me undergoing an ordeal, the more I think that it's my subconscious making everything up. It must be a metaphor for something. I just wish that metaphor would let me awake without a pounding heart, gasping for breath.

I wake up and Pauline's sitting on the side of my bed in her nightgown. Has she been sitting there the whole time?

She looks at me concerned. "You've been making sounds."

"Oh, it's nothing."

She puts her hand on my arm. "I'm cold."

She lifts off my covers and gets into bed with me. I lay back down and try to go back to sleep, but I can't. I freeze, suddenly uncomfortable.

"Um, can you go back to your own bed?" I ask.

She turns on her side. "No."

I try to close my eyes. "Why?"

She throws off the covers. "You're so selfish. How are you ever going to have a girlfriend?"

I hear the door slam as she walks off in a huff.

$$* \quad * \quad *$$

Sorting mail in the tiny mailroom with small windows that let in only a sliver of light, I remember Thomas's picture on the Danube. If we were really confined to this town, like Shaylee implied, there would have been no way Thomas and his dad could have taken that trip.

I look out the window to see a mail truck coming in. If Shaylee's conspiracy theories were right, no way could Thomas even order from a site like gbay. Last week I delivered a package of black new combat boots to him ahead of time. They had white laces. He was so excited to get it in two days. Two days rather than a week. I rushed processing for him. Even though I hate working in this shit customs office, I like the fact that I of all people have the ability to pull strings, to make things happen. I have that power. One day maybe I'll have even more power than this, outside of this room. I better have that power. One thing's for sure, if I'm working here at sixty like my dad was, I'll kill myself.

Shaylee is a conspiracist. That's what she is. I can't blame lowlies for thinking the way they do. It's not like they have our top Aryan education. As if we're stuck here. Us Aryans, being confined to a camp, a prison almost? That's laughable. No way any Aryan would put up with that. We descend from mighty warriors. There's no way they'd hold us here against our will.

Hans, a white-haired man who has been working here probably since the 1800s, comes over and drops more packages on my desk. I cringe. Since he's nearly blind, I've discovered that if I turn my chair around, he doesn't notice when I leave an hour early. I've even discovered a spotless way to do just that. I record the sound of myself typing and I just leave it on a loop. It stops at the hour I'm supposed to finish work. So far Hans hasn't noticed one bit. If he ever did notice, I'd just claim it was a glitch with my computer.

CHAPTER 9

"You're using me," Ava cries.

I finish my hamburger. "That's ridiculous," I say as I dip some fries in some ketchup. Some fall in between the car seat. *Oh well.*

"I'm your beard," she cries.

"That's ridiculous," I say. "You have no facial hair, unlike Helene."

"All you want to do is eat and you want me to chauffeur you around and you don't even like touching my breasts."

I reach a hand out and grab one of her breasts. "That's not true."

With my other hand I shovel more fries into my mouth. Gosh, these fries are amazing. I squeeze her breast, hoping that will suffice.

"Verpiss dich." She opens the car door and pushes me out.

"No need to swear like a lowly," I say, still chewing.

She swerves to miss a cat as she speeds off.

"Girls."

Scheisse. How will I get to Shaylee's in time? They'll kill me. Literally.

"Come back. I'm sorry," I yell.

I try to hitchhike but nobody stops. "Come on," I yell in frustration.

I realize standing here is getting me nowhere and so I decide the best way to get there will be on my own steam. I run and run, the wind blowing through my hair. My legs are aching. If only I had Thomas's steroid-built thighs. With relief I come to the sign I defaced. I look toward it, oddly, with pride.

My heart drops to my stomach. In front of the sign stand two officers. *Scheisse.* The eagle on their uniform means they're Upper Reichfield officers. For a second I think they're going to come for me but then I realize they already have a kid in a hoodie who stands there in handcuffs. A can of spray paint lies on the dirt. If they actually knew anything about art, they would have realized that the painting was painted with acrylics rather than spray paint. I laugh, suddenly feeling relief that I got away with something.

I look closer at my drawing and next to it I see the word, "Fucker." Oh so that's why they arrested that kid. They thought they caught him in the act. Ha. As if some lowly had my skill. I turn to leave and then I hear gunshots. One after the next. Bam. Bam. I turn back and the kid falls to the pavement.

I back away. Now I'm really running. I don't think they saw me. When I arrive at the house, I'm out of breath. I push through the swinging door. Shaylee sits on the couch with her phone in hand.

"They shot him. There was blood," I stammer, out of breath.

"You're late," she says coolly.

Out of nowhere, Hector knocks me to the ground. "What do you think this is? A hotel?"

I touch my cheek. I can already feel the bruise swelling. "Uh, no. For sure, a shithole."

Hector lifts his fist. Shaylee pulls him away. "Stop, he needs to paint."

* * *

As I'm washing the brushes, I look at the roofie in my pocket. Last time I didn't get to use it because of my unfortunate little episode. Maybe I'll get my chance later. I think about that vision of my doppelganger being shot and then the kid with spray paint being shot as well. I watch the red paint going down the drain. It's somewhat purplish. The smallest brush falls. *Scheisse.* It went straight down the drain.

Hector speaks to Shaylee about something in her unfortunate language. They must be having some sort of argument, though I can't really tell because everything in their language sounds like yelling to me. I hear the front door slam. Hector might have gone for a walk. I try to pick up the end of the paintbrush through the drain but I can't grasp it. Hector will punch me again if he comes back and finds out that in addition to coming in late, I lost one of his brushes. It's one headache he doesn't need, and another bruise I don't want.

Okay, Addie. You've done this before. I think about that time Pauline's mass of hair clogged the bathroom sink drain. It had only occurred to me afterwards that the bleached blond mess of fluff might have in fact been her pubic hair. Perhaps she dyes that too. That thought made me want to vomit. I had scrubbed my hands for a good forty minutes. Then, I soaked them in alcohol for another forty. For a week afterwards, I soaked them in a hydrogen peroxide bath and since I had touched everything in my room, there was no question everything had to go. The only thing that remained was my bed which I had sealed in a plastic bag. Mengela had to help me disinfect it with ozone.

I look underneath the sink. I unscrew the drain. I take the pipe off and my brush falls out. *Phew.* Then I notice that in the pipe there is something covered in a thin plastic. I pull it out.

"What do you got there?" I jump. I hit my head on the edge of the countertop. *Ouch.*

"What is that?" Shaylee looks at the plastic that I'm holding. I look at it too. Inside is what appears to be paper, maybe a small notebook. She grabs it from me.

She unwraps the notebook and sits on the couch. I follow her and sit beside her. "Gibberish?" She flips through the notebook.

I grab it. "It's German."

"You know how to read German?" she asks.

"Yes, don't you?"

She wrinkles her nose. "No, where the hell would I learn that?"

"In school, of course. It's part of the curriculum."

"Uh, no it's not."

"Yeah it is," I say but, then it occurs to me that perhaps the same standards of education aren't expected of lowlies. No doubt their language requirements are inferior.

I flip through the notebook. It looks like a diary of sorts.

"Well read it," Shaylee says.

"Okay." I start reading. The writing is faded but still legible.

"July 28, 1998: Today was the 101th time we attempted the procedure. Unlike prior attempts, this time it appears as if the egg has been successfully fertilized."

Shaylee looks at me impressed.

"It's just German." I continue reading.

"August 10, 1998: Miscarriage. Our efforts were in vain."

I flip the page. "August 13, 1998: It appears that the miscarriage may have been caused by someone trying to thwart our efforts. There has been a fire and we only have a small bit of the sample remaining as well as a birthmark. We will of course only use the purest sample and avoid the melanocytic nevus at all costs."

I continue. "July 28, 1999: Maybe it's a blessing in disguise that the fire destroyed what it did. It has allowed us to start anew. We decided to use the eggs of someone who has a higher degree of Aryan lineage and it appears as if we're making progress. Two eggs have been fertilized."

I flip through the book. She grabs my hand and flips the page back to a photo. It looks like a birthday photo except everyone is dressed up in white sheets except for a little boy. I look closer at the little boy who has a frown on his face. That boy looks oddly familiar. I flip the pages. The next page looks like the same kid. This time he's learning to ride a tricycle around a giant red symbol.

"Nazis." Shaylee wrinkles her nose.

"Nazis?"

She looks at me in astonishment. "Wow, you know German and you have no clue about German history?"

"I know a lot about German history, everything there is to know."

Shaylee laughs. "Well who do you think was responsible for World War II?

"World War II? We've only had one war."

Shaylee looks at me in astonishment.

"What? Stop looking at me like that." I wince. "What are Nazis? I can't possibly keep track of all the slang you guys use."

"Well they're kind of like you folk, only they kill people and they're hella scary. I can't believe they don't teach you that in history."

"I uh ... perhaps I was sick that day."

Shaylee grabs the book.

"Hey," she says excitedly. "This is so cool. This is like some cultural remnant. Maybe it's worth something?"

"Maybe," I say. I grab it back. I flip the page.

Now the kid is 8 years old and looks with that hairstyle, oddly a lot like me. I stare at the picture, examining the bone structure and the eyes. I flip the page. I continue reading.

"Dec 10, 2007: Our first choice is no longer. It was I who found him in the lab, dead. We got the mole and he can do no more damage.

However, we've been forced to our dismay to bring our second choice out of storage, specimen #397. I haven't let anyone know this but when the eggs were fertilized, there wasn't enough of the original sample to use for two eggs. This backup was in fact the inferior sample. The melanocytic nevus. I'm going to keep this fact to myself for if the others find out, who knows how they'll react? Maybe they will terminate this project altogether. With all the years we've invested, I'm not prepared to accept defeat."

Then there's some poetry scribbled at the bottom. I read it.

"How can a spot on the most perfect man be bad?
Rather a perfect imperfection.
Our Führer like a Sphinx rose out of shit to grandeur.
And this boy will rise up to liberate the sun."

This dude should really have taken a poetry class. Even I can tell that this poem is utter shit and I only have high school literature to show for it.

I continue reading. "Jan 6, 1995: I went to the lab to check specimen #397. For most of his life he's been sedated in a coma-like state on feeding tubes. Today is the day he'll open his eyes."

There's a picture of the boy on a table with tubes coming out of his mouth. For some reason when I look at that photo, I can imagine the room it was taken in. I can see the white ceiling with the crack in it, as vividly as if I was there. I have memories of voices talking over me. What are they saying? I can't make out what they're saying. That boy. Wait. Doesn't that boy look like me? Why does that boy look like me? Unless … he is me. I drop the book.

Shaylee picks it up. "Well come on. What? You're going to stop now?

What does it say? What does it say? Come on."

That's impossible. Maybe I'm imagining an uncanny resemblance. People do look like each other in this world. They say everyone has a doppelganger, right? That 'memory' before was probably just an overly active imagination. I am an imaginative person. Sometimes I read things and I see them like a video playing in my mind.

She places the book back into my hands, as if I'm telling her some bedtime story. Shaylee doesn't see the resemblance. Wait, but why would she? It's not like she even knew me as a kid. Beside the picture there is German handwriting that's larger than the rest, as if it's a declaration. I look at the scribble in German. I read it with confusion: *"I have absolute faith that this boy will become the Hitler we know."*

"Who's Hitler?" I say.

Then there's a picture of the boy who looks like me, this time at thirteen years of age. I haven't changed much since then. My face is the same but I'm now much taller. Again, that boy couldn't be me. It couldn't. Maybe I'm imagining it. Shaylee's eyes widen.

"What?" Shaylee laughs. "What the hell?" She grows more serious. "Is this for real?" She grabs the book. She looks from me to the book and from the book to me, her eyes narrowed. Maybe I'm not imagining it. Wait, if other people see the resemblance then ... could that boy, actually, be me? She looks from the picture to me and back.

"What. The. Fuck?"

She stands up. She looks from the picture to me and back again. "Fuck. What the fucking fuck?"

"Who's Hitler?" I ask again, my mouth dry.

"Well apparently you are."

I look at her blankly. She reaches into her pocket—and pulls out a switchblade.

"Stay the fuck away from me." She backs away from me.

I stand up. "Who's Hitler?"

"Stay the fuck away from me. We should have killed you before when we had the chance. Shit. I've never killed anyone."

"Hector," Shaylee yells.

I walk toward her. "Who the fuck is Hitler? Who the fuck is he? I'm not Hitler. I don't even know who the fuck that is, okay." I've never said fuck this much.

I look at her terrified expression. I turn around and walk toward the door.

She rushes in front of me, holding out the knife. "You're not leaving. Hitler was a monster. He killed millions of people; Jews, gypsies, what not. You'll kill us." Her eyes widen in fear, like those of a cornered animal. She locks the door.

"What? So you're going to kill me? You?"

I try to examine her expression to assess whether she has the willpower to go through with it, but the terror from before has already melted away, leaving behind nothing. A poker face. She's very hard to read.

"Listen, this guy Hitler, he must be pretty bad if you want to kill me that bad, but I'm not him, okay? I'm just a kid who wants to have a normal life, be a normal teen, get good grades. I have shitty parents. You probably have shitty parents too? Your genes come from them. Are you them?"

"My dad was a drug dealer from Chile who left us but he was no Hitler."

"Well are you a drug dealer?"

She stares at me, her jaw set stubbornly. I take a step toward her.

"Back up," she yells.

"And your mother?"

"I was raised by my aunt."

I take another step toward her. "I thought you wanted to kill me. Wouldn't that mean that you'd actually have to come close?" I take another step and another step. I walk straight up to the knife. "Well kill me."

I listen to her shallow short breaths. Slowly, I grab the knife out of her hand. She looks at me. I look at her. Her eyes widen with fear.

"I'm not going to hurt you."

I drop the knife. She looks down at the knife. With my foot, I kick it away. It slides across the room to the other side, the light glinting off its blade as it revolves to a stop.

She rushes to unlock the door. I push my way in front of her and lock the door. Her eyes widen further in terror. She runs to the back. Then I remember that there must be a back entrance as I saw Hector use it before. I run in front and jump on her, knocking her to the floor. I flip her around.

She's breathing heavily. I sit on top of her, holding her hands down. She's struggling to get free. This was kind of how I imagined our first encounter but now, I have no interest in sex. I'm more interested in knowing who the fuck Hitler is.

I speak very slowly. "I'm not going to hurt you. Stop struggling. Just tell me who the fuck this guy Hitler was, okay? Okay? That's all I ask and I'll leave you the fuck alone, okay?"

Her breathing calms down. I look into her eyes to try to assess whether she'll run if I let her go. "Deal?" I say.

She looks at me with astonishment. Confusion perhaps causes her fear to evaporate. She nods her head.

* * *

We sit on the couch. The place is a mess. The canvas is knocked over and paint is spilled on the floor. Hector could come back at any moment and if he did, he'd be pissed.

"So you're saying this Hitler was kind of like a bad guy?" I inquire.

"Kind of," Shaylee says with a voice that I think means she's being sarcastic. "I don't get how you can have no idea who he is. You speak freaking German. How can you not know?"

"Well I don't follow politics."

"This isn't something you follow. It's something you just know. Everyone knows it."

"Well I don't." I examine her expression and I can tell she's still freaked out.

"Okay I do look oddly like that boy in that photo, but it could be just a coincidence."

She grabs the book. She flips through the pages. "I never fail to notice ink."

She flips to the picture of the boy at ten years old. He has his face slightly turned to the side as if he's in some sort of school photo. She points at the boy's head, above his ear.

"A freckle?" I say.

"You're really not observant are you?"

I grab the book back. I look closer. It's then that I notice that it's not just a freckle nor is it just a mark. 3. 9. 7. The numbers 3, 9, 7 are printed in a small dot.

She takes out her compact. "Look!"

I look at myself. On me, where the "freckle" would be if it was me, is covered by my hair.

She takes out a razor from her bag. I look at the razor.

"No shaving cream?" I remark.

She hands me the razor. "Take it," she insists.

"No." I shake my head. I stand up. "Forget it. I'm not him. I'm not. I'm not him."

I back away toward the door. I notice the book on the table. I walk back to it and pick it up. Then, I back out of there.

I race home. I'm now on the street of my house. The same street that I've walked on since the age of nine. I walk down it, thinking of the times Thomas and I would kick the ball around, having fun. I remember where Father taught me how to bicycle. While most kids started with training wheels, Father thought training wheels were for sissies. He also pointed out that with them, I looked ridiculous especially since I was three years past the age where kids normally learn.

There's nothing like falling a million times and getting a thousand and one scrapes that makes you learn. And learn I did, faster than kids with training wheels though not without a broken femur bone.

As I approach my house, I notice something different. There are lanterns hung all about and music coming from inside. What's going on? I open the door.

Mother greets me. "You're late."

"Late?" I manage to get out, acting normally.

"For Pauline's engagement party, of course."

"Engagement, what? She's engaged?"

I walk inside as they cut the cake. It's pink on the outside and vanilla on the inside. This is just what I need to distract me from the whole ordeal of today. When on earth did Pauline get engaged? I look around for her. I can't seem to find her anywhere and then I see her. She's outside by the bee sanctuary. I walk outside and join her. She sticks her finger into the bee cage.

"So you're engaged, huh?" I say.

She looks up at me and brushes some hair out of her eyes. It's then that I notice her tears. Her eyes are red as if she's been crying for a while.

"Are you okay?" I inquire reluctantly.

A tear escapes and rolls down her cheek.

"You're crying," I say emptily. Why am I in this role? The last thing I want to do is have her cry on my shoulder, especially now after what I've been through today. Why did I not trust my better instincts and stay inside?

She looks up at me and forces a smile. "I'm just happy."

Phew. I turn around and leave. I sneak past everyone and go to my room. I close the door, letting out a sigh of relief. I open the book, studying the picture. People have doppelgangers in this world. I'm sure you could find two people in this world who look exactly alike, couldn't you? Everything is perfectly explainable. I touch my hairline.

The freckle.

No. I'm not going to go there. To give in to curiosity is just crazy. I'd be a crazy person to indulge such strange speculations. There's no way that boy is me in that story, which I'm sure is complete fiction. He was eight when he ... when he woke up, if that's even true. Well, if it was me I wouldn't have a memory before age eight but I clearly remember my mother in the kitchen baking apple pie.

Wait a minute, wait a minute. That's not my mother. That's June on, "Leave it to Hauser."

But I clearly remember my mother pushing me on the swing.

Wait, wait. No that was some kid on, "The Dick Van Diethelm Show". He thought he could swing to the moon.

I go into my mother's room and flip through our one album. We only have one as the rest got lost in the move. There's a picture of me as a baby. I'm in a crib and I'm smiling. Mom and Dad are looking over me.

Then there's a picture of me as a baby, crawling and nibbling on

Blondie's ear. I look closer, narrowing my eyes. Even Blondie looks different from my memory. Wait, Blondie wasn't a German shepherd. Did we have another dog?

"Looking over old pictures of your sister?" I jump. Mother rests her head against the doorway.

"Sure am," I answer. As if I'd really care that much but I'll go with it.

"You know, it's going to be a change with her getting married and all but it will be good. It's time." She sits down on my bed.

"Mom," I ask. "Who's that?" I point to the album.

She scoots over. "Oh you mean Blondie? You loved her so much."

I look up, confused. "It's weird. I remember Blondie, well … being a beagle."

Mom smiles. "No. That's silly. She was a German shepherd. You've just forgotten, I'm sure."

I'm confused. Wouldn't I remember having a dog ten times the size?

"Listen, we're all going to take a family photo. You missed most of the party. At least you can be in the photo don't you think, Maus?"

I go downstairs and take a picture with everyone. Then I notice Uncle Gerhardt by the piano, pressing a few keys. He used to drink and gamble a lot with my dad. There was a story about how one time he drank so much, he voted for a black guy for city council. Oh, I forgot to mention my uncle's color blind as well. "He wasn't black. He was purple," Uncle Gerhardt would proclaim. "So you voted for a purple guy," my father would tease. Uncle Gerhardt's likely on his fourth beer, by the looks of it. I can tell because at about his fourth, his face usually starts turning a bit red. Even if his judgement isn't always accurate, I'm sure he'd remember what kind of dog we had as it was always biting at his pant legs to take him for a walk. He'd at least remember if it was a large dog or small one.

He looks up. "Vonderful about sister's engagement, huh?"

"Hey," I say in a casual tone, "do you think Pauline would like a dog for a wedding gift? Like Blondie?"

He chugs some beer. "Oh you mean that beagle you had as boy? Perhaps ... but dogs are lot of work, almost as much as baby. You should ask—"

"Thanks." I run toward the stairs. I'm in my room. The book we found is on my bed. I take out a razor, my heart pounding in my chest. In front of the mirror, I shave that region, trying my utmost to keep my hand steady. The blade runs across my skin, removing from it the coarse strands of hair and revealing underneath—three numbers. *No.* It can't be. I look closer. In faded letters, it says, '3,9,7'. My hand is shaking badly. I cut myself. *Scheisse.* I drop the razor.

"Addie," I hear Mom yell, "Addie."

Scheisse. If they see me with my hair all messed up, they'll know something's up. I can't believe this. Who are they? Are they even my family? I look toward the door. Are we even blood-related?

"Addie. Come down stairs for dessert," Mom yells. Mom? Is that not my mother? If they see me they'll know. I need to do something.

I look around my room. On my desk is a brown crayola marker. I pick it up. I draw on hair. Now, my artistic skills have really come in handy.

I walk downstairs.

"Addie," Mom yells.

Everyone looks up from the table. I walk over and sit down in order not to draw suspicion. A piece of cake is put in front of me. I'm not hungry at all. Mom looks up from the table. If I don't eat, they'll know something's up as I never pass up cake.

I take a spoonful and shove it in my mouth. My throat is dry. It's extremely hard to swallow. I'm not the least bit hungry. My mouth feels like parchment. I start coughing and grab a beer. I hear Mother say, "Hey."

"Let him have it," Gerhardt shouts, "it's a celebration. Celebrate. Celebrate."

"I won't have my boy becoming a drunkard like his father," Mother persists.

"It's one beer." Gerhardt laughs.

I take another chug.

"Okay, fine. Just this once." She sighs.

I take the beer from the table and drink it. They all start singing a folk song. I think this one is called, "Da Unten im Thale," which translates to, "Down There in the Valley." Ten more folk songs later, everyone is tipsy and there are a lot of half empty beers lying about. I get up to clear the table.

Mother looks over. "Don't worry we hired help for that."

I smile. "It's not a problem."

As I clear up, I drink the half empty beers. One after the next. As I pick up the tenth beer, it occurs to me that such behavior could lead to a cold sore, couldn't it? Then I smile. Of course not, Herpes is not an Aryan disease. That much I remember from health class. It's only lowlies that get those awful things known as cold sores.

Everyone is still singing. It's hot in here all of a sudden. So many people in such a closed space. The door is open a crack to allow for airflow. I sneak off to the open door. I open it a bit more. I look to Mother who has joined in singing with Uncle Gerhardt. She's not looking at me. Now's my chance. I sneak out.

The block is completely barren. I make my way away from the commotion. I walk down the street and then I run. I run and run and run. I'm running through the Reichfield forest now. I cut myself on something. I can't see. I keep on running. Where am I running to? And then I know. *Shaylee.*

CHAPTER 10

I swing open the door.

"Shaylee," I yell.

I look around. Shaylee isn't here. Why would she still be here? What was I thinking? Of course she wouldn't. Why would she be here? It's like 4am. I walk inside and I sit down on the couch. I take the Rohypnol out of my pocket. I look at it.

I just want to forget. I just want things to go back to the way they were. I'm enticed to take the Rohypnol myself, my fingers itching in temptation. I listen. Silence. At least Hector's not here. But, Shaylee isn't as well.

"Why aren't you here?" I yell.

Why do I want her to be here this bad? Is she my friend? *No. Of course not.* Of course she's not my friend. She's a fucking flip. I … I just want someone to talk to. I want someone to tell. She's the only one who knows.

She knows stuff. She knows about me. That's it. She just knows. If it was anyone else who knew too, I'd want to talk to them. That's the only reason.

She's not my friend.

"Where the hell are you Shaylee?" I throw the Rohypnol down on the ground and stomp on it. I look down at the white powder. Maybe I shouldn't have done that.

Beside it is a paintbrush. I pick up the paintbrush desperately, as if I'm drowning and it's a lifejacket. I look around. There are no canvases. Hector was supposed to bring some new ones last time. Guess he forgot. I look around for something to paint on. An old chewed up baseball. A broom. Yeah, I could paint it for some witch theme park … or not. Some aerosol spray. Will they explode when painted? Hey … that might be fun. Then I see it. There's a large piece of wood on the back window, about sixty centimeters wide and fifty centimeters long. I remove it. Plastic still blocks the view so people can't really see in. I doubt Hector will notice.

I remove it and set it down, on the easel. Yes, this will work. I look at the blank wood. It's perfectly uniform. Nature's perfection. Somehow it annoys me. It makes it seem as everything is perfect. It is not. Everything is not perfect at all. I take the red paint and I sweep it across while letting out a giant sigh of frustration. I dip another brush in the black. I sweep it across again.

"Fuck it."

I don't care if I'm perfect anymore. Hey, I said fuck? A good Aryan boy doesn't swear. He must be perfect. Perfect? I should be perfect? Do I even care anymore? Who am I perfect for? For the people who engineered me to think the way I do? How do I even know what to think? I only think what they feed me, like some robot who has no will of its own. They have the power. Everything I do is because of them.

Yeah okay, I don't exactly think it's such a bad thing for that man Hitler to wipe out the inferior members of society, the elderly and the weak. It's fucking admirable. Wiping out sweet little old ladies and cripples with a heart of gold and gang members … well, maybe that's okay too. That's how society becomes stronger and not a cesspool like this shitty place but … I'm just a fucking machine that they created. Who am I to think I can even do. Any. Fucking. Thing. Original.

Am I inferior? Am I fucking inferior? A fucking inferior clone, a copy? Wow, I really am saying "fuck" a lot or rather thinking it. I take more paint and sweep it across the wood.

They've destroyed any career I might have had as an artist, not that I really wanted to be an artist as my main profession, or did I? Okay, it was always in the back of my mind. If I wanted to be an artist, being their product, anything I create, well, is their fucking product.

I. Own. Nothing.

I don't even own my hands. I look at them. *3. 9. 7. 3 fucking 9 7 397 397 397 397 Fuck them.*

I take my hand and smear it on the board. I look at my thumbprint. Nothing. Unique. Nothing. I make a saliva ball of spit. I spit on it. I look at my painting. I kick it, forgetting it's a board.

"Scheisse."

My toe. My toe. My toe. I jump around. Sunlight is now coming through the cracks in the window.

"What the fuck?" I hear.

I look toward the door to see Shaylee standing there.

"What the fuck?" She walks in. She looks at me jumping about. She walks to the wall and unplugs her phone charger. Then she notices the painted board lying on the floor. She looks from me to the board.

"Everything is a lie," I proclaim. I burst into tears. She looks at me, not knowing what to make of my crying. I don't think she's ever seen a boy cry before. I wipe my tears. Now I'm angry. She saw me cry. I'm angry at myself. Who the fuck am I? Am I a fucking boy who cries? A fucking baby?

Slowly, as if in a trance, she walks to the block of wood.

"It's shit," I say.

She picks it up. She picks up the knocked over easel and puts the wood slab on the easel. She backs away from it.

Snot is running down my nose. I wipe it away with my hand. My nostrils are now red and inflamed. She examines the painting, the flesh between her eyebrows crinkle in concentration. I can't understand why. Maybe she wants to rejoice in my failure.

"Hey," she says. A smile forms on her face. "It's—"

My voice is hoarse. "Terrible, I know."

She looks at it some more. "It's … genius."

"Ha. Quit mocking me. You can kill me now." I pick up the knife and hand it to her. "My art sucks."

She looks at the knife and laughs. "I'm not going to kill you. You've proven, well … that you're in fact … not him. You're not Hitler. Everyone knows Hitler was shit at art but you're not. You created this."

I look at her confused.

"You're not him." She iterates her words in a monotone voice, as if their contents are a fact, without a need to convince anyone.

"Get it?" She smiles, and for one shining moment, I believe her.

$$* \quad * \quad *$$

I expected Hector to laugh Shaylee out of the room but for the last ten minutes he's been talking about well … nonsense. Reminds me a bit of Helene, though minus the butchness.

He's trying to interpret my work and find meaning where there's none. There's no meaning. Doesn't he get it? There's nothing. I'm a clone. No soul. No meaning. My work is about as original as a xeroxed copy.

"I totally get where you're going with that. You're exploring the deconstruction of …" *Blah. Blah. Blah.*

He points to the canvas. "Here, you've channelled Duchamp."

"Hector," Shaylee asks. "How much do you think we could get for this?"

"Well … ummm that's the thing, he's a nobody. It's a great painting, for shizzle. But it's not like it's going to go anywhere. We could uhhh … hang it up on the wall. Like over there." He points to the area next to the window where I took the slab from.

"See." I stand up. "It's nothing."

"Shut up." Shaylee stands up as well. "It's fucking great. Hector, why does all our work have to be counterfeits? What if we started selling real stuff? Like go legitimate or something?"

"What are you saying?"

"Well like I could make stuff, you could make stuff ..."

Hector pipes in, "... and we could have an art show."

"Exactly." Shaylee's face lights up in a smile.

Hector laughs. "Are you fucking serious? We sell counterfeits, that's it. They pay the bills. We're not having a fucking craft fair and get what? Like fifty freaking cents?"

Shaylee puts her hands on her hips, her face determined. "But you said you like it."

"I do like it. It can go on the wall, like I said. But we're not in the business of art. We're in the business of counterfeits, got it? Now get back to work. Seriously. It's nice and all. Great for decor. Saves us time at having to shop at Reichfield Furniture Depot." Hector shakes his head as he walks out. "Shaylee, make sure this *artiste* shits out some counterfeits, that's your job."

Shaylee yells, "You don't have to remind me. I want a new phone."

He leaves. There's silence.

I look up at her. "See?"

"Well I think it's great." She looks at me. "Hey," she says, "if people knew your backstory it would for sure sell."

I smile. "Backstory. Hmmm ... my bio? A clone of some dude named Hitler who plays a shitty game of soccer?"

Shaylee rubs her chin. "Uh, you're right people would for sure never buy that …" Suddenly, she grins, her eyes narrowing mischievously. "But they would believe the shitty part."

"Ha." I look up at her, grinning back. "I am Hitler you know?" I show her the freckle.

She looks at me with an expression I can't quite read. I walk over to the knife, pick it up and hand it to her. She takes the knife and flings it into the wall. Wow, that girl got skillz. *Oh no.* I'm picking up some of their lowly lingo.

"For the last time, I'm not going to kill you."

"But I'm a monster."

She turns to face me. "Kiss me."

I let out a laugh. "Uh, excuse me?" She can't be serious.

"I'm serious." She looks into my eyes.

"Morning breath, I have morning breath," I stammer.

"I don't care," she says. "Hitler would in no way ever, kiss me. Prove you're not him."

"But uh, well I haven't flossed and I thought I proved that with that um … painting," I protest.

She puckers her lips and leans toward me.

"I'm not going to kiss you." My nose wrinkles. I put my hand over her face and push her away.

"Why?" she says.

I wince. "Because it's disgusting. You're a—"

"I'm a what?"

"You're a... you're a player from the opposite team and that's disloyal."

I get up and back out of there. "Bye, I'll see you later. I'm going to be late for class."

She smiles. "Weirdo."

CHAPTER 11

As we train at practice, every time I think about kissing Shaylee I want to punch something. I look up for a second. Coach looks astonished. I'm actually doing amazing today. Maybe it's the anger. Kiss her? Me, an Aryan boy kissing a flip? Is she serious? It's so insulting. How ever would she think that I'd sink so low?

Okay. The sex part. I was going to have sex with her but in my defense she was going to be unconscious. Kissing is different. Kissing implies love or at the very least like.

I keep on having to remind myself, Addie, she in no way is your friend. She's some flip who is bullying me into making counterfeits for her, that's all. She's not even that hot. I picture her running on the field. Her small and perfectly shaped A-cup breasts bouncing. Her ponytail flipping from side to side. Her angular chin. Rain beating down on her face and her shirt. A smile as she kicks the ball into our net. Shaylee looking at us, defiant. Full glory and all.

No. Stop it. Stop thinking about her. She's a flip.

She's a flip.

She's a flip.

She's a fucking flip.

Why am I suddenly saying fuck so much?

Coach blows the whistle. Thomas comes up to me. I notice an irritation near his mouth.

"Is that a cold sore?" I ask.

"Are you serious? Herpes is not an Aryan disease."

Thomas puts his hands on my shoulder. "Addie we might have a chance now of winning this thing," he beams.

"What are you talking about?"

Thomas smiles at me, confidently. His smile reminds me of the time when we were kids and father thought Thomas was some sort of prodigy. Thomas was extremely annoying. He talked exactly like my dad who was from a different generation.

"Horsefeathers," Thomas would say when he didn't believe something. "It's the bee's knees," he'd say as he bit into some of my dad's black licorice.

Part of me wonders if he's still annoying and if I'm just immune to it now. Sometimes I think, why am I even friends with this flachwichser? Then at other times, for some odd reason, I think that he's the only person I want to see.

"You could be our soccer champion with the way you're playing. We could take them together, Addie."

I let out a laugh. "Are you serious? Me, a champion?"

"Yeah, someone's gotta be it, so why not you?"

He looks at me strangely, as if he can see my potential—and I'm flooded with suspicion He's never seen my potential before. Why is he suddenly looking at me like I'm a leader or something? Wait. Does he know?

Could he? Who's in on it? Are they all in on it?

Is he even my friend? Do I have friends? Have I ever even had a friend? Why am I thinking like a freaking girl? She's rubbing off on me. Stop it, Addie. Stop it. You're a man. You don't care about friends. The only thing that matters is soccer and destroying the competition, not art and definitely not Shaylee.

You're only friends with her for one reason. To take down the competition, that's it. You're going to find out what makes her great and destroy her. In the back of my mind, there's a thought. I try to push it down but I can't.

Doesn't it change things now, knowing what you know?

What if everything is a lie? Why does soccer even matter anymore? I'm just a cog in the system. A machine to do exactly what they want.

* * *

I get back my art assignment and it has an F written on it. F?! Are you serious? How can my art get an F?

"Fuck," I yell. F is for Fuck.

Everyone turns to look at me and then I remember, Addie doesn't swear. I must be Addie or I'll draw suspicion. Who's Addie? Addie is someone who doesn't swear, someone who lives by Aryan rules. When Addie gets angry he stands on a desk and yells, but he doesn't swear. Never. Addie would never swear. If I'm not careful, I'll mess up for sure. I don't want them knowing that I know. As long as my discovery remains a secret, I have that advantage.

The shocked Aryan faces of my classmates are still staring at me, their mouths opened comically. I get up on my desk and yell in German, leaving out curse words of course, because authentic Germans don't swear. At least not in public.

*　*　*

On my way to Shaylee's, it occurs to me that even my thoughts aren't my own. If they aren't mine, whose are they? This dude named Hitler's? This society's? Hitler for sure wouldn't kiss Shaylee. He'd rather burn off his lips first or freeze them with liquid nitrogen. When I arrive, I find Shaylee painting on a hat with gold acrylics.

"Are you going to wear that?" I ask pointedly.

She looks up. "Maybe."

Business is going so well that Hector has been coming in later and later. Shaylee says he's drinking with his buddies or doing motorcycle tricks or both, not that I care. I'm just glad he's gone.

It's important he's gone for me to do what I'm about to do. I stand beside her. My palms are clammy. I'm going to do this. It's not like she's Ava. What does it matter if I screw up? Without thinking, I pull her toward me and try to kiss her, as I've seen on the silver screen. I barely make it to her lips when she takes a quick step back, yanking her head away. Even in a moment of acute rejection, I'm impressed with her extremely fast reflexes.

"What the fuck? What are you doing?" she yells.

"Proving to you that I'm not Hitler."

She looks at me and smiles. She takes a step closer. We're now an inch apart. She touches my cheek and looks into my eyes. Suddenly, there's a loud crash. She pulls away. We turn our heads toward the window. We rush to it and look out. Thomas is laying on the grass.

"Thomas?" I yell with surprise.

"You know him?" She looks at me with confusion. I run outside.

"Thomas," I yell.

Thomas gets up. "What's going on Addie?"

"I can explain." I walk toward him.

"Stay back," he yells, "I don't know you."

Thomas hurries off to his car. I run up in front of him, blocking him off.

"Addie, what the hell are you doing? You've gone completely mad." Thomas reaches for the keys in his pocket. He pulls them out. Flustered, he drops them. I reach down to help him. He slaps my hand away. "Don't freaking touch me."

"Thomas. Listen. It's not what you think."

Thomas glares at me. He gets into his car.

I run up to his car and put my hands on the window. "Just let me in, I can explain."

I hear the doors lock. The engine starts. The car pulls out. Thomas's tires screech. He nearly runs me over as he speeds off.

CHAPTER 12

All night I worry about Thomas telling everyone what I did. Nobody will ever look at me the same. I'll probably be kicked off the soccer team or worse … bullied off. Ava will for sure hate me. This really screws everything up. Now, no more art. I won't be able to make or sell any of my paintings. Okay, even though they're imitations of someone else's, it still gives me some satisfaction. And Shaylee … it's not like she's my friend or anything. Of course not. But she knows my secret. She's the only one who knows. And that, well, it means something.

What's my backup plan? *Come on Addie. Think.* What if I told everyone that she drugged me? Hey, I have the Rohypnol. No. That won't work. They could test my urine. They'd find it negative for everything. Then, they'd know for sure that I was lying. Then again, they might take my word for it and not test me. Also, it wouldn't hurt to take the Rohypnol as a sleeping pill. I am having difficulty sleeping. I go to my dresser drawer and take it out. I pop it in my mouth and chew.

Wait, if I tell everyone that Shaylee drugged me, well, she won't want to see me again, now will she? Maybe they'd even kill her? Would they do that? Well, we did put their former captain in the hospital, but murder goes beyond what we do, doesn't it? I think of the police officers shooting the boy beside my painting and his graffiti. Well, they must have shot him for doing something more than graffiti, of course. They wouldn't shoot him just for graffiti, would they? No, that's crazy. He was a ruffian. So what if he looked twelve? A verbrecher can be twelve. Twelve year olds can rob liquor stores.

No more Shaylee. It hits me. I slump down on my bed. What's wrong with me? Why am I thinking about her so much? Why do I care? It's Ava who should be on my mind constantly. She's what every guy should want. I close my mind and try to picture Ava naked, as if that will distract me. My mind returns to Shaylee. No. I can't stop seeing Shaylee. I have to see her. I need to see her. She's the only one who understands, who sees me for more than me. Suddenly, disgust overtakes me when I think about how much of a monster I was for ever even contemplating drugging her. I would never even think of doing that to an Aryan girl. How could I have reduced her to nothing? She's the only one who gets it, who makes me feel like I can be anybody, even someone different from what I was raised to be. My body feels heavy, as if all the energy, as if the very blood in my veins is draining out of it. Why do I feel so tired?

And then I remember the Rohypnol. *Scheisse.*

I fall to the floor.

*   *   *

Moments before I arrive at school the next day, I'm pretty sure that Thomas has told everybody. However, when I arrive, everything is completely normal. Nobody is giving me looks even with the bruise on my forehead. Perhaps they think it's from soccer rather than collapsing on the floor.

"What?" a boy in 7th grade says as he passes me. It's then that I realize that I'm the one giving people weird looks.

Does nobody know? Why didn't Thomas tell anyone? And then I remember the bottle of DI-X that fell out of his pocket that time we were playing soccer. Thomas was supposed to stop taking it after they found out the adverse side effects. One of the side effects includes body-wasting syndrome, down the line. He made me promise not to tell and I obliged. Ha. I have something on him. There's no way he'd tell on me. I could get him and his father in serious trouble. I smile.

I catch up to Thomas in the locker room at break. "We need to talk," I say and pull him aside.

Thomas quickly removes my hand from his shoulder and brushes off his jacket.

"Listen, I have a plan—"

"What? To get an STD? To get contaminated with non-Aryan DNA?"

They taught us in Biology of the White Race that it's possible for DNA to transfer during the act of intercourse and possibly even kissing, which is why it's important to choose a partner of the highest calibre. Shaylee was very close to me. As she spoke, saliva particles could have travelled into my mouth. Worry washes over my face. Then I remind myself what I learned in basic science, that Aryan DNA is stronger than non-Aryan DNA. So Aryan DNA would for sure win in the DNA war, wouldn't it?

"Thomas. We didn't kiss."

"Well it sure looked like you were going—"

"I know how it looked but I have a plan. A plan that's greater than what you saw. A plan to bring that flip down."

Thomas shakes his head, his face crumpled in a mixture of skepticism and disgust. "By kissing it?"

Okay. I didn't think so far. There's silence. Crap. I have to fill this silence. The fact that he didn't tell anyone means that I can rectify things, right? *Think of something, Addie. Think.* And then it occurs to me.

"Thomas, Thomas. A woman is all heart, right?"

Thomas takes a step back. "I wouldn't call that thing a woman."

"Just go with me, okay?"

He looks away, but then looks back toward me.

I continue, "Listen. Just listen. Sure, you can beat someone up. But, to really destroy someone, you have to get to their heart." I gesture to my heart, pleased that I managed to incorporate a gesture. According to a book on persuasion that I read, people believe you more when you use gestures.

"And that's what I'm doing, okay? I'm going to make that bitch fall in love with me."

His face is frozen in confusion. I can't tell what's going on in his head. Then, he turns abruptly and walks away.

I yell after him. "If we're going to win this season, it's not enough to simply beat that chick up. Who knows? Maybe they'll replace her with someone better? What if they replace their whole team with hybrid Filipino-Chilean, devil-worshipping, voodoo-wielding scum?"

He stops. His arm lifts. He rubs his chin. Am I getting through to him? He turns around and walks back toward me. "You're saying this is all an act?"

I smile. "Of freaking course. I had to take my mom's anti-nausea medication so I wouldn't vomit when we kiss."

His nose crinkles in disgust.

"However, we didn't kiss. I didn't get that far. You interrupted us. It's good you did because one more second and I would have vomited all over the place." *Nice touch, Addie.* I congratulate myself. Is he buying it? "Next time, I'll know to take twice as much," I add.

Thomas looks at me. His expression softens. "Wow, that's terrible, Addie. Just terrible. Sorry you had to endure that."

Ava walks by with her friends. I look at them. "Seriously, in a perfect world, she would be the only gal I'd ever lock lips with." I use Thomas's lingo to build rapport. I continue, "Sometimes you have to do things that disgust you for the greater good." I raise my hand in the air, high in front of me as if raising it to a higher power, a higher cause. "For Reichfield."

He copies me by raising his hand straight ahead in front of him. "For Reichfield," he echoes. He puts his hand down. His nose crinkles. "Gosh Addie. What a great man must endure for success."

*　*　*

After practice, I walk into the locker room and see students huddled in a circle and whispering. I walk up to Karl and Heinrich and look over their shoulders. There's a circular vat.

"So how do we do it?" Karl asks.

Thomas looks on his phone. "You think it would come with an instruction manual?"

"What's that?" I ask, peering over.

"Just a present," Thomas adds from behind me. I jump. He pulls me aside. "Good news. Thought of a plan that will mean you won't have to tongue kiss with that flip after all."

"Plan?" I walk back to the vat and attempt to open it.

Thomas slaps my hand away. "You want your hand to fall off?"

"Thomas, what's in there?" I look at him.

"Just a present." Thomas smiles.

"Liquid nitrogen?"

"Ooh, that would have been brilliant," Thomas beams.

"Nerve gas?"

Thomas smiles. "Patience. It's a surprise. You like surprises, don't you Addie?"

"Thomas."

"It's a gas Addie but you'll just have to wait to see which one." He laughs. "Get it, a gas?"

"Thomas," I say, trying to control my voice. "Listen, I thought we agreed.".

His eyes narrow. "You really want to tongue kiss with that flip, don't you? You want to grab her charlies? You want to caress her casserole?"

"What, caress a casserole?" I laugh, but even to my own ears, my voice sounds hollow. "No. I want to eat a casserole, maybe."

"So you admit it?"

"What? No."

The other students look at me. I pull Thomas aside. "Listen, what I want is to defeat them. If you kill them, we can't exactly do that now, can we?"

Thomas rubs his chin. He looks toward the nerve gas. "Oh come on, it will be jolly fun."

Suddenly, I have a strong urge to do what I did when I was ten which was shove a wooden stick up his ass. Almost forgot. Blondie had bit Thomas and Dad shot her to protect me. I remember it now. I guess I had blocked that incident from my memory, being that it was extremely traumatic. I had been so upset. It was Thomas's fault. If he hadn't taunted her ... I hated him. Oh how I hated him. One night I had gotten my revenge by dosing him on the painkillers Pauline had received for the removal of a rotten tooth. Strange he has absolutely no recollection. Yet, funny that I could have forgotten that. It was quite amusing watching him try to sit on the stool the next morning and eat his pancakes, in those rifle-patterned pajamas that he always wore.

"Jolly fun," Thomas beams.

I smile with frustration. "What about defeating them, smearing their blood across the field? Wouldn't that be fun too?" I say, hoping to get through to him somehow.

Thomas rubs his chin again. I notice that he's growing a bit of a goatee but not a real goatee. More like stray pubes. I feel like ripping out those gingie pubes with my bare hands. It's almost as aggravating as Helene's chin hair.

"Wouldn't that be fun, Thomas? Wouldn't it?" I ask, trying not to sound too eager. "Defeating them?"

His eyes light up. I think I'm finally getting through to him.

"Well," he begins slowly, "this is funner. Seriously, Addie. Imagine their faces after the game. They'll cheer. Then they'll get on their stupid bus and then boom. They'll choke and all be dead." Thomas drops to the floor imitating choking and asphyxiation. The other boys laugh.

"Thomas," I yell. Wow, that's the first time I've actually yelled like that, with such a deep tone. Strong but stern. I sound authoritative. He stops rolling around on the ground. He looks up at me, his voice silenced, his eyes in awe. I can feel the power surging through my fingertips. "Thomas, we're not going to do that."

Thomas or the other players might very well think I'm this guy Hitler. If they do, maybe they'll listen to me? "We're not going to do that because it will be more fun guys, won't it? To torture them first?" I look to the other players for support.

The other players stare back at me. *Will they stop? Will they listen? Scheisse, if this doesn't work, I don't know what will.*

"Okay," says Karl or Heinrich. Always confuse the two as they are both the size of whales.

"Let's torture them first like Addie says," yells Mengela.

"Addie, we should just kill them." Thomas stomps his feet. "Then we can focus on our studies and get into like, I don't know, Harvard?"

I shake my head.

"Addie, come on, you're making a mistake," Thomas protests.

"Really?" I look at Thomas. "Am I? Well the other players don't think so."

Thomas looks from me to the other players. I can sense his disappointment. "Fine," Thomas utters. He stomps off.

"Put the vat somewhere where he can't find it," I say to Heinrich or Karl. Fortunately, the other fat one comes over and now it's safe to say both of their names. "Thanks Karl. Thanks Heinrich," I add.

The fat kids pick up the container. I feel like I'm in "Alice in Wonderland" with Tweedledee and Tweedledum carrying dangerous chemicals that can leak out at any time and kill us.

"Where should we put it?" They ask in unison.

I look at them coolly, completely in control.

CHAPTER 13

I watch Ava as she swims in our "olympic-sized" pool. I used to think it was impressive until we visited North Prep. With the amount of funding they receive from the government, it made ours look like a dinky blow-up pool in someone's backyard.

Ava pushes herself out of the water, taking in one large gasp of air.

I smile at her. "Hey."

"Oh hey, Addie," she says apathetically. She takes in a large breath.

"Ava," I yell. Too late. She goes back under.

She does another lap. She comes back and takes a big breath of air.

"Ava," I yell.

She's about to go under but stops. "What?"

"So what are you doing later?"

A crease appears between her eyebrows. "Addie, I'm sick of this."

"It's just... umm, I need a ride."

"Oh, so that's it?" She says with one side of her mouth raising.

"And I really like spending time with you," I add with mock-sincerity.

"My friends say you're using me. Are you using me, Addie?"

"No."

She looks at me.

I hold her eye contact. "But so um, could you—"

"Could I what? Chauffeur you somewhere?" she yells.

"Well, uh, the thing is, I've been meaning to get my license—"

"Not my problem." Ava jumps up and is about to go under.

"Ava," I yell. "I really like spending time with you. It's just I also like to multitask."

Ava smiles. "Well so do I, just without the task of being your bitch." She dives into the pool and swims away from me.

As annoyed as I am that her newfound sense of independence is an inconvenience, I'm somewhat impressed.

*　　*　　*

Hector decides to treat us out for ice cream today as we sold five forgeries for "a killing" and Shaylee won the game. Again. This is the first time I'm celebrating with the winner from the opposite team. If someone sees me here, I'm dead. Then again, who from Upper Reichfield comes to this part of town, anyway?

I feel like such a traitor. I have to remind myself that it is Reichfield who betrayed me, not the other way around. They manipulated me. They exploited me, making me their little science experiment and historical harlot. We'll just pluck this boy out of history, take his genome, gear him up like an atomic bomb, not once asking if he minded. Do I mind? I didn't ask to be born. I didn't ask to be used. I didn't ask to be exploited. They want to cleanse their society of filth? Call a garbage man. I keep on having to remind myself that what I once considered filthy and disgusting, may not in fact be so. I look at Shaylee. Some chocolate ice cream falls on her lap.

She looks down. "Shit." She dabs at it with the stiff napkin.

Hector sits across from us, playing some game on his phone. It looks like high action. I'm still amazed at the technology lowlies possess. On our phones, we can play solitaire.

"Shaylee," a girl yells from across the picnic tables.

Shaylee looks up. "Oh, hey Yvonne."

Yvonne. That girl from the bus. She walks over to us.

"Hey Parce, who's this?" Yvonne looks me up and down as if sizing me up. At first I'm offended that this chick doesn't remember me. Then I remember that in her defense, I was wearing the mascot head.

"Oh, this is Addie," Shaylee answers.

"Strange name. What happened to him?" Yvonne looks at my drenched shirt.

"Yeah, what happened to you?"

"Had to run, remember? My ride, well, it didn't work. Was going to be late and stuff."

Yvonne looks at me confused.

"I ran," I repeat.

Yvonne blinks. "Oh, right."

"If the boy's late, I punch him." Hector laughs.

Shaylee and Yvonne share a smile with an expression that reads, "I can't believe he said that."

"Gotta run. My grandma needs me to do some cleaning around the house. So let's catch up later, Shay." Yvonne gives Shaylee a hug and then leaves, but not before glaring at me. A glare that warns, "hurt my friend and you're dead". I feel like this girl would definitely have given me problems had I used the Rohypnol on you know who. Good thing I dodged that bullet. Sometimes things don't work out, but other things do. For example, I'm sitting here eating this wonderful ice cream cone. Cone tastes a bit stale-dated, though.

"Raisins, are you serious?" Shaylee laughs at my ice cream.

"It's killer," I say, trying to mimic her lingo.

My flavor is called Spanish Siesta. I had never heard of such a flavor and was in the mood to try something atypical to prove once again that I am not a product of my genes. It feels good. Hitler would never have ordered this.

A cool breeze touches my neck. I was hot a second ago and now I'm feeling cold but this ice cream is too good. Why don't we get these types of flavors in Upper Reichfield? I take another lick.

A tanned player from Shaylee's team comes over dressed in his soccer uniform. His thick neck protrudes from his v-neck jersey and appears to be as large as his head. He's wearing a headband to keep his greasy, shoulder length, brown hair off his face. On a guy who wasn't as buff, the headband would look girly, but with is broad build, he manages to almost pull it off. The red and white dotted mittens however, he cannot.

A dog barks. I look down and see a pitbull in a sports jersey and a baseball hat growling up at me. I jump back.

Cayan looks at me and wrinkles his nose. "Stinky." He pulls the leash. The dog moves closer to him.

Wait. Did he call me stinky? I hate this guy already. No doubt his dog smells worse than I do. Wait, no that's not entirely accurate. Judging by the looks of it, the dog is way more pampered than him. It's thus reasonable to assume Cayan smells worse than his dog on a regular basis. I doubt he even flosses. I, on the other hand, only smell bad because I had to run five miles in order to be on time.

"Who's the bag of B.O.?"

"Just a friend Cayan—"

"Just a friend." Cayan repeats, smiling. He reaches out and hugs Shaylee in a headlock that looks somewhat aggressive but at the same time oddly sexual. For a second, I feel a pang of resentment, of uneasiness. *You're not jealous, Addie. You're not.*

Why this dude's still wearing his soccer uniform is beyond me. It's Tuesday. Thomas and I know full well their soccer schedule. It's Mondays, Wednesdays, Thursdays and Fridays. Tuesday they have some weird meditative shit. We had to learn this because we had to plot a time that would work for both of us to poison their former captain. Cayan must sleep in his soccer briefs. Either that or they're his permanent underwear that he never takes off.

"Hey Rendos." Shaylee pats the pitbull. I'm guessing Rendos is his name.

A few girls come over, smiling in a sickly-sweet manner. "Oooh can we take a picture?" a slender girl in an oversized sweatshirt with long brown curls asks.

"Sure." Cayan holds up his pitbull.

Her friend snaps the photo. I'm not sure what's going on.

"Rendos is famous," Shaylee says to me.

"Famous?"

"Yeah, Instamatic."

"Insta-what?"

"Can he sign it too?" The girl holds out her phone, showing him what I'm guessing is the picture she just took.

"Ugh, he can't really write," Cayan says.

"Why not?"

"Well, he's a dog." Cayan thinks to himself. "I know."

He takes the girl's phone. Then he takes Rendos's paw and holds it up. He takes a picture. Then, he fiddles with the phone in some graphics program. He hands the phone back to the girl. The paw print is now superimposed on the picture.

The girl's face lights up. "Wow, thanks."

"No prob."

Rendos's fans leave.

Cayan reaches into his bag. He takes out his phone. "Look what I got." He places it in front of Shaylee. He reaches down to pet his mutt. "You hear that? I can make you look even better in pics, Rendos."

Shaylee grabs his phone and examines it. It's even more high tech than the futuristic phone that Shaylee gave me. What secret technology do the lowlies possess? No doubt they stole it from our top German scientists before they released it. All technological advances come from us. The only problem is lowlies and other inferior kind have used their witchcraft to hijack our biological superiority. They do this through mind reading. This often leads to them releasing tech before we do. No wonder Werner, our top scientist, couldn't predict the trajectory of their soccer balls.

I have a flash of Shaylee laughing at me in her car, "Witchcraft? No, you guys just suck." Wait … if I was lied to about my DNA, could I have been lied to about the superiority of our tech? I mean, no doubt there are top German scientists. There statistically would be top scientists in any given population. However, what if there were top scientists from other cultures as well? I feel like my brain is going to burst. *Other cultures?* My inner voice yells, *Addie, wake up. There's only one culture, the German culture.* How can I be thinking like this?

Cayan holds up Rendos's paw. "Hey Shay, that signing thing. It could become really marketable you know." He kisses his pitbull. "You hear that Rendos, you could be big biz for me, even more than you already are."

Shaylee hands Cayan back his phone. "Wow, how did you afford that?"

"Got some more tutoring jobs," Cayan responds.

"Tutoring." I smirk.

"Something funny?" Cayan looks at me sternly.

"No. I just might be in need of a tutor. It's providence. What do you tutor in?"

"Math," Cayan answers.

I'm shocked. I wouldn't trust this guy with counting anything other than drugs or drug money. "Did you say meth?"

Cayan's lips turn downward and his eyes narrow. "Like I said, buddy. Math."

I have to keep myself from laughing. There's no way this guy can count to three.

"You need a math tutor?"

"Maybe," I say.

"You should ask Shaylee. She's even better than me." He puts his arm around her.

She punches him in the shoulder. "Aw thanks." He pulls her close.

Now Shaylee. Okay, Shaylee I can believe. From the looks of it, she seems to excel in everything, even though I hate to admit it. But this sitzpinkler? Come on. It's not even his heritage that makes me doubt him. If he was some Aryan boy, I'd be just as doubtful. I have a sixth sense for stupidity.

I hear cheers. I turn around and see a throng of soccer players from North Prep. What's going on? This wasn't supposed to be all of them celebrating, just a private celebration of my defection. Now, I really am a traitor. Wait, if they recognize me, they might rat me out to my school. I pull down my hat. It's getting dark but fuck it. Hey, I said fuck again. *Stop it Addie.*

Cayan leaves. He comes back with five flavors of ice cream on little spoons.

"You're so adventurous babe." Shaylee grabs Cayan's ass.

It's getting really cold, all of a sudden.

Cayan sits down and plays with Shaylee's hair like a girl. I think he might braid it. I'm surprised he doesn't braid his own hair. No, he probably does. Shaylee looks into Cayan's eyes and smiles slowly.

Wait does she actually like this sitzpinkler? I watch them chat for what feels like an eternity. Suddenly, I realize what I have to do. Ice cream represents more than the dessert. It's an allegory for a real man. Real men try a lot of flavors. Real men are players. I get up. I push my way through the line of soccer players waiting their turn to order.

"Hey." A soccer player midget from North Prep sneers.

"I'd like to try that one." I point to Crème Brûlée. The girl behind the counter gives me a taste on a little pink spoon.

"... And also that one ... and that one ... and that one ..."

I come back to the table with a few spoons of ice cream after trying all eighty flavors. Okay, I only tried seventy-nine because player #78 punched me in the face. Now in addition to a sweat drenched shirt, there's a high possibility I have a black eye. I feel the capillaries in my eyelids dilating.

I sit down in an alternate reality. Am I sitting at the wrong table? I look around. No, that's Shaylee and she, for real, has her tongue in his mouth. I look at her ice cream that's dripping on the table beside her. It drips on her lap. It's then that I feel a bit nauseous. How could an Aryan boy of my caliber have sunk so low? It's then that I feel a tear escape and another tear and … *Scheisse, I'm cold.*

"Are you crying?" Shaylee looks up, from her long passionate kiss with sitzpinkler.

"Uh, no. I'm just cccc—"

"I think he's trying to say he's cold," adds Ceyan or Cayan or whatever the hell his name is.

"Cold? It's not that cold, is it Cayan?"

Why am I so cold? It's mid-fall, barely sixty degrees. Wait. Maybe, it's the sweat. Sweat cools you down. I remember the one survival day we did at Reichfield in the winter. The instructor taught us to build igloo-like shelters called Quinzees (though improved by us Germans as we added space for rocket launchers). He told us, "If you freeze you sweat." No that's not right. It was, "If you sweat, you … "

I feel myself falling over. The ice cream shop tilts and blurs as I slide off the bench onto the dirt floor and start shaking uncontrollably. Cayan gets up.

"Don't touch him, he's epileptic," Shaylee yells.

"I'm nnnnnnnot," I manage to get out.

Cayan looks at me. He looks at my drenched shirt.

"Hey, it's the sweat man. If you sweat, you freeze." He must have taken a survival course too.

Next thing I know, I'm in Shaylee's van. Cayan looks in the back at my head, nestled in the plants she refers to as ganja. The fluorescent light emits no heat at all. I feel like I'm going to die. No doubt I have hypothermia. There's a scratchy blanket around me. Then out of the corner of my eye, I notice a snail crawling toward me. The snail crawls into my ear.

"Nnnn … Nnnno … No," I whisper. I try to lift my hand to brush it away but I'm too weak. I imagine it snacking on my brains, slowly dissolving them before I get home.

Cayan looks behind at me. "Get into bed with him," he jokes.

"Yeah uh, hells no." Shaylee winces as she stops the engine. She comes around and pulls me out of her van. "He'll be fine." She pats me on the back. I stumble up the path to my house and collapse at the front door.

"He's so weird." I hear her say as she gets back into her car.

Shaylee must feel some guilt because she gets back out of her car and runs up to the door. Then she rings the doorbell before retreating back to her car. I know she really likes me under everything. I know. But then I see her pull Cayan to her and kiss him before speeding off.

* * *

My fists clench in my sleep, but I'm very much enjoying this dream. I'm making ice cream and people are screaming, literally. The giant ice cream scraper blade rotates. North Prep's soccer team run for their lives and there's a giant snail following them. Blob, blob, blob. I think this should be called, "Spanish Siesta Part Two." Raisins fall around them like snowflakes. *You should be enjoying this circus. Clowns. You can't outrun me forever.* The first to fall under the ice cream blade is Cayan. He screams.

Hugely satisfying. I almost have an erection. Then all those bastards in line get their turn. I'm laughing. The snail is laughing too. The snail survives. I wonder if I'm actually laughing in non-dreamland. I feel something against my shin. What's touching me? Something's touching me. The snail. My eyes shoot open. I throw off the covers.

No. It's Pauline's foot. She runs it up my leg, affectionately. I sit up and look over at her. I stand up quickly. I'm in my boxers. Why am I in my boxers?

I wince looking at the bare shoulders of Pauline whose freckly skin is somewhat glowy. "Are you naked?"

She wraps the sheet around her. "Not fully."

I see a snail crawling on her shoulder. Phew. At least that's out of my ear. I look at her bare shoulders again and she's for sure not wearing a bra. I feel Spanish Siesta coming up in my throat.

"You were so cold, like ice. Mom's not home."

I feel like I'm going to throw up.

"What the fu—" I mutter. I turn around looking for my clothes or my bathrobe. *I hate you Shaylee. You got me here. My life was good and now I'm, now I'm ...*

I look in the mirror. "Oh my gosh, I'm black."

∗   ∗   ∗

Hanging out with the lowlies is turning me into a negro. There's a giant freckle on my face and it wasn't there before. It just appeared. I've been marked. Now, everyone will know. Everyone. It must have been caused by my feelings for Shay— I don't even want to admit it to myself. There's no way an Aryan boy like myself could like her.

Pauline comes into the bathroom as I'm scrubbing myself with a bristly brush. My skin is red with irritation. Good. I deserve it.

"It's just a freckle," Pauline says with her hand against the doorpost. There's a slight glimmer in her eyes. She leaves. I hear her go down to the kitchen.

"It is not just a freckle," I yell. She doesn't understand the magnitude of this. If I turn negro, then I'll be the negro version of this man Hitler. Hitler's supposed to hate blacks. Oh no, I'll be stoned by the people who hate him as well as the people who gave birth to me.

And then a thought occurs to me. A thought I push out of my mind as quickly as it comes, that it would be easy if things just ended. No. Absolutely not.

Addie you're not a quitter nor are you suicidal. You're not weak like Jared. They won't find you hanging from a pole.

I look in the mirror again. Maybe Pauline's right. Maybe it is just a freckle.

* * *

Thomas touches my neck. "Are you wearing makeup?"

I slap Thomas's hand away. Pauline's powdery thing did wonders even though it's slightly the wrong shade.

Coach looks up at the heavy clouds in the sky. The dark sky makes the field look like an even brighter shade of green. She takes out her remote control and presses a button. The clear dome surrounding the field closes with a low mechanical hum. The hum of the dome is overshadowed by thunder in the distance.

"Ten push-ups," Coach yells.

Thomas does them with ease. I can only manage five and then I do the lady kind.

He looks at me. "Are you serious?"

Hypothermia really took a toll on me.

His nose crinkles. "Are you growing weak?"

"No," I insist through gritted teeth. Even so, my arms give way under my weight. I can't even do the lady kind. *Ow. Scheisse.* I feel like not enough oxygen is getting into my muscles. Maybe I'm lacking in some essential nutrient. Maybe I'm losing my Aryan lineage.

"You like her."

"Shut up."

"Fifty burpees," Coach yells.

I feel like my body is ninety, brittle and feeble. I feel like my muscles are marshmallows, light and useless. This is why technology needs to advance. I need an exoskeleton of metal; one that can do burpees like a soldier.

"You do, you're stuck on the flip. You want to make whoopee with her."

"Whoopee? Shut up."

I'm amazed that Thomas can continue to have a conversation with me while doing a gazillion burpees. It's like he's superhuman … but in a steroid taking way. Today he's wearing blue short shorts and a tight-fitted black shirt and I realize how out of proportion everything is with his body. His upper half is twice the size of his lower half. I always thought girls liked that type of thing. However, one time when we snuck into a lowly bar, just for fun, in order to laugh at the degenerates, one girl who actually could have passed for an Aryan saw him and winced.

"His head is so much smaller than his body," she said.

Then this Filipino chick started grinding really hard on his leg. The horrified expression on Thomas's face was priceless. And so, we were out of there. To each their own.

"Jumping jacks. Ninety," Coach barks.

"You li—"

I put my fingers over his mouth. "Shhmouth."

"Jumping jacks," Coach yells.

Thomas and I do jumping jacks.

"You like that mule," Thomas continues. He won't let it go.

Coach takes a phone call.

"Listen Thomas." I pull him aside. "Your paranoia is getting to me. If you must know, I was sick the other day. Why was I sick? Well I was spending time with that mule and my dick got hypothermia. If I liked her, would that happen?"

Thomas grows silent. He presses his lips together sullenly, as if he doubts my story.

"Listen, if you don't believe me, you can ask Pauline."

"Gross, you're that close with your sister?"

"No dude, listen. My other body parts got hypothermia as well. It was a whole body package, one brought on by having to fake attraction for that degenerate."

"Oh, sorry bro—"

"I don't like that I have to do this, but some things are important." I put my hand up in the air in salutation. "For Reichfield."

Thomas stands there, taking in my story. He opens his mouth. "How's your dick?"

"Defrosted," I answer.

"Good, because Ava wants to go out with you again."

"What? Really? Why?"

"She just does."

I shake my head. "We have nothing, nothing in common."

"Oh come on. That dame? She's smokin' and you know it." Thomas beams with excitement.

I definitely don't feel the same level of excitement. I could use a lift but I'm quite liking not having to pretend to like her, especially when I absolutely don't. I look at Thomas. "Well if you like her so much, why don't you go out with her?"

CHAPTER 14

I'm almost finished painting "Sunflowers" by Gottfried Schultz. The door swings open and Hector comes in. He picks up my canvas and places it aside mid-brush stroke.

"Good news boy, today's your lucky day."

Shaylee looks up from texting on the couch. No doubt she's texting with that greasy ignoramus.

"Did we sell more?" She asks.

Hector's eyes bulge. "Oh we're going to sell a lot more because a trove of new Franz Marc's were discovered."

"What?" Shaylee perks up.

"Yes, they were discovered beneath the floorboards of his studio," Hector says with jumpy enthusiasm.

"Well give me them," I say. "And I'll copy them," I add, not fully understanding why he thinks I'll find this news exciting.

"Can't."

I pause, confused. "Then how will I copy them?"

Hector points to his head.

I wince. "I'm not psychic."

"No boy, you'll create them."

"Hector, I don't understand. The paintings were found, right?" Shaylee comes over.

"They were 'found.'" He holds up two fingers to imitate quotation marks.

"Oh, 'found.'" Shaylee smiles. "I get it."

"You mean you're creating them?" I ask. I smile, skeptical, and then my smile turns into a frown. "I uh, wouldn't know where to begin."

I think of all the times Helene looked at my art disapprovingly. There would always be silence, a withheld breath, a slight breath out, a shake of the head, a hand coming up and then going down, another withheld breath, a rub of the chin, a shake of the head, a twitch of the nose and then a frown. This sequence would repeat and repeat. I'd always wait for her to say something but most of the time she wouldn't comment, she would just move on to Steinfeld. Steinfeld, the Jew she loved. Even if he painted a dot on a canvas, she would say it was brilliant or existential.

"Yes you can and you will," Hector bellows like it's life or death. My life and death.

"Hector, I paint still lifes, still lifes. Abstract art, it's not my specialty."

"Not your specialty?" Hector's eyes are doing that bulging thing again. I read somewhere that's caused by a problem with your thyroid.

"But that painting before?" Shaylee looks at it, hanging near the window.

"A fluke. I don't get what you guys see in it anyway. It takes way more work to paint something accurately."

"We have pics for that," Shaylee intercepts.

"Even if you guys are right, that my abstract mess is somehow considered high art, I can't …" I shake my head. "It was a fluke." I think of Helene saying, "What are you smiling at?" when I submitted art that I thought was great, that she returned with a G.

"A fluke?" Hector's eyes are bulging so much that I imagine it possible that one of his eyes could fall out at any moment onto the floor. He should really get his thyroid checked.

I stammer, "I was upset, emotional, drunk maybe, mad. It was a moment."

"Listen boy, you'll create the painting or your whole team will know you're a traitor, got it?"

I look down, full of worry and apprehension.

"You're going to make us rich," Hector beams.

CHAPTER 15

I sit in front of the blank canvas, staring at it vacantly, my heart sinking. Shaylee is outside with Cayan on the patio and the house is a complete mess, much more than usual as Cayan's power tools are everywhere. Two large rectangles of particle board lean against the wall and there are architectural drawings scattered about. When Shaylee asked Cayan what he was building, he told her it was some kind of puppy mansion for Rendos. I could never hate a dog, but this one I come close to hating as it looks almost identical to Cayan. It's like they transversed out of the same birth canal. The dog probably emerged first followed by Cayan dangling off his paw like some leper. Rendos you should have shook your leg, left him in there. Fortunately, Rendos nearly bit me last time he was here so Cayan stopped bringing him.

I hear Shaylee and Cayan laugh together and I cringe. Supposedly they're studying. The first thought that occured to me was, "lowlies study?" I refrained from saying that. Shaylee would have punched me. *See Addie, you're learning. You're opening your mind to the possibility that not all lowlies are stupid.* Cayan lets out a giant belch and laughs. My fists clench. My paintbrush drips a drop of blue on the floor. *Scheisse.*

Copying Franz Marc's signature style will take a lot of practice. I need to completely immerse myself in the world of Franz Marc. For the purpose of this project, my identity is fluid. I will take on the personality of Franz Marc. I glance out the window to the patio. *Is that sitzpinkler touching her leg? Addie, focus. Franz Marc, remember?*

I glance at a few paintings on a high tech computer pad device that Shaylee left beside me. The technology that lowlies possess is phenomenal. Smoke wafts through from the patio. I hear Cayan laugh. I cringe again. *Focus Addie, focus.* The painting that speaks the most to me on Shaylee's pad thing is called *Tyrol.* It's a cubist piece. We studied cubism briefly in the art history component of German Art. However, I've never actually painted in it. The jagged and sharp lines of the cubist landscape is what speaks to me the most. Tyrol is the place that I live in with my life turned upside down. *The Fate of the Animals* also speaks to me. I feel like one of those animals, lost in a cubic hell. Everything is a jagged edge and I'm the biggest one of all.

The day when Shaylee came in and saw the piece that I had painted, the only thing I produced that was my own creation, I hate to admit, was one of the best days in my teenage existence. For the first time, I felt validated as being more than just my genes. I thought I had felt validation before as a kid but it was then that I realized that I hadn't.

When Mother had praised me for winning in "Flight of the Valkyries," an RPG, she wasn't praising me, she was praising him. Him. That dude, Hitler. When I had been praised for getting an A in History and Superiority of the White Race, an interdisciplinary subject combining mixed media, she was once again praising him. One time I had drawn on a mustache so that Thomas and I would appear older. We did this in order to get into that lowly club. Dad had caught me coming in late. Yet, instead of yelling and slapping me across the head, he embraced me as if I had done something noble. For the longest time, his reaction had bewildered me. That was until I had discovered that this man Hitler, had the exact same mustache. The point is, nothing that I was ever praised for was due to me or anything I had done. It was due to my genes. It was due to who they wanted me to be.

The way Shaylee looked at me when she saw my art that day was the first time anyone had ever really seen me. Maybe that's why I like her. I stand up and push the chair away. *Shut up. Shut up, Addie. You don't like her ... Or do you?*

In the middle of my conflict and confusion, I hear her laughing outside—and within the unrestrained sound, loud and free and soothing all at once, I find my answers.

I'll paint her laughter. That's what I'll paint. I sit back down. I dip a thick brush into canary yellow. I smear it across the canvas, the brush alive, nearly tingly in my hand. Now, the canvas is not empty, like my life. My life's no longer an empty genome, an empty formula, an empty machine. Shaylee, you've seen me. You saw something in me and now you'll see something in me again and once you do, it will be me and you on that porch. The old Addie would have felt disgust at liking a lowly but this Addie is the real Addie. This Addie is not a product of his genes. This Addie can choose to like someone he'd never like even if at times it makes him want to vomit. What a great way to say verpiss dich to the powers that be in this shit town. *They think they're God. No, all they are are people who think they can control me but they can't. I control me.*

I dip into the black paint with a small square brush. This stroke will represent my inner desire to dig my own nails into my neck every time I envision Shaylee's thick muscular legs or her long black hair rippling in waves as she storms across the field like a Valkyrie. I see her eyes filled with passion, desire and hate. She hates me, I sometimes think when we collide on that field. Part of me hates me too. I hear her laugh again. I take my fingers and run them up and down against the black, smudging it. I wipe them on my face. War paint.

"You'll like me Shaylee." I dip my brush into white now and I paint strokes of light breaking through the darkness. I hear Cayan's laugh. I want to punch my fist through the canvas. I dip it in red and I punch toward it, stopping at the moment of impact. Just my knuckles touch. *Huh.* I look up, that worked. It created an interesting texture. Art is expression. I get it. Something Hitler never got, did he?

Hitler had wanted to be an artist but all he painted from what I saw was still lifes. He didn't connect to the fact that life is not still. Life is ever changing. I can change. Every moment things can change. One day you're up, the next day you're down. You can't let people push you down.

I think of soccer and all the times that I fell. All the times that we lost and let them have the upper hand. I know full well I could have the upper hand now. I know how to channel my anger. I'm not their tool. I dip my brush into black and mix it with white. Then, I add a speck of blue and a speck of red and it whirls into a reddish, purplish brown. The color of life. The color of a boy who's living and breathing more than the automated processes these so called "creators" have programmed into him.

I'm possessed now. I have a Norse song in my head. It starts, "Drøymde mik ein draum i nótt." This means, "I dreamed a dream last night of silk and fair furs." It channels through me. It's a song I heard once before. It continues, "... and in the dream I saw as though through a dirty window the whole ill-fated human race, a different fear upon each face." It's the song that I'm creating. It's my war chant. I feel it. It continues with different verses. I'm doing great up until Cayan's shit song comes on, some fast repetitive hogwash that competes with my war chant. Ughhh, I want to punch that arschloch, trying to ruin everything. He won't ruin this.

I dip my fists into orange and red this time and punch. I punch and I punch. Then, I draw slim lines with a round brush in order to mimic Franz's style. The painting has to be mostly of lines or it won't pass. I know this. By drawing lines over the circular fists, I can blend two periods of his style. *The Three Horse's* circular cubist style and the linear cubist style seen in *Tyrol*. My classical Nordic warchant will win against Cayan's fast-paced, cheap anthem. I drown it out and paint and paint. I dip my fist into paint again for one last punch. The song finishes in my head this time at its loudest. *Peace, if it is to be found, is where one is furthest from the human noise.*

"Wow," Shaylee remarks, looking at my painting. I was so entranced that I didn't even notice her come in.

I'm about to punch.

She pushes my fist back, not realizing it's my technique. "Don't, it's awesome. Isn't it awesome, Cayan?"

Cayan speaks on his phone.

"Fluke? My ass! Addie, it's really awesome." Shaylee beams. She looks down and notices paint on her hands. She goes to the sink and washes the paint off. "Addie, it's really great," she says. "Maybe your best yet."

I smile. Suddenly I'm getting more attention than Cayan.

She walks closer to the canvas and looks at it. "Addie, you're amazing. Isn't it amazing Cayan?" Shaylee turns her head toward Cayan.

Cayan puts down his phone and takes a look. "Yeah, whatevs."

"Addie, it's great." She puts her arm on my shoulder and rubs it. I feel my cheeks growing hot. Suddenly, I can't speak.

CHAPTER **16**

I think this is payback for that time I shoved a stick up Thomas's ass. I'm being anally raped by him shoving Ava up mine. How did I get on this "date"? Thomas tricked me by telling me he had a surprise. Then, when we got to the field after driving for ten minutes in his car, I was all excited. There was a horse.

"A horse," I exclaimed. He knows I love animals.

However, when I noticed Ava was sitting in the saddle, any previous excitement slid off my face. *Oh.* I'm in no need of this bullshit and why's she even here? Last time I saw her she told me she didn't want to see me. What? Is she really that desperate?

Sitting on his horse, Thomas looks down at me suspiciously. Maybe he thinks I'm gay. *Oh no.* I think again of that kid hanging from that pole. I've forgotten his name already. I can't have Thomas thinking I'm gay. I pretend to look at her breasts. Thomas notices. Good. He approves.

I get on the horse reserved for me, a light brown horse with a strip of white on his forehead. Thomas tosses me a polo stick. I catch it. He briefly explains the rules but I tune out, still annoyed with him for bringing Ava.

We play polo. As I barely paid attention to the rules and can barely focus now with my level of annoyance, I'm not really on par today with my athletic ability. Also, I can't get this horse to move in a straight line. It must sense how I want to escape. Oh how I do. *Jump the fence Horse. Jump the fence. Let's go.* I briefly consider doing that but then I realize that my phone is in Thomas's car and I need to check if Shaylee left any messages.

Ava reaches down from her horse to hit the ball with her polo stick. Thomas's horse races up beside her. She swings the polo stick sending the ball through Thomas's goal. She cheers. For a second I think, this chick reminds me of Shaylee and I'm kind of into her. Maybe, I should give her a chance? However, not even seconds later, Thomas's horse farts in Ava's hair, making it air blown. Then I think, uh no, I may be a clone of Hitler but she's a cheap knockoff of Marilyn Monroe. Horse got it right.

* * *

In Arts and Aryan Thought, I stand in front of my painting. I'm so excited that I can't contain myself. I feel like a hyper pre-teen girl. My painting is nearly identical to the painting I gave to Shaylee. My genius will finally be apparent to everyone. My stomach jumps about, which is almost like the way I feel around her. I feel like I'm radiating light. It's as if I'm a human glow stick, the kind we used last Heldengedenktag.

This is the day that I'll be recognized. Affirmation. Everyone will see that I have what it takes, that I can shine in more than just soccer. I imagine the look of disbelief on Helene's face. A thought occurs to me. What if it's too great? What if she thinks I paid someone to paint it for me? I take a breath, reassuring myself. If she thinks I paid for my masterpiece, then I can just demonstrate my skill in front of her, can't I?

Students enter, carrying their canvases. I spot Thomas's. I let out a little laugh. His painting is a still life of a soccer ball on a grassy field. I know he doesn't even like art and that he's just taking it because his dad wants him to be more well-rounded. Another laugh escapes from my mouth. I muffle it so Thomas doesn't notice. I know I shouldn't want him to fail but I'm quite happy that I'm miles ahead of him in something. In soccer, he's a far better player than me. I know it. I'm under no illusions. I've had a few flukes, that's all, but he's more consistent. If our team was somewhat capable, instead of sucking, I'm sure he'd be the star player of a winning team.

This is my arena to shine. I glance around the room at some of the artworks. There's Steinfeld's. *That Jewish bast—* Oh wait, I forgot, I'm supposed to stop myself from saying racist shit. *That Jewish bast—* Well I'm thinking it, not saying it, right? Makes it better. *Okay Addie, now you're really going to try to like this guy. You're going to go up to him and make friendly.*

I walk up to Steinfeld. "Hey," I say. I look back at Thomas who gives me a look that reads, "Have you lost your mind?"

"Hey," Steinfeld responds, in a scared tone. Perhaps, he's anticipating me doing something to him like the last time where Thomas and I had tripped him. He had fallen into a giant puddle of mud, ruining his artwork.

"Nice collage," I say. I lie. It's a mixed media collage of what looks like pictures of hair.

"Thanks," Steinfeld answers suspiciously.

"Hair?" I ask. "Your mom's?" *Oops.* That was an accident.

"Squirrel tails. I took the photos myself with my SLR."

"Squirrel tails," I mouth.

Helene comes in with her flowy skirt and citrus-mint perfume. I take a whiff. They say when you walk by shit and you smell it, a part of you is actually tasting it through inhalation. So in effect, I have tasted Helene. Suddenly, I have the strong urge to amputate my nose. I make my way back to my painting and stand by it, proud.

"Okay class, show me your stuff," she says with a toothy smile and cruel eyes. Her mouth is salivating. She's just waiting to tear someone apart. Usually that someone is me. Well today will be different, won't it? When she sees my masterpiece, she'll realize that she was wrong all along. All around the room, students stand by their canvases. I stand by mine excited to get the recognition I finally deserve.

Karl looks at mine. "Wow," he says. He gives me the thumbs up. I smile. This is going to be great.

Helene walks around the room, praising students works and then she gets to me. She stands in front of my canvas. Her nose twitches as usual but I ignore it. She walks closer to it and then walks away. I'm pretty sure she's mesmerized. I smile. This is my moment.

"Addie, it's uh, it's uh … What's the word I'm looking for?"

"Brilliant ... revolutionary?"

"It's uh—"

"Groundbreaking?"

"It needs work."

My jaw drops open.

"It seems as if you are trying to capitalize on the abstract art deco movement. It's almost as if instead of channeling the soul of a true artist, you're how do I say this Addie, without hurting your feelings ... you're trying to make something to sell at "Heimlich's Sofa Land & Decor" for fifteen dollars."

My eyebrows raise. "What?" I yell.

"Which is great," she adds, "but not like real art, you see."

"Excuse me?"

"Students what do you think?" All the students in the class come over.

"I think it has potential but—" Ruprecht says.

"I don't know it's missing something," says Mengela.

"It looks as if you're trying to copy Rembrandt," Ava says. "Sorry Addie."

Okay, Rembrandt? Rembrandt? No it does not look like that Ava. Rembrandt never painted anything abstract. Don't pretend you know anything about art. You said that just to seem smart.

"It looks like desktop wallpaper I'd have ... or maybe not. It's a bit too busy," says Werner.

"Karl," Helene continues, "What do you think?"

Good. Karl can stand up for me. He liked it. He said, "wow," after all.

"I um ... I um ... I think maybe ... it needs work."

"Karl. You just gave me the thumbs up," I exclaim.

"Yeah," Karl adds. "But what I meant was ..." Karl does the thumbs up sign. "Good try but needs work."

Thomas puts his hand on my shoulder, as if to comfort me. I shake it away.

"Now, class, let's take a look at Steinfeld's work. Isn't it superb?"

We don't respond because we of course hate him, because he's Jewish.

Helene beams looking at Steinfeld's vomit on canvas (which would be better), "Unlike Addie's, it has, how do I say this ... soul. Perseverance Addie, that's what you need. Perseverance."

Helene turns to the class. She walks up to the blackboard. She writes "Preserverence" across it. "Preserverence. They did this study with toddlers and marshmallows. A toddler was put in a room and a marshmallow was placed on a table in front of them. That toddler was told that they could have that marshmallow or wait .. and get two. What do you think happened?" She looks to the class.

Steinfeld raises his hand.

"Steinfeld."

"Most of them ate them," he answers.

"Exactly," Helene answers, "but not all. The ones that waited, well in life they rose to the top of their professions, teachers, lawyers, doctors ..."

"My dad's a doctor," Steinfeld adds.

Good for you, I think bitterly. My dad is dead.

"And artists. They became artists," Helene adds looking at me. "Perseverance," she repeats.

I smile. I imagine that word in big toy block letters, toy block letters I'd stone Helene with to death if there weren't repercussions. Perseverance, Helene. Preser-fucking-verence. No Helene. I don't lack Perseverance. I just want to create something that surprise, I actually want to put on my wall. Not a collage of freaking squirrel tails. I'm surprised he didn't use real squirrel tails. That psycho.

∗   ∗   ∗

I escape to the bathroom for a breather. Steinfeld's there taking a leak. *That fucking Jew.* I'll shove his circumcised dick up his anus, as if it would be long enough. I stand beside him as he urinates into the urinal. I unzip my pants in order not to arouse suspicion.

When will I do this shoving exactly? Should I do it mid-pee? Or wait until he finishes and wipes? Why is he urinating like a waterfall? He must have drank some serious apple juice.

Hurry up, you Jewish cocksucker. I glance over at his urinal. It's then that I notice something strange. That sitzpinkler isn't circumcised. Wait. I thought all Jews were circumcised. This makes completely no sense. They tell us in Biology 101 that the way to recognize a Jew from an Aryan, is to look for the circumcised flesh.

Then a thought occurs to me, wait … is this dude even Jewish? Is this just another ploy to manipulate me to hate Jews? Are Jews really the enemy here? Is this cocksucker part of them, the society that created me? That nose. What if he's not Jewish at all but Italian? Or what if they gave him a nose job? That honker could be some plastic prosthetic.

Steinfeld zips up his pants. I'm just standing there, mid-thought. He gives me a strange look and it's then I realize that I'm just standing there with my dick in my hands and not peeing. I guess I was lost in thought. How could I even have grabbed his dick to do the shoving up the anus part? As if I would hold two dicks in one hand like a dirty schwul.

"Verpiss Dich," I shout at Steinfeld who stands there, giving me a strange look. He flinches. It's then I realize that the swine understands me. Of course he does, he understands German as he's only faking being Jewish. No need to even translate that as "piss off" as I had been doing before for his courtesy.

Piece-of-swine is still standing there. It's then that I notice his blonde roots. He dyes his stringy hair brown. He's really Aryan. I'm right. He's not a Jew at all. I bet he's wearing brown contacts. If I punch him in the eye, could I knock one out? *Stop looking at my dick man.* I zip up my pants and suppress the urge to punch him in the face as I have better things to do. Steinfeld backs out of there as if he's expecting me to attack without first washing my hands twice with a frothy soapy lather.

Wait. If he's just an actor, do I even want to beat him up anymore? Or do I want to beat up the guys who hired him? Wouldn't it be better to shove their dicks in their mouth like one shoves an apple in a pig's?

Who created me? Was my creator my father? If he was, then why is he gone? Then I remember that Hitler's father had died when he was young. I found this out in the mini bio Shaylee showed me on wiki something. I have to ask Shaylee to show me that thing called the internet again. Is Mother faking her illness too? Perhaps she is. I sigh in relief. Why did I sigh? Why do I care? She's not really my mother. She's just a surrogate. If I met my creator, I'd ask him one thing, "Did he love me?" Can one truly love a science experiment? *C'mon Addie, are you growing soft? No.* I tell myself. *I'd ask him that and then I'd kill him.*

CHAPTER 17

"Ugh." I pick up my canvas and throw it in the trash. I must have thrown out five canvases. If I throw out one more, Hector will punch me in the face as "supplies aren't cheap."

I can't do this. I can't do anything. I can barely play soccer. In the back of my mind is a voice. *But there's one thing you can do, Addie.* I know what that is. Embrace my genes. Become him. *Shut up,* I tell myself. But the thought is still there.

"Dry spell?" I look up to see Shaylee standing over me.

"I can't do this. I'm no good."

"Are you serious? You're amazing, we've sold so many paintings because of you. Look, I got this new phone." She shows me her phone. It's even more high tech than Cayan's.

"Yeah well, they weren't mine. They were copies. I am Hitler and I suck as an artist."

Shaylee hits me on the top of my head. "Scheibenkopf."

I let out a little laugh. "Where did you learn that?"

"You're learning my language. I'm learning yours." Shaylee smiles. "Anyway, Hector liked your art and Hector doesn't like anything."

"But you're l—" I'm going to say "lowlies" but stop myself.

"We're what?"

"You're lebensmüde."

"Did you just call me a swear word?"

"Uh no. It just means you're trying something that will most likely fail … meaning me. You think there's hope for me, but there isn't."

Shaylee walks away. She brings the painting that I did the other day back. "There is hope, here."

"Really?" I say. "I brought in one just like it. If it's as good as you say, why did my entire class tell me it was shit?"

"Well maybe they're all in on it, huh? Ever consider that?"

"All of them?" I shake my head. "Do you know how crazy that sounds? Like my art teacher, Helene is some closeted white supremacist or Nazi, how you referred to them? She's the farthest thing from that, you know, from what you told me. She wears patchouli."

I look at the painting that I painted the other day, that Shaylee loved. It actually reminds me of a mix of Boccioni with Franz Marc.

"It's good," Shaylee says, "like really."

I look back at the blank canvas in front of me. "So, okay then … what do I paint today?"

She walks over to one of my discards. She picks it up. She puts it on the easel.

"This is what they want you to be." She gestures to the artwork, if it can be called that.

"A hot mess." She looks at me. "Now change it. Improve on it. Turn this hot mess into gold."

I dip my brush into crimson red. I mix it with blue to form a rich purple and then I paint. I paint until I'm satisfied. I step back.

"Not bad." Shaylee smiles.

"But not great?"

"You just need confidence. Stop looking at me for approval."

"You don't think it's great?"

"No, I like it."

"But you don't love it?"

"Let me tell you something." She pulls up a chair and sits across from me, her gaze straight and honest. "When my older cousin, who's actually more like a brother to me, was training me growing up, when one of us would get the ball in the net, do you know what we'd do?"

"Cheer."

"No, we wouldn't say anything. We just continued playing like it didn't happen."

"We get medals." I shrug. "For just about everything."

"You get medals for nothing."

Hey, I think with a flash of resentment. But then I reconsider for a second. We are a losing team, why do we get medals anyway? Players get medals for nonsense things too like "Field Presence". What the hell is that?

Shaylee continues, "Me. I'd score the craziest goals and so would my cousin and you know what, there was never any high fives. It was just back to the game. Back to the battlefield."

"Battlefield," I repeat, savouring the word, the corners of my lips slowly lifting in approval "So where is your cousin? He sounds like a great guy. I'd like to meet him."

Shaylee looks down, her shoulders suddenly limp. "He's in the hospital."

"I'm sorry, is he sick?"

"No… someone from your school poisoned him."

"What," I exclaim. "That's horrible."

"See." She stands up. "You're 100% not like them. I know it."

Poisoned? I think to myself. How terrible.

And then, with a cold jolt, I remember … it was me.

CHAPTER 18

In the pit of my stomach, I feel something I've never felt before. Guilt. But it's only because I like Shaylee. If I didn't like her, I know I'd feel absolutely nothing. I'm going to make it up to her. I'm going to do something great.

"You okay?" Thomas asks.

I nod.

I feel like I'm more in my mind today than in my body. It's then that I remember that I'm in my uniform. The game is about to begin.

The temperature of the field is lukewarm. The sky's covered with threatening grey clouds, but the air is warm with the occasional cold blast of wind. The perfect conditions for a storm. I wait on the field with anticipation. I eagerly await Shaylee's entrance, her muscular legs running as she takes her position.

And there she is. Shaylee, running onto the field. I want to cheer but I suppress myself. I'm such a traitor. A hand reaches out and grabs Shaylee's fingers. *Scheisse, It's him.* It's Cayan. Sitzpinkler. He's holding her hand like he's her freaking boyfriend. Wait, I thought he was just some fling. Something she'd forget. Could they actually be dating?

A deep sadness grows within me. Throughout most of the game I'm not myself. I can't concentrate. Thomas passes me the ball but my mind is somewhere else. Coach pulls me. I find myself sitting off to the side watching our downfall. Could they actually be dating? Thomas looks at me. It occurs to me that he must now think that my plan is not working. Their team is better than ever. I look like a failure to him too.

I watch as Shaylee scores goal after goal and then Cayan that sitzpinkler, scores one too. They kiss. *Schwein.* My fingers curl into a fist. Suddenly, I'm not sad anymore. Anger rises within me.

Two big gaudy letters, "NP," flash in like plane guide lights on the board, 3 to 0. Cayan. Who could have such bad taste? Wait, if she has such shitty taste in men, who's to say my art is even good? It's all a freaking lie. She's a freaking lie and what she has been spewing is a lie. I'm no artist. She's just messing with me. And suddenly I want to scream. No way Cayan is going to shine. I'm going to plough his sitzpinkler head into the field.

I turn to Coach, "Let me go in. We're getting crushed."

Helene frowns. "You were unfocused before—"

"I'm fine," I snap.

Helene sighs as a player kicks a ball out of bounds. The other team begins to substitute players. Coach might think I suck in art but she knows full well that aside from Thomas, I'm the only other decent player. Helene nods.

It's not just a game to me. Not anymore. Anger fuels me as gasoline fuels a war tank or stealth bomber. I can't get the thought of Shaylee kissing that arse out of my mind. Dirty swine. I'll show you. Shaylee will see that I'm way better than that sitzpinkler.

I pound down the field, ripping the ball out from underneath one of the North Prep players. Then one of their players jump out at me and I'm able to maneuver around him. Every obstacle seems to fall out of my way as I make my way to their goal. Shaylee comes up behind me but I'm able to maneuver past her. I race down the field with the ball and lob it past the goalie. Reichfield's first goal of the game, 3 - 1. My team cheers. I run back to them. For the first time I feel like a champion.

It feels good but I'm focused more on Shaylee. I look toward her. She looks as if she's taking me more seriously now. Game on. Even with the success, my fellow teammates are exhausted. They trudge their way to the center of the field at an abysmal rate, and aren't looking too good. It is up to me.

The whistle sounds and the match continues. Shaylee and I spring into action, each vying for the ball. I kick the ball to the right, spinning it with my feet above Shaylee's head. Then, I race down the field. Two red, blue and white uniformed North Prep players coordinate with each other, attempting to corner me. I move my leg as if I'm about to kick directly into their faces. The players cringe, covering their eyes. With that distraction, I knock them down and slam past them. I wait for the referee's whistle, but I hear none.

Now it is just me and the goalie.

I can hear Cayan yelling at players behind me. I grin and kick the ball. The ball curves and thumps as it passes the goalie and hits the net.

3 - 2.

I jump in place, feeling the adrenaline rush into my fingers and toes. I can feel Shaylee's eyes on me. She has never seen me this victorious before. For the first time, I imagine her looking at me with respect. Sure, she thinks I'm a decent artist but never have I beaten her. I can do this. I can win. Time is running out. As the referee blows his whistle, I have a feeling it might be his last. I need to act now.

North Prep has the ball, with Shaylee leading the charge. Shaylee corners me, looking for an opening. I kick my feet in, my size and agility an advantage as I slip through Shaylee's defense. We fight down the field, slowly getting closer and closer to North Prep's goal. Shaylee kicks the ball out of my reach. She turns to take it and return it for a goal.

I slam into Shaylee's back, throwing her to the ground. The watching North Prep crowd gasps as Shaylee crashes and slides in the mud. I clench my jaw, jumping past Shaylee, waiting for the whistle and the subsequent red card. After a long, tense moment, I realize nothing's going to happen. I charge through, grabbing the ball and firmly kick it into the goal as the whistle blows.

3-3.

I smile. I can see Shaylee off to the side, covered in mud, swearing and cursing to herself. She is no longer holding Cayan's hand. Victory. Cheers break out from my team. Reichfield supporters rise up, giving me a standing ovation. The team rushes toward me, and their hands slap my back, ruffle my hair, and lift me in the air.

I look toward Shaylee, not being able to take my eyes off her. Shaylee yells, "It's only a tie." A laugh escapes her mouth. "It's only a tie," she repeats.

Well, Shaylee, it may only be a tie this game, but this is the beginning of your team's downfall. However, don't worry Shaylee, it won't be the end for you. I'm sure you'll be very happy as my art assistant. You can give me motivational pep talks and say slogans like, "If opportunity doesn't knock, build a door."

CHAPTER 19

Shaylee slams the door. "What was that?"

I add a few brush strokes to my painting. I look up and smile, "What?"

"You know what."

"I don't know whatever you're talking about," I say, focused on the canvas.

She grabs me by the ear.

"Ow," I yell.

She plops me down on the couch; the same couch we were sitting on when we discovered the book.

"I played a good game, that's all."

"That's all? What about pushing me in the mud?"

"I didn't push you. You fell."

She glares at me, fuming.

"I thought you'd like some competition. Weren't you talking about that the other day, your brother winning and all?"

Shaylee leans over me and fake punches toward me. I cover my face. The door creaks open.

"Guys." I look up to see Hector standing by the door. "They love it, look." Hector opens up a briefcase and empties it. Wads of cash fall out.

"Oh, my." Shaylee reaches down at the cash, mesmerized. "For his paintings?"

Hector smiles. "For one painting."

Shaylee's jaw drops. "I don't believe it … why so much?"

Hector shrugs. "The other buyers were just amateurs, nouveau rich, easy to be fooled by talks of a heist."

"And these?"

"These are real museum buyers. We're talking big museums. London. Paris. They think it's legit. I think the guys who hired us may have even bought off a few art historians. The story they concocted, must have really fooled them."

"How much is here, ten thousand?" Shaylee asks gleefully, throwing the money up in the air. For a moment, she looks like an overjoyed child.

"Ten percent. That's just the down payment." Hector smiles.

"Ten percent," I exclaim, my mouth dropping.

"You mean, we get a hundred thousand?" Shaylee asks, incredulous.

"Yes," Hector confirms.

"Before the dealer?" she asks.

"After."

"Well, what does he get?" Shaylee asks.

"He gets one million and his other partners also get about that. I think there's five of them or more … maybe ten. Doesn't matter. We get one hundred thousand."

"Wow, it seems like nothing in comparison but then again, it is a hundred fucking thousand. I could buy like a million new dresses." Shaylee beams with excitement.

"We split it, remember?" Hector looks at her sternly.

"How much do I get?" I ask.

Everyone is silent.

"Come on Hector, we have to give him something," Shaylee protests.

"You get to keep your face." Hector smiles, but his eyes remain cold.

"Oh come on, Hector," Shaylee pleads.

Hector leaves. "Five thousand," he yells behind him. "In total … for the series."

I smile, genuinely pleased. That's five thousand more than I've ever made. If this continues, I could even quit my job at the soul-sucking customs office.

* * *

I walk down the street I grew up on. Everything feels different now; happier, maybe. I'm so absorbed in my own headspace that Thomas manages to make me jump by tapping me on the back. He must have been behind me that whole time. How long was he walking behind me for, I wonder?

"Hey," I say, smiling at Thomas.

"What's up with you?" Thomas asks in an accusatory tone.

"Nothing."

"Well, you seem … different."

I try to play dumb. "I do?"

The space between his eyebrows crinkles. "Yeah, happier, maybe—"

"Well, I just got a paycheck."

"Is that where you came from? From work?" Thomas asks.

I nod.

"Oh," he says. "Because I thought I saw you coming from Lower Reichfield."

"Well, I was … but first I go to work, remember?"

"Really, I didn't see you there."

"You were there?" I gulp.

"Yeah," he says, "ordered something on gbay."

"What did you order?"

"Some new shoes." Thomas looks at me suspiciously.

"Well, you must have just missed me."

He sighs with relief. I see his facial muscles relax. "Well good, I hope you're not happy about spending time with that flip."

I clench my fists and unclench them. "Listen, of course I'm happy. Why wouldn't I be? I'm fooling her and she's eating it up like candy. To her it must seem like some forbidden love story. Flip falls in love with the Aryan boy." I chuckle. I need to get him off my back for good. I need to make him feel guilty. "Thomas, your level of suspicion is really bugging me. The fact that you could even imply that I could like that flip is grounds for me to punch you in the face." I walk away leaving him standing there. I hope that works.

"Addie," Thomas yells.

I continue walking.

"Addie."

I turn around. "What?"

"I'm sorry," he calls after me.

I smile.

✳ ✳ ✳

Ava looks different today. For one, she's dyed her Aryan blond hair to brown and she's dressed differently. She reminds me of someone, though who, I can't quite place.

"Hey." She smiles weakly. It's then that I notice a bruise on her wrist.

Thomas notices the bruise as well. He looks confused and maybe even a little angry.

Helene's giving some stupid lecture on deconstructionism, whatever that is. I don't understand it. I actually feel like it is in German. Although if it was, I'd for sure understand it and I don't. *Helene, Helene, if I'm really so awful at art as you believe, would I have sold my painting for over five million?* The side of my mouth goes up in contempt.

Helene you are so wrong. I shouldn't even be in this class. My skill is beyond yours. You make me feel stupid. You make me feel like I suck and now, look at me. My artwork will hang in a museum and yours will only ever hang in this class or your crummy apartment. How can she be so tasteless as to not recognize genius? I smirk.

Wait. Wait a minute. What if she isn't tasteless? What if she knows I am great and knew all along? What if she's supposed to discourage me the way Hitler was discouraged from pursuing his dream? Shaylee told me Hitler didn't get into art school because of some teacher. That some Jew got in instead. I look at Steinfeld. Suddenly, it comes to me. *Scheisse. This is a setup.* Could it be? I look from Helene back to Steinfeld. Hope-crushing art teacher. Fake Jew. Hope-crushing art teacher. Fake Jew. I can't wait to tell Shaylee and share with her the extent of their corruption.

$$* \quad * \quad *$$

Soccer practice finishes. I'm alone in the locker room as I took a moment to argue with Coach over our tactics, which turned into a much longer moment. Everyone has gone home except for me. My thoughts are going a mile a minute from soccer to this whole conspiracy. I'm wondering how deep this thing goes? *Is everyone in on it?* I turn on the shower. Hot water beats down on me. *Ow.* Too hot. I turn a bright beet red shade all over. I flick it in the other direction. Cold water comes shooting out. *Scheisse.* I quickly turn it off. Now, I probably look even more like a lobster. No doubt my monumental lower extremities in my trunks are now all shrivelled up to the size of that midget soccer player of North Prep.

I back up and jump when I feel the semi-naked body of someone behind me with boobs. *What the?* I turn around and it's Ava. She's in her bra or a skimpy swimsuit if it could be called that.

"Hey."

I take a step back. "Think you made a mistake. You're in the wrong locker room," I say calmly.

"Oh, it's no mistake," she says as she takes a step closer to me.

We're now standing millimeters apart, face to face. I've never stood this close to someone on purpose. Ever. I take a step back. She takes a step forward. I take another step back and now we're waltzing around the shower room, in some semi-nude dance. I'm not sure what's going on. I smell like body odor. I need to smell lemony sweet for Shaylee. *I just want to take a shower, bitch. Why won't you let me take a shower?*

I look at Ava's sleek hair that she probably styled with a flattening iron. That might have taken her a good forty minutes. Pauline spends hours just going over the same piece again and again. She does this while watching some tasteless film noir. I'm sure she imagines herself as the sexy femme fatale. I feel nauseous. I reach for the shower lever. I turn it on, this time in the middle. The water comes out. I'm figuring if she's anything like Pauline, she won't want to mess up her hair. But wait, if it's only one faucet, she might stay and watch me. I really do need my alone time to wash all my extremities. I scamper to every faucet and turn them on.

She smiles vindictively. "Kinky."

I can't make out the look in her eyes. It's a blend of mischievousness and something else. Water pours on her and now she's completely drenched. She brushes back her hair with her fingers.

Why won't she leave me alone? What should I do? I'm at a loss. *Think Addie, think.* As I'm thinking, she takes steps toward me like a viper. *Think, Addie.* Finally she has me cornered in the corner like some mouse, by a predator. I'm scared. I put my hands up.

"Addie," she whispers, her voice sultry and sickening. "Addie, look at me."

I can't. I look away.

"Addie." She takes my chin and points it toward her. My eyes are closed and fearful.

"Addie," she says. "Open your eyes."

I keep them closed.

"Look at me," she whispers insistently.

I open one eye. "If I do that, will you leave me alone?" I inquire.

She nods. I open the other eye. I look at her, and my eyes fall to her breasts, glistening with water. Suddenly, I feel my man part, although shrivelled from the cold, come alive. *Oh no. Don't.* Why is my biology betraying me?

"Not now," I yell, looking down.

"What?"

"I wasn't talking to you," I say.

"Okay," she says coyly. "Let's not talk."

She puts her finger on my mouth and kneels down.

CHAPTER 20

I exit the locker room and I'm a mixture of elated versus disgusted with myself. One thing's for sure, I think of Ava in a new light. I may even look forward to seeing her now and again. I like to organize things in my brain, and Ava never fit into a category. She was always floating out in space, yet somehow annoyingly in my life, due to Thomas. Now, I can put her into a category. The same category as chocolate cake, beef jerky, "I Love Landra", snow days, and toasted peanuts, though not in that order of course. At some point I'll have to return to this and try to figure out exactly where she fits in for my own peace of mind. Does she fit above beef jerky or toasted peanuts? Hmm ….

I sit across from Shaylee at the house. I paint a few brushstrokes on the canvas.

She looks over at me. "You look as if you're deep in thought."

"I am," I answer vaguely, confirming her question and giving nothing more.

"About what?" she inquires.

"Oh, nothing."

I *am* deep in thought. I'm wondering how I can get her mouth to where Ava's was on my schwanz. Of course, I won't tell her that. I'm afraid she'll actually hit me. The more I think about this, the more I'm distracted. I need to concentrate. I look down.

"Not now," I whisper to my pants.

Shaylee looks over. "You like someone?"

"What? That's crazy." I feel my cheeks go hot.

"You do." She perks up in excitement.

I like you, I think to myself but of course, I don't say it.

"So who's the girl?" she asks.

"She's—"

"I knew it."

"She's nobody."

"Well, nobody's got you awfully glowy."

"Glowy?"

"Yeah, could tell the moment you walked in there was someone."

"Oh," I say. "Well, there's this girl," I say looking into her eyes. They're a lighter shade of brown, not quite russet. I gulp. "In my school. She's—"

"Please tell me it's not some dumb airhead," she sighs

"Of course." It now occurs to me that I have to actually think of something besides what she did that I like. "You'd like her. She changes her hair a lot."

Shaylee cringes. "Wait. You're attracted to her because she changes her hair?"

"One reason—"

"What else?" she interrogates.

I gulp, my mind blank.

"Next time, point her out to me. I like to see who people are attracted to. You probably have some sort of type—"

"Doubt it." I shake my head. "Wait. How will I point her out to you if we're on the opposite team?"

Shaylee thinks. "Turn to face her and then scratch your neck on both sides."

"Like a secret code?" I smile, all thought of any other girl disappearing from my mind.

"Exactly."

* * *

At the soccer match, I do the secret code, motioning to Ava who's standing off to the side. She actually looks better today than usual. I still can't quite place my finger on it. Shaylee gives me a weird look. She's distracted and we tie once again, but this time not due to my skill, I hate to admit it, but due to her distraction.

At the house, I spend most of the time painting in silence. Today, Shaylee's less talkative than usual and spends the whole time texting from the couch. I figure she's mad at me for scoring the goals I did. She likes to win. I get that. I'm happy that she's so pissed. I'm getting a lot of painting done today as there's less distraction until, she breaks the silence.

"Do you like me?"

My heart jolts as if it's been electrified. I look up, trying to control my voice. "Excuse me?"

"Do you like me?" she repeats.

"Why?" I ask as my face grows hotter. I gulp.

"It's just that girl you pointed out, you know she kind of looks like me, don't you think?"

"Looks like you?" I say. "Are you serious?" An Aryan girl look like Shaylee? That's craziness talking. But then again … Now that I think of it, Ava did just dye her hair brown. It was also longer with extensions and curled, kind of like Shaylee's. Is that why I … my mind flashes back to the locker room.

"Well, I hope you don't like me. You know we're just friends, right?"

"Of course," I say hoarsely

"Good." Shaylee smiles. "I like having you as a friend. Plus with your mad art skillz, you make me a lot of money." Shaylee resumes her texting. She looks up again. "What's that girl's name anyway?"

"Ava," I say.

She laughs. "Ava, huh? You like an Ava?" Then her face grows serious. She pulls a chair up and sits in front of me. "Ava, her name is Ava?"

"Yeah, why?" I ask.

"Ava?"

"Yes." I nod my head.

"Ava?"

"For the final time, YES."

"Eva Brown, that ring a bell?"

"Uh, a girl I met ten years ago was named Eva Brown, I think. Haven't seen her since. The other Evas—"

"The other Evas?" Shaylee's eyebrows go up. "How many Evas were there?"

I think to myself. "Hmm … about ten or twenty, maybe? But come to think of it, they spelled their names with an 'E' rather than this Ava who spells her name with an 'A'. Weird."

Shaylee lets out a little laugh.

"When Ava number twenty-two first came to our school, she had brown hair rather than blond. I actually thought she was cute at first, unlike the others who seemed like copies."

Shaylee mouths to herself, "Wow."

"I took an interest in her but the second I did, she turned weird. She dyed her hair from brown to bleached blond like the others and started to be all … how do I say this—" I wince, thinking about how clingy she became.

"Thirsty?" Shaylee suggests, leaning forward.

I look at her, confused. "I wouldn't know. I mean, she didn't have a water bottle on her."

She ignores me. "Desperate?" Shaylee asks, her face serious.

I nod.

"So there were lots of Evas?"

"Yeah, I think the most amount of people who ever tried to befriend me were named Ava or Eva. Isn't that weird?"

"Ya think?"

"What's the probability of that?"

Moments later, I'm looking at a picture of Hitler's Eva Brown. Hitler was dating a girl named Eva Brown. The exact same name as the first Eva. When I think back, I think that it was only the first Eva that had the last name Brown or any last name to think of it. The other Evas just went by Eva. I never knew their last names. When it got to their name in class, the teacher would just say Eva and end there. That always struck me as odd, especially because she said all of our last names.

"Do you see what I'm saying?" Shaylee says.

"Uh, that there are a lot of Evas?"

"No. No. They are manipulating you. They want you to choose an Eva."

I think to myself. Is she right? Was what happened in the locker room a manipulation? If it was, it was a pretty good one at that.

The space between Shaylee's eyebrows increases. She rubs her chin. "It's just strange. If that was their plan, why were there so many of them?"

"So many what?" I ask.

"Evas."

"Hmmm ..." I think about it for a second and then I smile. "Well, maybe because I didn't exactly like them."

"Seriously?" She smiles.

"Yeah, they were … almost too perfect, if there could be such a thing. Normally, I like perfection but in this case ..." I wince. "Yeah, I don't know, it was almost like those artificial displays you see in museums—"

"Displays?" Shaylee asks.

"When we went on this field trip to the Reichfield Museum, there was this display of clay apples, oranges and bananas as well as all this other fake food. Beside it was a nutrition chart, but none of the food looked appetizing."

Shaylee laughs. "You wouldn't want to break your teeth on a clay apple?"

"Exactly, but it wasn't just that, even if that food was real, no doubt it would give you dysentery or something like that. Your body would just know it was wrong for you, even if it looked great."

"I hear you. I want someone real," Shaylee says, "who farts but not all the time because that would be irritable bowel syndrome."

I laugh. "Well Cayan, he smells really bad so you got that going for you."

Shaylee hits me playfully. "It's obvious you don't like him."

I hold my breath. "Is it? Maybe I just don't think he's good enough for you." I look into her eyes.

Shaylee gulps and looks somewhat uncomfortable. She looks away. "Well, all those Evas couldn't have been completely horrible," she says, changing the topic. "I mean, they must have chosen girls who were at least hot."

"Yeah, they were," I admit, "but I didn't think much about that. Of course, everyone wants someone who they're attracted to for sure, and they were all great, smart, talented, beautiful. Only, it was as if someone was insulting me with a cheaper version of what I really wanted, you know? There were just too many Evas, and I guess, I wanted someone more, well, unique."

"Unique. It's funny you say that—"

I tilt my head to the side, smiling. "Because I'm a clone?"

"Yeah." Shaylee smiles back. "But it's weird, at the same time you're not. You have way more individuality than all those Evas."

"You think?" I grow excited.

"Yeah." Her smile widens.

"You want to hear something ridiculous?"

Shaylee nods.

"About a dozen of Evas put me on the spot one time in sixth grade."

"How so?"

"They gave me this paper with a picture of all them. They said, circle the girl you like the most."

"Wow, what ever did you do?"

I smile. "I gave it back to them with the words written across, 'I hate ALL of you.'"

Shaylee throws her head back and laughs. I laugh as well. We laugh together for the next ten minutes, one of us starting again just as we'd stop, infecting each other with giggles and laughter and snorts. If Hector came in now, he'd think we were high on drugs.

Shaylee stops laughing. She breathes in, wiping a tear from the corner of her eye. "Still, can't get over you rejecting what was probably the hottest girl in school." She shakes her head in disbelief. "Man, you're picky."

"Yeah, don't forget the others too."

"Wait." Shaylee grows serious. "Ava. You like an Ava or an Eva. You can't like an Ava."

I feel my throat tighten. "It's just attraction. Nothing more."

"No feelings?"

"Of course not," I say, suddenly wondering if I could have … *No Addie, don't go there.*

"Good."

CHAPTER 21

I'm in a field, looking for a hubcap. The hubcap that just flew off Thomas's car. We were just driving around, having fun, speeding and whatnot, and now we're doing something else. Ava picks up something and I can't believe what she's holding. It looks like a used circular aluminum baking tin. She thinks it's a hubcap. Is she serious? I don't know whether to laugh or cry. Do they really think I'm this stupid to go for someone who doesn't even know what a hubcap is? Shaylee would know what a hubcap was for sure.

I get Ava to follow me and we let Thomas look for the hubcap. I lead her behind a bush. Now's my chance. I can ask her if her last name's "Brown" which might draw suspicion to myself or ... I can just pull down my pants.

"What are you doing?" She looks around.

"We have time," I say. If the ones who created me are using me, I'm going to use her. She smiles. She kneels down and I'm in my own world.

I'm going to get something out of it. It will be her heart I'll break instead of Shaylee's.

"Addie," I hear Thomas calling. "Addie," He yells.

I hear his footsteps approaching. *Go away. I'm almost there.*

"Addie."

He'll be here in a second. Finally, a release. I quickly zip up my pants. He catches me zipping them up. I blush. Ava stands up quickly. He knows he interrupted something.

"I found it," he says. His eye twitches.

Do I hear a slight tinge of hatred in his voice? Do I see a slight sneer in his expression? A thought occurs to me but it can't be. He's the one who has been forcing Ava on me. There's no way he's … jealous? Is Thomas jealous? Does he harbor feelings for Ava? That's not possible, is it? And then we're in the car driving and Thomas is back to his old self, telling a joke about a Filipino, a Mexican and a … I tune out. Maybe I was just imagining that look of jealousy. It was dark. Maybe I saw something that wasn't there. There's no way he's jealous.

$$* \quad * \quad *$$

It's just moments until the game. I'm all ready. I can feel the blood coursing through my veins. A few of us stand off to the side waiting for the other players to arrive.

Karl comes over. "You see that?"

"What?" Annoyed, I look at his chin blubber shake like jello. I wonder why he's talking to me. It's not like we're even friends.

Karl motions to a Latino player from North Prep who leans his shiny new bike against the bleachers.

"What?"

"He stole it. You think we should tell someone?"

"Helene?" I look toward the area off to the side where she usually sits.

Then a thought occurs to me. I look back at Karl. "So how do you know he stole it? Did you see him?"

"No."

"Wait uh … I'm confused. Did someone steal a bike?"

"No."

"Wait … so why did you say—"

"That's what they do. They steal stuff."

Right. Right. I let out a nervous laugh. Why does this bother me? It's not like it would have a few months ago but anyway, it annoys me for some reason. *Shut up Karl. I don't have time for this.* I look around for Shaylee but I don't see her.

I see Pauline off to the side. She motions to me.

"What?" I grimace. Another annoyance.

She motions to me to come over. I try to ignore her but she's like a fly in the corner of my eye. Reluctantly, I walk over.

"What?"

"Where were you?" she asks, in an angry tone.

"What are you talking about?"

A concerned expression passes across Pauline's face. "Yesterday, I went to the office and you weren't there—"

"Oh, I stepped out."

"Yeah, that's what I thought but then Hans said you were right over there. He pointed at someone else."

"Well, Hans is crazy," I add.

"Oh. So are you going to be at work today if I drop by?"

"Of course." I ball my fists. "What's with you checking up on me anyway? You think I'm lying?"

"No. That's not what I said, Addie."

"You should just care about the money I bring home. Do you bring any money home, Pauline? Are you helping Mom, or are you too busy planning your wedding?"

"That's not fair, Addie. I told Mom and—"

"You told Mom?" I clench my fists. The woman who's faking sick. The woman who's not my mother, who wants the worst for me, who could destroy me?

"You told Mom?" I repeat, trying to hide the anger in my voice, to not arouse suspicion.

"Yeah, she said she'd have a talk with you."

Coach whistles. I run off. I'm furious. How dare she check up on me? Why is it her business what I do with my time? It's not like she works or does anything besides invade my space. We're just siblings, that's all. In a different world, I wouldn't have to associate with her at all. We wouldn't even be friends. I just imagine her wrecking everything for me. Suddenly, paranoia takes over. If Mom finds out I'm doing art and actually enjoying myself with Shaylee, she'll ruin everything for me. She might even pull me out of Reichfield and homeschool me. No. I finally have friends. A real friend.

Shaylee takes the field. She kisses Cayan. I feel a surge of anger move through my veins as if I'm Aryan Galactic Warrior when he comes out of hibernation for the first time. I storm onto the field. Damn you, Pauline. To hell with you, Cayan. Verpiss dich Karl. Bodies fall around me as I kick the ball with laser focus, and suddenly, the world falls from concern. I'm fully connected, fully present. I've never felt so alive. The ball and I are one. It moves with me like an extension of my limbs. Everything flows into place. I'm not paying attention to the score. The game must have ended and I don't believe it. My team, they're cheering; cheering for me. Thomas has tears in his eyes. We won. We didn't just tie. We won because of me.

* * *

Thomas and Ava pull me to "Elsa's Dairy" to celebrate our "winning streak." I have a lot of art to finish but it can wait until tomorrow. For now it will be malts for all to celebrate. They put mine in front of me and it's more tangy than usual. Thomas is the happiest I've seen him in quite a while. The only time I saw him this happy was after we poisoned Kero. He took credit for it. Granted, it was his idea but we both worked together, kind of like now.

"Did you see that, Addie? Did you see them fall? It's prophecy," he beams.

Ava takes a sip of her strawberry malt and gets a malt mustache. She blushes and wipes it away. Normally, witnessing any imperfection in the female form, especially Ava's, would annoy me. Yet, today I find her display of frailty kind of endearing. It's nice to have some contrast. Ava looks into my eyes. It's the first time I really notice how blue they are. So Aryan. Even with darker hair she's stunning. Now, why don't I like her again?

CHAPTER 22

Mother is out of her room for the first time in a long time. I thought at first she'd have a talk with me about what Pauline told her but then I notice the balloons. At first I think it's for Pauline's engagement but then Mom brings out a giant black, red and white present for me. This is the biggest box that I've ever seen. How did she organize things so quickly? It's like she called "Party in a Box" or something.

"Pauline said you skipped work."

I tense up. "Oh?"

"But I figured you were just practicing," she says with a hint of suspicion.

I gulp. "Of course." I smile nervously. "You know we won?"

"I know," she says with a smile. "By one point." She reached out and rubs my shoulder. I relax. "Next time you'll completely decimate them, won't you?" I wince. *Is nothing ever good enough for her?* She continues, "It's about increasing, Addie. Getting better. Setting a challenge for yourself."

I nod. I look at the present in front of me on the living room floor. I undo the bow, which falls away listlessly, without resistance. I open the box. Inside is, I don't believe it, new soccer jerseys for the team and one for me.

"Maybe this will give you some motivation."

Mine is a black and gold with a curious symbol on the upper right. I think I remember seeing that symbol somewhere, but I can't be sure. It reminds me of a wheel of blades rotating, kind of like my ice cream dream.

"Thanks," I beam, elated. Now we look official and powerful.

Anne comes in. "Mom, why does Addie get a present, they only won by a point, a flipping point?"

She doesn't like the attention taken away from her. Good. Later, I'm practicing moves in my bedroom that I'll do in the next game. I jump around, pretending to kick an invisible ball.

"Mom." I hear Anne yell in a high-pitched scream. My body tenses up as if I'm going to be attacked. "This isn't fair," she whines. "Addie's so loud."

I don't hear what Mom says but then I hear Anne yell, "But Mom, I can't sleep. This is ridiculous. Addie—" She pauses. I imagine she's about to say, "Addie doesn't do anything," as usual, but she stops herself and sulks. I hear her stomp back to her room. I smile to myself.

*　　*　　*

As I ride through Lower Reichfield, something's different. Off the hill to the right, there are usually tons of lights on at this time, but for some reason today, it's dead. Power failure, I think. No doubt, the lowlies couldn't make ends meet to pay the bill.

I arrive at the house and start painting. I'm amazed at how productive I am today. I have five more paintings to go. I beam as I paint. I never before felt such extreme confidence. It's a bit destabilizing, like a rush of electric current. I feel as if I'm hovering above everyone in this town. Why shouldn't I be above them? I'm better than most people, smarter than most people. I use both the left and right sides of my brain adequately. It's hard to understand how people could be happy doing such mediocre things when they could be truly excelling like me.

Shaylee sits on the couch and texts. "Why isn't that girl responding?" she says aloud to herself.

"Who?" I ask.

"Yvonne," she exclaims. "So weird."

Shaylee leaves her phone on the couch and comes over to look at my artwork. The space between her eyes wrinkles along with her nose. "Um, are you feeling okay?"

"Never better." I dip my paint in sky blue and add a few expressionist brushstrokes.

"Huh. Well, I just think I should tell you that this is utter shit."

My mouth goes dry. I cough. I feel anger, resentment and then a thought pops into my head, dark and resentful. *She wants you to fail, Addie, like on the field. She's threatened by you.*

"Excuse me? I think you're just letting your loss interfere with your taste."

Shaylee laughs dryly. "You think so?"

She pulls up a chair and sits beside me. "You want me to tell you why this is shit?"

"Please do."

"There's no feeling, no emotion—"

"Really?" I say. "What would you know about emotion? You like someone who is beyond stupid—"

"Cayan?" she says, raising an eyebrow. "You know he's actually applying to do an MBA?"

"Well I'm sure that's what he tells you. Hey, maybe he isn't so stupid."

Shaylee swallows her anger. "You know what? I don't even have to tell you it's shit. I can show you. One sec." She walks to her phone and picks it up off the couch. She types something. She comes back and shows me something that looks somewhat like my painting.

"Great minds think alike." I smile.

The right side of her mouth raises in contempt. "It's a craft project."

"So?"

"By an old woman in her sixties who wears holiday sweaters year round and has cats. Lots of them."

"Is she an Aryan woman?" I ask.

Shaylee kicks my chair post.

"Sorry. It's just if she was—"

"Trying not to be Hitler, remember?"

"Right." I nod. Aryan should be out of my vocab. Wait, it's a staple. What will I use in replace of it?

"Do you get what I'm saying?" she asks.

"That some non-Aryan woman ripped off my idea?"

She speaks slower as if she's frustrated. "For one, she didn't. She did it before you and second of all, it's shit. It's crafty. Do you get what I'm saying?"

"Crafty?"

"Yes."

"Okay." I clench my fists.

* * *

My mind's completely not in soccer practice. I suggest a few plays for the next game but when they come out of my mouth, I realize how stupid they sound.

"Addie's brilliant," shouts Karl. The other players agree with him.

Mengela, who is a great defense but not a strategist, also smiles in agreement.

"You think?" I ask.

"Of course. Addie knows best," Werner adds.

I look at Thomas and he's silent. Thomas for sure knows that what I suggested is utter shit. Yet, he's not speaking up today for some reason. He's looking at Ava who's giggling with her friends.

After practice, I walk up to Thomas. "Thomas, do you really think what I suggested is brilliant?"

He gulps. "Of course."

"No you don't." .

"Listen, Addie. Why don't we talk about this later?"

"Why?"

"Well I just have some things I want to take care of. Okay?"

* * *

I come to the realization that I have to tell Shaylee how I feel. Keeping all these feelings in isn't good. Now that I'm a star, no doubt she'd choose me over Cayan. I can for sure kick Cayan's ass in soccer now. It's like I've become an Aryan Warrior of the Galaxy overnight — okay not an "Aryan" Warrior. Shaylee doesn't want me to use that word, remember? Remember that, Addie. If you're going to use words like "Aryan", for sure Shaylee won't want to date you. Wait, date? Do I really want to date a non-Aryan? I look at myself, feeling like the ground has been yanked from under my feet. Am I really this person?

Shockingly, I don't feel like throwing up as usual. I used to think that a man who settles for someone non-Aryan is a man without faith, without standards. But this Addie, this Addie, is not that Addie. This Addie is just going to go with what he feels. That's it. *Addie, when you stop analyzing, you live life.* It's like in soccer. Those bursts of anger helped me win the game. The anger stopped any thought process I had. I just gave in to a feeling and went with it, rather than letting my thought process and my judgments interfere.

Something in me has changed. I don't know when it happened. Maybe it was the time that horse farted in Ava's face. Was that it? Or were there seeds of it a lot earlier, when Thomas and I had snuck into that lowly bar? I still remember that. Two girls watched us come in. They weren't bad looking. One could have passed as Aryan with some hair dye as her eyes were a bright blue.

The blue eyed one looked at Thomas. "Oh look there's a Gingie ..."

Thomas turned bright red and his freckles were more noticeable.

"I'm not a Gingie," he yelled. "I'm not a Gingie."

The girls laughed at him. Maybe it was then that I started to question everything Upper Reichfield told me. If Thomas could be so threatened by two girls, who is to say that the things they want me to believe are even true? Is Aryan really superior? There is a chance that it very well could be better, of course. Yet, how do I know what's real when the people who made me want me to succumb to their will? When they want to use me as their tool? I'm just a hammer to them, or a nail. Just a freaking tool that they can use and manipulate however they please. Aryan or not, I'm going to make up my own mind about what I like or do not like. No one is going to program in me a set of standards to live by. I'll live by my own standards and do as I please. No one will control my life. Only me.

✳   ✳   ✳

"You're coming with me," Pauline shouts when she catches me after practice, heading in the direction of Lower Reichfield.

I turn around and fix her with a gaze as cold as ice. "You're crazy."

She smiles sweetly. "I'll tell Mom you're not going to work again and that you're not at practice."

Moments later, we're at some bridal salon and Pauline's trying on a dress. It looks like a straitjacket which is so appropriate for her.

"You should totally go with that," I say, in as convincing a tone as possible.

"Really?" She beams.

"Really." I nod. I look at my watch. "Great, you've found a dress. Now I can go." I stand up.

She stomps her feet. "Stand with me Addie."

I sigh. I get up and stand with her in front of the mirror. She pulls me close to her and holds my arm as she would hold the arm of her husband, her hand wrapped around my lower bicep.

"This isn't right." Pauline grimaces.

The bell on the door chimes. I turn around. Ava walks in, rustling through her bag. She takes off her coat.

"Sorry," she says to the other salesgirl who puts on her jacket and leaves. Ava puts a name tag on her chest, looks up and around the store, and makes eye contact with me.

"Addie?" Her eyebrows raise in surprise.

"Ava." I smile. It's funny, all this time I knew so little about her. She just was someone who gave me pleasurable moments. Now, I see that she has a life too, and a job.

"This isn't right," Pauline exclaims. She looks toward the counter. "Do you have a suit for him?"

Ava nods. "One sec." She comes back with a few suits.

Pauline looks through them. "No, No, No." She slaps them away. "Do you have one a groom would wear?" Ava looks at her, confused. Pauline gulps. "I want to see how I'll look next to my groom."

Ava nods. She turns back and smiles at me. She understands how weird this is. I smile back at her. We're both in on a secret. We both know my sister is absolutely nuts and there's nothing either one of us can do about it.

Ava brings me a nicer suit. I humor Pauline and change into it. I stand in front of the mirror while Pauline fixes her makeup. Ava brushes her hands down the sides of my pants to smooth them. Then she fixes my jacket. A tingle moves through me. Ava stands next to me. She's wearing a white camisole and her hair is up in a braided style. Suddenly, I'm aware of how beautiful she is. In the back of my head, a thought arises.

It's because Aryan is better, Addie, you know it. You do.

Suddenly, I can see our life together. In a flash it hits me. I could marry Ava. One day we could move out of this shit town together. Instead of being the soccer star of a shit town, I would become a soccer world champion and she would be by my side. She'd look great by my side. Everyone would love her. She doesn't have the hard edges of Shaylee. She doesn't have a personality that takes getting used to. With her beauty, people would fall at her feet, instantly.

My sister finishes fixing her makeup. She stands beside me and pulls me closer to her. If I try to move away, it will make it worse. Ava smiles at me. Pauline puts her arm around me. I feel nauseous and use all the willpower I have not to throw up. These dresses are expensive.

Pauline smiles. "I like this one."

It's then that I shift my attention from Ava to Pauline and notice what dress she's actually wearing. It's horrendous with frills everywhere and long strips of white fabric that have additional frills. Everything combined makes her look ten times fatter. That. And also a lot like an octopus. If I cared, I'd tell her but I'm just glad she found one that hides her body well.

Ava looks at Pauline with sympathy. "Well, why don't you try on a few more to be sure?" Ava goes to the clothes rack and sorts through some more dresses.

No.

"Ava. It's alright, she likes this one," I yell after her.

Ava brings a few more to her.

"How do you know what you really like it until you have something to compare it to?" Ava hands Pauline dresses and pushes her into the changeroom.

Ava looks at me, a mischievous grin taking over her face. She unzips my pants and bends down on her knees. I'm all excited but then I hear the bells on the door. Someone's here.

I quickly zip up my pants. Ava tries to stand up but can't. Her hair is caught in my zipper. *Scheisse.* We hear the bells again. The person who came in, probably saw nobody and turned around and left.

Pauline flings open the door of the dressing room. As if it couldn't get worse, my eyes are now burning. She's in a wedding dress if it could be called that. It should really be called a wedding skirt. Her saggy breasts hang out with just triangles of beaded fabric covering her nipples. Thankfully.

She looks down at Ava who is bent down near my crotch. The hair. Right. In my zipper. Temporarily distracted by the horror. Fortunately, Ava thinks quickly. She's holding up the end of my pants.

"Adjustments," she says. She smiles at Pauline.

"What do you think?" Pauline asks with a whine to her voice that's even more annoying than usual.

"I think you should try them all on just to be sure," Ava says in a reassuring tone. I have new respect for Ava's acting ability.

Pauline lets out a huff and heads back into the stall.

Ava fidgets trying to get her hair free of my zipper. She's tugging. I hear the bells on the door chime again, making me jump. Ava jumps too.

"Ow," Ava screams. Half of Ava's hair is stuck in my crotch, not just a small piece but a huge piece. It's like she shaved off her hair with my zipper.

"My extensions," she yells.

Oh great, now I got hair extensions for my crotch. I rip Ava's hair out of my zipper and hide it behind my back. She feels her head and looks in the mirror. I think I see a bald patch. It must have ripped out some of her hair as well. It's like she's been scalped. I hand her the weft of hair I've pulled from my zipper.

"Scheisse." Ava holds up her extensions to the bald spot.

Pauline opens the door again. Ava flings herself around so Pauline doesn't notice the bald spot. She holds the extensions behind her back. She's now standing next to me.

"What do you think?" Pauline asks.

"Why don't you try more to, uh, compare?" Ava smiles a half smile, which looks painful. She fidgets with her hands.

"Ugh, okay." Pauline sneers. She stomps back into the changeroom.

Ava stands closer to me, our sides touching. I might be imagining it but I feel Pauline's eyes on us as if she has laser vision and can see right through the changeroom stall. .

Pauline yells, "I told you I liked the first one." The door of the changeroom flings open and Pauline storms out. "The first one. I know what I want and I can't unzip this."

Ava comes over and helps unzip her. Back freckles galore. Pauline storms back to the changeroom. I hear her rustling to get the dress off. Ava's hand touches mine. Pauline flings open the door to the changeroom. Ava steps away from me. Pauline looks from Ava to me and from me to Ava. It must upset her how much better looking Ava is in comparison to her, even with the bald spot.

"Let's go," Pauline barks. Her mouth turns downward in a frown. She takes my arm and pulls me away from Ava.

＊　＊　＊

I'm really late. If I don't get there soon, I'll be in trouble. I ride faster and faster. There's a yellow ribbon ahead. It fences off the turn I usually take to get to Shaylee's. I brake quickly and come to an abrupt halt. A Lower Reichfield policeman stops me. I'm angry.

"What's going on?"

He walks up to my bike. "You can't go through here."

"What? Why not?"

"There's been an accident."

"Well come on, let me through. I'll go around, I promise."

"It's the whole area."

A man in a hazmat suit and gas mask walks toward us. He takes off his gas mask. "You can't go through here."

"What happened?"

"This area is off limits. I'm not at liberty to say."

I realize I'm not going to convince him. I back away with my bike and ride off. I'll have to find another way and I do, but not before going through an area that looks even more run down than the route I normally take. I'm glad I'm going fast. When I finally get to the house, I'm over an hour late.

"Sorry," I pant, out of breath.

Shaylee sits on the couch next to Cayan. Her cheeks are red. She's crying. Cayan holds her.

Shaylee looks up at me. "It's Yvonne."

CHAPTER 23

Cayan fills me in that there has been a gas leak. He works for the gas company so he got the news before everyone. The authorities don't want to create mass panic. He's not supposed to tell anyone about it until they rule out sabotage, but he's telling us. I hate him a little less. I like being in the know.

"A whole neighborhood?" I ask.

Shaylee nods. "Oak Ridge."

"That's horrible." I gulp. This is something that Thomas and I would rejoice at before. A thought occurs to me that maybe Thomas was involved but then I wave it away. There's no way he could get that much gas for a whole neighborhood. There's no way. Also, I doubt even Thomas would have the guts to do something so mass scale. What? And sacrifice his future at Harvard or a top German school?

Shaylee cries. I feel like I should feel bad, but I don't. I didn't even know Yvonne really. I met her once or twice in real life. Then, she was in my fantasy getting sucked under that ice cream blade. I remember it now. I smile.

"What are you smiling at?" Shaylee wipes away her tears, suddenly angry, her eyes flashing.

I gulp. "It's not a smile," I say. "Sometimes when I laugh, people think I'm crying."

This is true. Mother was always confused when I was a kid. She would come over with bandaids when I was laughing at "Aryan Galactic Warrior." It took me awhile to figure out that she had thought that I injured myself by pretending to fly by jumping from the couch. I demonstrate my laughter and try to make it sound like crying.

Shaylee looks at me blankly along with Cayan.

"Same thing with smiling," I say. "I'm sorry." I put on my sternest face. "I know what it's like to lose a friend, to lose family. It's horrible."

Shaylee knows better than anyone that I know what it's like to lose someone, to lose the entire family you thought you had. To have it just have been a charade. We have that secret. She nods. She leans on me and cries.

* * *

Anne hates me more today than usual. I can't figure out what I did to her exactly besides for existing. Tears pour out of her inflamed, red-veined eyes and I think she's been yelling for ten minutes. I don't know exactly how long it's been because I've tuned out. A few times I heard the word, "room". I figure this is about the gift. Mom gave Anne a pearl bracelet for her birthday and Anne was elated. She put it on and paraded about as if she was some princess. I just thought about how great that would look on Shaylee and so I took the bracelet and gave it to her. Shaylee hugged me and thanked me for the friendship bracelet.

I don't know how Anne realized it was me. Did I leave something behind? And then I remember, the bras. I took out some of her bras and laid them on the counter. I think I even tried one on just for the fun of it. I thought it might go great in addition to the gift. I put everything back of course … or so I thought.

Oh wait … A memory of slingshot, underwear wars. I couldn't resist. I think I broke a porcelain owl and parrot and maybe a goat. My sister has way too many china things lined up on her shelf just asking to be shot. I don't have a problem shooting them, because they're not real of course. It's not like I'd ever shoot a real goat.

Anne's crying. It suddenly occurs to me that she's the exact opposite of Pauline. She flings all these horrible insults at me, "selfish", blah blah blah, "lazy", blah blah blah, "unmotivated", blah. So different than Pauline.

Pauline thinks I'm the greatest but in a way that makes me uncomfortable. At a family party, she referred to my chin as chiseled and once when I was headed to the bath, her eyes lingered longer on my abs than I would have liked. I think the perfect sister would be a vastly different breed.

Anne's yelling has now taken on a maniac tone. Maybe I should have played underwear wars with Pauline's underwear, but that wouldn't have been half as fun. They're all granny panties. Just the thought of that makes me want to ... I feel like vomiting. Why is my stomach so weak?

"What's wrong with you?" yells Anne. "You're such a freak."

Eventually Anne calms down and it's dinnertime. Mother actually decides to join us today. Anne decides not to cook on account of exams as well as being upset. She also believes she's suffering from some allergy to wood mites and has wrapped the wooden kitchen chair in cellophane. Instead of Anne treating us to goulash and onion soup, Pauline makes us something she calls, "her specialty." We sit around the wood table. I look at the canned tuna that has a hole in the top. I pick it up. *Scheisse.* It burned me.

Anne looks at the can of tuna. "Are you serious?" Anne gives Pauline a cold, condescending look. She gets up from the kitchen table and brings a box of cereal back.

"This is great, Pauline," Mom says in a tone so cheerful it can't possibly be real. Besides, I know she doesn't mean it because Mother's cooking is top notch, or rather was top notch before the breakdown, but I guess she wants to be encouraging.

"Thanks," Pauline says brightly. "Learned it on a field trip."

Oh yes, now I remember. That was the field trip where I learned to build that quinzee. It's then that I notice that part of our wall is black. Instead of using the stove like a normal person, Pauline apparently decided to light a fire. In the kitchen, on the countertop, nonetheless. In the wilderness, soldiers do this. They take the top of the can off. Then they cover the tuna with toilet paper and light it. Apparently Pauline thinks we're in the bush.

Pauline graciously removes the burnt toilet paper pieces left over from Mother's can but leaves me to fend for myself. My can is also only partly opened. The can opener must have failed her somehow. I touch the can. It's burning hot as if she threw the whole can into a fire. I get up and walk to the counter in search of a can opener or something. I see a bowl with charred bits of newspaper on the countertop as well as a few roles of toilet paper laying about. Anne had the right idea by getting cereal. I open cabinets looking for something to eat. There's barely anything there. I forgot, it was my turn to get groceries. Pots and pans are scattered about. I have no idea why she needed so many pots and pans for this. In the bush, soldiers cook tuna this way precisely because they have no pans. Then, I remember the newspaper. This must be her second attempt.

Pauline looks toward me. "Seconds, Addie?"

"Uh—" *No. Say no.*

"Sorry I didn't make any ... well, I tried."

Phew.

I spot the can opener next to the toaster. Fine. I'll eat what's put in front of me. I'm looking for a kitchen glove, something to hold the can with as I open it, and then I look back. Of course. It's on the table. I walk back to the table and pick up the can with one mitt. With my other hand, I try to use the can opener to open it fully. *Scheisse.* It slips. Pauline reaches out her hand to catch it. Her hand sizzles but she doesn't seem to notice or mind. I'm sure she'll have third degree burns but she just goes back to eating as if it's nothing.

"Thanks," I say.

Anne stares blankly at us, crunching on her cereal. I try to grab it from her but she pulls it away.

"Mom, Addie won't let me study," Anne says, looking tired.

Mother gives me a disapproving look.

I look up. "I'm practicing. I need to practice, don't I?"

Anne pushes her chair back. "Practice? What does he do besides kick some stupid ball around? As if he's going to get into college with that." She scoots forward on her chair. She sticks her hand in the cereal box and takes out a handful of granola with marshmallow shapes. She picks out the marshmallow shapes leaving behind the granola.

"Anne, don't be mean. Your brother's trying."

I glare at Anne. She eats the cereal, crunching ever so slowly. "Who bought your cereal?" I ask.

She stops crunching. "Well, you wouldn't have that job without Dad's connections."

"Speaking of connections," Mom says, "Pauline has a job too—"

"So now you, Anne, are the only one without a job," I say to her.

"I'm twelve. You're seventeen. Working in some crummy office is probably all you'll ever do. You'll be just like Dad."

I push the chair away from the table. I'm nothing like him. He was a drunk and he would yell at us all the time. I thought he hated me. Though one time, when I was a kid, I had forgotten to wear the helmet he had gotten me. He had gotten me the helmet because I was always jumping off things trying to be Aryan Galactic Warrior. One time I landed splat on my face after running and trying to jump off the kitchen counter. He had come over and picked me up and rocked me in his arms. Then all of a sudden, he turned cold, he dropped me and got up. Maybe it was all an act too, the meanness, I mean.

"What's Pauline's job?" Anne asks. "Is it singing related?"

Lots of people think my sister has a great voice but I'd rather listen to a tone deaf homeless person belting out our school anthem.

"No, but it's related," Pauline says. "I'm going to be an announcer ..." She takes a bite of the tuna. "...for Addie's team, isn't that great?"

"Wait, how is that related and second, ugh no, why?" The last thing I want is to hear her squeaky voice over the speakers any more than I already do.

"Well to be a singer you have to be loud, right ... and heard? So, I'll be heard and Addie, I just feel like we've been growing apart. I feel like you've been somewhat distant. This will give us more time to spend together, won't it?"

That's great. I lost my appetite. On the one hand, perhaps maybe she'll stop wearing those short skirts now that her lower half won't be visible in the announcer booth. Yet, on the other hand now, I'll have to hear her as well as see her face on the large screen they just added. Before, if I didn't look toward the Reichfield bleachers, I could almost block her out.

"How did they make you announcer?" I say.

"Oh Addie, don't you know I have hidden talents?"

"She banged the referee," Anne says.

"Anne," Pauline exclaims innocently. "Need I remind you, I'm engaged." She flashes her glass engagement ring. She gets up and takes our dishes and dumps them in the sink, probably breaking a few. They clank against the pots and pans. I don't want to think of my sister banging anything. Pots and pans, Pauline, that's all I want to think of you banging. Ever.

*　　*　　*

I figure Thomas will grow suspicious if I don't continue to hang out with him as usual, so I show up at Elsa's Dairy. It suddenly occurs to me how ridiculous it is that this is the place he chose to work as he's lactose intolerant. I remember a time he confused his lactose pills with steroids and apologized the whole time for the gas. He tried to make a joke of it too. "What a gas," he kept on saying.

As I walk into the dairy, I hear a commotion.

I hear Thomas. "You guys have to leave."

Shaylee and Cayan sit in a booth. Thomas in his manager's uniform, stands over them.

"This is a free country," Cayan protests. He stands up and walks toward Thomas. Even though Thomas is a lot more muscular than Cayan, Cayan is a foot taller. Thomas backs away.

Shaylee stands up and pulls on Cayan's shoulder. "Come on, let's just go. I told you we should have gone to the one around the corner."

Cayan shakes her arm off. "This one's nicer. And I'm not done." Cayan pushes Thomas. "Apologize to her." He takes a step closer to Thomas, sticking his chest out menacingly. His voice drops to a growl. "I said apologize."

Out of the corner of her eye, Shaylee spots me by the door.

Thomas calls to me, "Addie. These lowlies think that this place is for them? Isn't that funny?"

I don't think Thomas recognizes Shaylee. She's wearing her hair up today and looks more feminine. Also, I think Thomas thinks all lowlies look the same. Cayan has his back to me. People are looking. If he looks up and recognizes me, it could cause problems.

"Hysterical," I say, muffling my voice so Cayan doesn't recognize it. I back away around the corner to the gentlemen's room. Shaylee glares at me.

I hear the clang of the door chimes. They've left.

"Do you believe that?" Thomas comes over. "Lowlies, in our place?"

"Yeah, completely ridiculous. You'll have to disinfect that table."

"Twice. I know." Thomas walks into the kitchen and returns with a bleach solution. "You think this will work?" He sprays some on the table and wipes furiously with the paper towel. Then he sprays the booth and scrubs it.

Thomas looks up from furiously scrubbing. "Hey. That girl. That girl kind of looked familiar. Wait, Addie, isn't that—?"

I nod.

He stops scrubbing. "Well I don't get it, you want to break her heart and she's with some other dude?"

"I know. My plan's working though, it's just taking time."

"But she's with him. Listen, Addie, if it's not working you should abandon ship. I mean, it's like you're giving them ideas. Soon all lowlies will think they can show up here." Thomas throws down the paper towel.

"Thomas." I put my hands on his shoulders. "I know what I'm doing."

"Do you?" He looks at me skeptically. He looks at his hands. "Good thing about this bleach, it's making me even more Aryan."

* * *

I'm babysitting Anne tonight while Mother goes for some treatments with her acupuncturist. She's trying some holistic approach with some naturopath. Babysitting to me is just an excuse to catch up on "Leave it to Hauser." So, that's what I'm doing. Anne's twelve. Why does she need a babysitter or more importantly why does it have to be me? Pauline's out somewhere, maybe with her fiance or the referee.

Mom looks at me. She sighs. "I don't like going to a Jew but they say he's the best so, it's worth a shot." It's then that I remember reading the mini bio of that dude Hitler on wiki-something. He blamed the death of his mom on some Jew. More manipulation.

Mom tells me she's leaving and I fake concern. "Addie," she says, "by the way, I hate to ask this of you now, you're obviously busy."

"Obviously."

"But Addie, I didn't find the paycheck where you normally leave it."

I sigh, ball my hands and get up. I run upstairs and I come back down with the cash.

"This time Hans gave me cash," I say. I put the cash in her hands and walk back to the TV.

"Cash?" She looks at it, surprised.

"Yeah." I nod. "Something about being out of cheques." I gulp.

I hope she buys that. I would have gotten a cheque from Hans had I not left early. Now, I'll have to wait until next week. Instead I have to give her my hard earned money, money I earned from painting. I sit down in front of the TV once more, this time annoyed.

"Addie," she says.

I turn away momentarily from June on "Leave it to Hauser." She stands there, awkwardly. I think she expects me to hug her like I normally do. I really don't want to miss my show. I get up and give her a hug. I sigh and watch TV over her shoulder. I always thought Mom reminded me of June. What a lie.

I wonder just how long I have until she fakes her death. Wait … that night. After the argument before my dad died, she had said something on the phone. "It doesn't make sense. He wasn't supposed to die then." Then. She had said, "die then." It was all a setup. Maybe something had gone wrong. Maybe my fake father had accidently drank himself to death too soon.

Anyways, I've come to the painful realization that she could care less about me. I'm just the breadwinner to her and after her faked death, I'll have to take care of everyone. I'll even have to make food for Anne. Babysit Anne full time. She'll be thirty-three and living at home, I know it. Even though she talks about independence and studies all the time, she needs someone around to pick on, to boost her confidence. That person will be me. No guy will ever put up with her amount of criticism. I'll be babysitting a thirty-four-year-old. Suddenly I'm angry. I want to punch something. I feel my eyes water.

"Oh Addie, don't worry. I'm going to be alright," Mother says.

She thinks I don't want to let her go but what I really want is for her to be June. To actually care. She pulls away from our embrace and I force my angry expression to turn back to neutral.

After Mom leaves, I hear a knock at the door. Did she forget her keys? I open it and see Shaylee standing there. Shaylee. I step outside and shut the door behind me. I pull her aside.

I look at her, confused. "Are you crazy?"

"You have some nerve. I thought we were friends and you let that dickhead treat me like that."

"Who?"

"Your friend. That gingie mancunt."

"Oh, Thomas."

"Addie, I thought you were different but there, you know who I saw standing there? I saw him, Addie. Him."

"Don't say that." I raise my voice. I cover my mouth and talk in a whisper so Anne doesn't hear. "I'm nothing like him."

"Really? Then why didn't you stick up for me, huh?"

"Listen, I'm sorry … It wouldn't have made a difference."

"Well, it would to me." She turns around and walks back toward her car out front.

"Shaylee," I yell. "Shaylee."

I run across the lawn in my socks. I grab her arm. She turns around, furious, her eyes bright and accusing. "I'm sorry. I should have stood up for you. It's just I didn't want to blow my cover, okay? Can't you see that?"

She breathes in. She's still angry, but I see her calming down. She throws my arm off and gets in her car and drives off.

CHAPTER 24

We win another game by two whole goals and I'm ecstatic. I notice that North Prep is short a few players. I hate to think that it's because of the accident with the gas leak. Of course it's not, Addie. You're just improving. Now's your time to soar in everything. Shaylee wasn't at her best today though. For some reason that makes me mad, almost disgusted. Do I like her less? Perhaps. I mean what kind of person lets their feelings interfere with winning? That's just weak.

Speaking of weak, the veins in Helene's forehead are bulging more than usual. I think she's threatened by me for some reason. She must feel her job slipping away as the players start listening more to me. Of course they are listening to me, why wouldn't they? I deliver results. I get them the goals they want. Thomas, Karl, Mengela and I are like a team of four. We ride through the field on our horses. We execute judgement against the players of North Prep — who will live and who will die? Or who will get a ball to the balls?

That was Mengela with Player 17. For a second, I thought Mengela felt guilty. It was strange. He even offered medical services to the other team. Like they would take him up on that after he was the one who caused that injury.

On the sidelines, I watch as Mengela takes out his notepad. He looks over at the player who got hit in the balls, who hobbles off the field, toward the parking lot. It's then that I understand that all he wants to do is document stuff. Documenting pain gives him pleasure. Perhaps he's drawing a diagram of the amount of pain caused by a blow to the balls or how slow a guy walks when that happens. He'll probably color code it later with highlighters.

*   *   *

When I arrive at the house, I can't find my art supplies anywhere. Nor can I find a fresh canvas. Shaylee normally has one already propped up for me. Shaylee's not here. Neither is Hector. I'm all about ready to leave when Shaylee bursts through the door. She pulls me to the couch and shows me a news report on her phone. A dark-skinned female reporter stands in front of what looks to be a disaster site.

"Today there was another serious gas leak and a fire in Lower Reichfield. Authorities say they now have the situation under control. The areas that were affected were Red Cloverfield and Dippermoose. Casualties are estimated in the thousands. Injured number in the hundreds and are being treated at Lower Reichfield Mem—" Shaylee puts her phone down.

"Scheisse," I say. "I hope you didn't know anyone."

"Addie, it's them."

"Them?" I say with a confused smile.

"Them. The Nazis. The ones that created you."

I think about it for a second. I mean it's entirely possible that it is them. It could be, but then again the ones that created me have remained hidden. It just doesn't make sense. Nothing like this has ever happened before. They are relying on me to become this man, Hitler. He started things. He set into motion that thing called the Holocaust. It wouldn't make sense that the ones that created me would act without me. They created me, after all. They're relying on me to lead them. They take their orders from me, not the other way around. It doesn't fit with their methodology.

I turn toward Shaylee. "Listen, it was probably an accident. Or if it was some racist, it was probably just a few hooligans. I wouldn't worry about it."

She turns to face me completely, her brown eyes incredulous. "Are you serious? A few hooligans? You talk about this as if it's no big thing. Three whole entire neighborhoods have been demolished in the last month. Do you really think it's just a coincidence?"

I shrug my shoulders, as if trying to dismiss my uncertainty. "Well, it's just I haven't heard anything … There hasn't been any gossip from anyone in my school."

The space between Shaylee's eyebrows narrows. "Doesn't mean—"

"I'm sure if Thomas were involved, everyone would know it. There's no way that blabbermouth could ever keep silent."

Shaylee's mouth turns downward. Her eyes narrow. "Addie—"

"Perhaps it's gang related. Why would you jump to the conclusion that it's—"

"Nazis?" Shaylee's eyebrows raise. She breathes in. "I see, it doesn't affect you. This. Doesn't affect you—"

"Sure there are Nazis. Even without Nazis, it's not like there aren't shootings here every week, right?"

Shaylee's eyes widen. Her nostrils flare.

I touch the base of my neck. "And who are those shootings caused by? Ruffians, verbrechers, hooligans, what not—"

She scoots closer to me. "Addie, I have a theory—"

"Shaylee." I throw my hands up in the air. I stand up. I look at her. I place my hands on my hips.

"Hear me out. This is a soccer town, right?" Shaylee looks into my eyes.

I nod. One side of my mouth flinches. I look away.

"That's what people care about, right?" She continues.

I nod. I look back at her.

"More than anything?" She stands up and walks toward me.

I'm confused, apprehensive and annoyed all at once. "What are you getting at?"

"Three goals. Three towns." Her eyes gleaming with certainty.

The collar of my shirt feels tight. My mouth feels dry. "Shaylee, that's ridiculous, and we beat you five to three so that would be five goals, not three, if there was truth to—"

"No." Shaylee shakes her head. "No. You've exceeded us by a total of three goals. Think about it. When you tied, nothing happened but when you won—"

"Shaylee." I shake my head.

"When you won. Oak Ridge. Wiped out. And now you win by two goals and two towns are demolished. Hear what I'm saying?"

I laugh. "Shaylee, I think you're just imagining it."

"Imagining it." Shaylee throws her hands up in the air.

"Or maybe you just don't like losing. Listen, what happened is horrible but what you're suggesting is just crazy."

"Addie, listen to me—"

"No, you just don't like it that I'm winning. You're trying to mess with my mind so you're the star once again. Well you're not the star, Shaylee."

Shaylee's shoulders hunch. She sighs. "Fine, Hitler. Go."

"Don't call me that."

"Hitler," she taunts, her nose crinkling.

I calmly walk past her to the door. I slam it, leaving her standing there alone.

CHAPTER 25

It's Pauline's wedding and I'm in a cheaper version of the uncomfortable suit that I tried on at that dress store. I think she may have picked it up for me second hand. I'm amazed she got the right size. Come to think of it, maybe I shouldn't be so surprised. I remember that one time I was undressing in my bedroom. I had opened my closet door to find her sniffling and crying into my trousers. There was a snot stain right in the middle of the crotch. I was so annoyed because it was my last pair of clean pants. Mom had taken to her room with another bout of depression and it wasn't as if she could iron or wash me a new pair.

Mom actually looks a bit happier today and healthier than usual. She stands next to Pauline in a purple two-piece. Pauline and her soon-to-be husband are going through their vows. The priest asks if anyone objects. Pauline glances at me and she doesn't turn away for a whole ten seconds. Do I have food on my face? I've been snacking on potato chips to make the time go quicker. *Take her. Take her please. Away from me forever.* If anyone objects (as if that would happen), I'll punch them in the face. Wait. The referee dude. Where is he? I look around, panic seizing my heart for a moment. *Scheisse.* He better not be here. You're not objecting, buddy. I'll kill you with my bare hands. Fortunately, no one objects. I smile in relief. Oh no. They kiss. No time to look away. I feel that afternoon snack coming up. I try to repress it. I can do this. *No I can't. Oh no.* I vomit all over the five-year-old in front of me.

A woman exclaims, "Did you just vomit on my kid?"

I think this is my call to exit, gracefully. No doubt Pauline would want me to dance with her or something like that. Now, I have an excuse. Stomach flu. I tiptoe out. Pauline's married and she's out of the house. *Yay.*

"Addie?" I hear Pauline's voice.

"I'm sick. Gotta go." I back right into Mother.

"You're not going anywhere," Mom says. "You need to be here for your sister."

"I have a—"

Mom feels my head. "You don't have a fever."

"I do … It's just not feelable." I point to the kid covered in vomit being lead to the washroom. "Look. That's all me."

Anne comes over. "I always feel better after I throw up." *Verdammt nochmal Anne.* She only said that because she knows I don't want to be here. It's revenge for keeping her up at night. They all look at me with a look that says "You're staying." *No.*

After the party and Pauline forcing me into some slow dance, Mom and I return home. The cabernet causes Mother to crash immediately, but

I'm wide awake. I go to Pauline's room and survey it for possibilities. This would make a great studio. I move things around, making noise.

"Addie," I hear Anne yell. I ignore her.

My easel could go in place of Pauline's frilly bed, by the window. This could work for me. Finally, I get it looking the way I want and I'm pleased. Pauline's remaining stuff sits in a corner in the room. I cover it with a sheet. That will do. Then I hear the front door spring open and something crash. *Scheisse.* It's a burglar.

I walk downstairs with a can of bear mace from my school camping trip. I hear footsteps come around the corner. I spray the bear mace.

"Ahhh," Pauline screams and falls over the couch. Her legs go up along with her gown. I move my hands to my eyes. Unfortunately, I can't cover them in time to avoid catching a glimpse of her purple G-string. I will never forget that awful image. *Damn you Pauline.*

"Addie," she yells.

"Oh shit," I say, trying to fake empathy. I stand there, bewildered.

"Addie, get me water."

I go to the kitchen and empty a can of spritzer on her face.

"Ow. Water not club soda."

I find a bucket used to water the flowers. It has some dirt in it. I fill it up and throw it on her. She screams again as it's probably quite cold. I'm amazed we didn't wake up Mom. She must have been very out of it. I sit with a drenched Pauline on the couch. Her eyes are bright red from the mace. I doubt she can see much. I envy her blindness. That G-string image is still on my retina like the negative of some photo.

Anne stomps downstairs. "What the fudge is going on?"

I look up at her. "Es ist nichts. Go back to bed."

"Verdammt nochmal, you're going to wake up Mom."

"Get the fuck back to bed, Anne," Pauline snaps.

"You guys are so selfish," Anne huffs. She turns around and stomps back upstairs.

Pauline starts to cry. I don't want to be here. I don't. I really don't. *Get me out of here.*

Pauline sobs. Snot runs down her nose into her mouth like the Rhine. "Obscene things. He was trying to do obscene things to me, Addie." She sobs. "Obscene things."

"Oh," I say. In actuality, I couldn't care less and it's quite annoying having to fake any form of empathy.

"Obscene—" She sobs.

"Things," I say, not caring one bit. I just like to finish a sentence. I couldn't care less if her man were to lock her in some dungeon for days. I say "her man" because I've already forgotten his name because he has absolutely no relevance in my life. *Take her. Away. I don't care where to. I don't care if you do nasty things with her. Just don't tell me about it. In fact, take her away and never bring her back so I can forget her name too and that G-string, most of all.*

Mother comes downstairs. "Pauline, what's going on?" she asks, groggily.

Great, my out. I get up.

Mom sits down next to Pauline and Pauline sobs to her the whole story.

"Obscene things," Pauline's cries on Mother's shoulder.

I manage to sneak away but not before I overhear that those obscene things were merely the act of procreation. And Shaylee thinks I'm weird? It's like they raised that bitch in a time capsule. How can you not know how babies are made? Okay, we never really had any official biology courses as it's not proper to talk about private matters like that, but come on ... are girls really that daft? Then I think of Ava and Shaylee and I realize, no. No they aren't. My sister is just a freak of nature, more so than me. Two freaks. One household.

I begin to think about why my sister is so messed up. I mean, if she didn't want to marry that guy, why did she? I take a moment to contemplate that fact. Wait a minute, if they are trying to create this dude Hitler, could Pauline be a part of that too? What if the only reason she got married was to imitate Hitler's life so that I become him? If I was with Shaylee, I could ask that question on that thing called "internet." If that's true, it would mean that their plan to make me Hitler was much bigger than I had thought. It would mean that more things in my life were purposely there only to make me become him. Ava. Pauline. What if soccer too? No. That's crazy. But what if? What if it's supposed to build some sort of Aryan aggression in me somehow? What if those "accidents" in Lower Reichfield, the accidents that wiped out entire sections, weren't accidents at all? What if they were somehow related to that dude Hitler? Somehow to me as I'm his clone? Could Shaylee be right?

CHAPTER 26

Sexual thoughts have turned my mind to mush. Maybe Shaylee's right. Maybe my recent art really does suck. What if those early successes were just flukes? What if I can never deliver ever again? One thing that is comforting though is the feeling I get when I walk through Reichfield High. Everyone knows me now. Everyone smiles at me as I pass. It's like I'm a celebrity. I get to my locker and discover it filled with gifts, nearly spilling out of the metal enclosure. A random girl walks by and flashes me her G-string, peeling her clothes down ever so slightly, and it's a G-string that I actually don't mind seeing.

I change for practice and suddenly realize that I'm the only boy in the locker room. Is practice cancelled? Or maybe I'm late? Maybe this is the day that the clocks have switched and no one bothered to tell me? Confused, I make my way onto the field out of the tunnel. It's empty. Where is everybody?

It's then that I notice a large and new, two-story, glass building replacing three quarters of the bleachers. Did that just pop up overnight? The walls are tinted. I'm curious. I walk to it, confused yet curious. All of a sudden, the walls magically untint and reveal the whole team inside. I jump. The walls retract upward like a garage door. Then, Reichfield fans run out onto the field, singing our school chant. I spot Ava who moves to the front and does a cartwheel, the edges of her skirt swirling in the air like those of a pinwheel. Pauline follows and tries to copy but can't quite get her feet up high enough. I look away, this time in time to avoid viewing any undergarments. I look back and Pauline's on the grass. She shakes her wrist. Must be a sprain. I smile.

Our fans sing, "To Reichfield High stand, we sing our chant of praise. Our life and light she's been to all throughout her days." Pauline gets up, brushes herself off and joins in, albeit on a completely different key, discordant even from this distance.

Thomas rushes toward me with his shoulders back and his hair gelled more than normal. He runs his hand through his stiff copperish hair. "Addie, what do you think?"

"I don't get it." I shake my head, confused. "What is this?"

"VIP, Addie. That's our VIP area. Not only that but we get a brand new, renovated locker room where we'll be able to change and get ready, and it's all because of you."

"Where will people sit?" I ask, still confused.

"Watch this." Thomas takes out a remote control and untints the second story. Inside are rows and rows of chairs. It's like they moved the bleachers inside this building. They upgraded everything overnight. Literally, overnight.

"The ministry saw our steady improvement and approved our grant."

"No way," I say. This is great, especially now. After the last game, players from North Prep got rowdy when we won. If we continue our winning streak, which I have full confidence we will, we'll definitely need a protected area in case a fight breaks out. No doubt the glass is bulletproof.

"And guess what?" Thomas beams. "A reporter from Reichfield Today will be here to cover the game."

"That's awesome."

Thomas bounces in place. "And get this Addie, his family is close with a top-notch German school. If we look good, we can improve our rankings and maybe all get scholarships—"

"Really?" I'm in disbelief, my fingers tingling with the thought of possibility.

A scholarship would allow me to leave this town. Not only leave but go somewhere great. This could be my way out.

*   *   *

I must have, as Shaylee would say, "a shitfaced grin" glued to my face. I'm in my own world walking through the parking lot of Reichfield High. I gasp when suddenly I'm pulled into Shaylee's van and she drives off at high speed.

"Hey Parce," she says with her eyes focused on driving.

"What the hell?" I yell.

"Well, I didn't want to risk being seen."

"You could have texted."

"Yeah, I could have, but you're like in 1812. You would have replied a month later."

"Ten minutes," I say. "Ten minutes."

She hands me a can of Panta, a knockoff, orange soft drink that has the logo written upside down. It's then that I realize that Lower Reichfield must get knockoff rejects of canned foods from China. Not only knockoffs, but a knockoff reject. I'm surprised it doesn't have a dent in it and come from a food bank. I don't get it. Shaylee can now afford more upscale food, thanks to me. As well, she can purchase the original instead of this knockoff. Doesn't she realize what I do for her? Where's the gratitude?

She pulls up on a cliff overlooking Oak Ridge or one of the other fenced off neighborhoods, by the look of it. She tosses me a gas mask. I hesitate. How do I know if it even works? Might be a knockoff too. She gives me one of her, "Just do what I say or else," looks. Frankly, I'm more scared of being killed by her. I put it on.

I see the sign for Oak Ridge, the first neighborhood that had an accident. It really doesn't surprise me, the accidents. I mean, Thomas and I learned from an early age how inferior lowlies were at making stuff. We watched a video in Civics where they built balconies only to have them collapse. Thomas and I shared a good laugh. Those were good times. Simpler.

Now that I think of it, something always struck me as strange. In the video, when one of the black lowlies tries to put up a chandelier and it falls down on his head, the shot pans from his head to his waist. Then it pans to the ground. Between the panning, for a split second, I thought I saw a white hand. It could very well be another manipulation. Then again, watching Shaylee drink her knockoff Panta drink makes me wonder if maybe that video was right. Maybe lowlies just don't do things right. Maybe the gas leak was because of their inferior technology. I don't know what Shaylee's hoping to find here.

We sneak past the yellow tape. The neighborhood's completely deserted. It reminds me of something post-apocalyptic. I feel as if the draugar are going to come get me at any moment. At this spot in the valley, you're really aware that you're in the lower part of Reichfield, not because it's any worse than any other part but because you can see how the cliffs surround it. One cliff off in the distance has "Lower Reichfield," written in large letters. Underneath, a motorcycle sticks out of the rock. It's made to look as if the motorcycle somehow drove out of it. Seems about right that it would be an accident how anyone would ever end up here. On a different note, it's an amazing feat how they actually got the motorcycle up there. Sure, some lowlies probably died in the process. Trial and error.

"This is cool," I say.

"Cool?" She punches me, her eyes piercing. "Cool? My friend died here. Idiot." She walks ahead of me.

I follow behind her. "Sorry ..." I try to remember points from a video Shaylee showed me about sensitivity. "I'm really sorry. Listen, I'm sorry if

I offended you. I just meant that it reminded me of the video game I sometimes play with draugar—"

"Draugar?" The glare in her eyes intensifies and her mouth stiffens.

"Zombies."

"Again, my friend died here," she yells.

"Sorry."

We stand in front of a house. It actually looks nicer than a lot of houses you'd find in Reichfield. It's yellow on the outside with flowers in the windowsill. We walk inside. I turn to the right to face the open kitchen. On the floor is a broken teacup. *Wait.* Lowlies drink tea?

I turn to the right and walk toward the living room. Shaylee walks into the kitchen and kneels down near the teacup. I look at the mantle on the fireplace. There's a picture of Yvonne and what looks like her grandma.

"Addie!" she yells. "Addie!"

I run into the kitchen with a poker from the fireplace.

"What the hell?" she yells, looking at the fireplace poker.

"Draugar," I say. "Thought you needed help."

"Again," she says.

"Your friend died here," I respond.

"Right, Addie. Look." She points to an area under the sink. A large hose comes out of a large hole in the wall. The hose starts large and then becomes slightly thinner and then goes into another hole in the wall, likely connecting to the stove.

"What are you doing?"

She twists off the hose. There's a knob on the top of the hole. She opens up the knob. I don't understand what she's doing. Then, she takes her lighter and a big flame comes out from it.

"So? They have an outlet for gas. That's normal. People cook with gas you know?"

"No Addie. The hole. It's weird how big it is. It's like they wanted the house to fill with gas as quickly as possible, so nobody could get out."

"Shaylee. I think you're reaching. I mean, it's the kitchen."

"Right." Shaylee runs out of the room. I hear her footsteps on the steps.

I sigh. This is pointless. This time would be better spent with me working toward painting another masterpiece.

"Addie," she yells.

"What?" I run upstairs to the bathroom.

Under the sink, there's another similar hole. This hole doesn't have a hose. Only a lever. Again, she does the lighter trick.

"Perhaps this bathroom was at one point a kitchen?" I say, speculating.

Shaylee grabs my shirt and pulls me down the stairs. We walk out the door, down the front steps. She looks around the block. She chooses a house, a red brick one across the street. She pulls me across. We enter the house. She pulls me to the upstairs bathroom. She opens the cabinet under the sink.

"Shaylee," I protest.

"Addie, look." Sure enough, there's another identical lever. We walk out of the house. "Addie, you have to promise me that you're not going to win another game."

"Are you crazy?" I say. "This isn't proof."

"What proof do you need?" she says. "Another neighborhood, dead? Me, dead?"

"Shaylee. I'll …" I think of how I'd feel if she were to die. I don't know what to name it, but my chest clenches, and it's painful. "Okay. You're right. I'll lose."

"Promise me, Addie," she yells, looking at me with puppy-dog eyes. She's never looked so vulnerable.

I grow solemn, realizing what I have to do. I nod.

CHAPTER 27

Guess it was too much for me to expect to excel at both soccer and art. It's now that I have to choose. I love winning at soccer but if I really sit down and ask myself what I want out of life. If I tune into my soul, if you could call it that, it tells me the thing I already know. That art is my calling. Art is what I should focus on. Art is my path, even if it means never succeeding. Even if it means never getting the same acknowledgment that I get at soccer. Hitler went with what he was good at, perhaps because he couldn't handle rejection. He needed everyone to cheer for him, like they cheer for me on the field. My last art piece sucked. The rest of my art could suck as well. I could live life never getting the acknowledgment I crave, but so what? So fucking what? It's my life. It's not theirs. They might have programmed these genes but I choose … me. I make the choice and I can choose a different path.

We're on the field. I know what I have to do but will I be able to do it? The high-pitched whistle signals the start of the game. I jump forward, feeling a sense of adrenaline race through me. I kick the ball to Thomas. Thomas pounds down the field, expertly navigating through the red, blue and white North Prep players.

I huff, running to keep up with Thomas. The rest of the Reichfield players fall behind, looking at the two of us, tiredly. I shake my head, sighing. Nobody deserves to be on a team with such pathetic players.

I just hope that Thomas and I can hold out for them. Even though I know what I have to do, at least I'll make Reichfield look as if we gave a good fight. Thomas yelps as his foot slips against the ball as he attempts to pass. The soccer ball wobbles toward me. Suddenly, something lean and quick moves in between us, snatching the ball away. It's Shaylee. She kicks the ball in the other direction.

Rounding on her, I kick the ball out of Shaylee's reach back toward Thomas. I narrow my eyes and run toward Thomas. We near the goal. Cayan, at the goal, backs up, trying to keep his eyes on both of us. Thomas kicks the ball toward me. I pass the ball back deliberately too hard, and the ball careens out of control. Shaylee rushes in, taking the ball. We watch as she runs with it, toward a goal. My team groans.

"Dude, what was that?" Thomas calls from the other side of the goalie box.

"I'm sorry," I yell.

The game continues. My teammates, thinking that I'm the strongest player on the field, pass me the ball. Consistently I "lose" the ball to Shaylee or to another North Prep player although, not enough to make it seem as if I'm not trying. Either that, or I "miss" the ball at the most inopportune moment. Statistically, I must make it look like I'm trying but that I'm not at my best so that they come to the conclusion that I'm either sick or tired.

I wince as I watch Thomas score a goal, tying the match. I glance at Shaylee. She shakes her head. *No.* I was trying to make it look like we were trying but now my "trying" might backfire as we may actually win this thing. If that happens, I'll be Hitler. I'll have been the cause of another neighborhood being destroyed, of lives being lost.

The next round starts, and Thomas gets the ball. Suddenly, he trips and falls flat on his face. A wiry and short player from the other team grabs the ball. He looks a little surprised that he has it as he runs down the field. I pretend to chase him, but I don't intervene when he lobs a kick and scores a goal, propelling North Prep ahead. Humiliating, to lose to such a dummkopf.

The clock is ticking now. There is less than a minute left in the game and North Prep leads by 2 to 1. I can feel the pressure begin to weigh on me as they set up for the next round. How could I just let my team lose? I hate this feeling. Losing in such a cheap way feels even worse. I can feel bile piling up in the back of my throat. I can also feel Shaylee's eyes on my back, but I don't turn around.

The whistle sounds. Thomas snatches the ball and runs down the field. We only have a few seconds left before the end of the game. I catch Shaylee's gaze. She shakes her head.

I grunt, running down the field. "Thomas. Over here," I yell.

Thomas glances at me. I see hesitation in his eyes but he also spots the two red, blue and white uniforms coming to corner him. He passes to me.

I sigh in relief. I freeze for a moment, looking down at the goal. I can do this. I can tie and save all those lives or I can score a goal and have everyone love me. I close my eyes and kick. Time seems to stand still, everything moving in slow motion. I open my eyes as the ball leaves contact with my foot. It soars through the air, arcing downwards toward the goal. It falls and bounces off the post.

I groan, sinking to my knees. I can hear North Prep celebrating. I've lost … and the only person I can blame is myself. I look up. In Thomas's eyes is a look that goes beyond disgust. Of course he's angry with me. Yet, for some reason this look strikes me as more than the anger that comes with disappointment. It's a look of pure hatred. A second later, the look disappears and is replaced with the sadness that comes with defeat.

*　*　*

Shaylee's not responding to my text even though I did exactly what she had asked and lost. You think she'd be more grateful. After the match, I was so demoralized and was looking for a way to cheer myself up. I couldn't handle losing for nothing and so I punched mascot-boy out again. Then on the bus, I tried to kiss Shaylee again, dressed as him. Unfortunately, I forgot to take off the head, which resulted in a beating. Her other teammates looked up at her beating up the mascot and were confused. She responded that she still had some aftermatch aggression that she needed to release. What is it with girls? You do what they want and they beat the shit out of you?

She's probably chillin' with Cayan or something. *Answer your freaking text.* It would be so easy to get rid of him. I could so do it too with the help of Mengela. Yet, then again who knows, maybe it would make Cayan into a martyr or something? Maybe she'd idolize him to the point where nobody could ever compare. Or what if she went into a bout of depression? How would that serve me? She'd be completely no fun to be around. I'd be delegated to "girlfriend" and have to listen to her bitch for hours. Nope.

Maybe I could set him up for cheating instead? I could pay a random girl who goes to Shaylee's school, I could. Then again, who knows if that girl would even be trustworthy. Too big of a risk that it could get back to Shaylee. I thought of just smearing lipstick on his collar like in a film noir movie. I even tried with Anne's lipstick in shade Vixen XXL.

The reason I chose Anne's instead of Pauline's was because I didn't want anything of Pauline's near my lips, ever. Unfortunately, Anne walked in while I was kissing an old undershirt. She yelled, "Mom." Instinct took over and I flung her lipstick across the room. I thought I had confiscated all the evidence, but Mom walked in to find the undershirt covered with lipstick marks sitting beside me.

"Someone's popular," Mom said with a smile.

"Mom, he took my lipstick. Mine," Anne yelled.

"Anne, at some point you're just going to have to accept that your brother's growing up."

This made me oh so happy. I'm the star and she isn't. I can get away with taking her things … taking anything. It's me in the spotlight. Yes, Anne that is something you're just going to have to get used to.

Anyways, there's no way I can believably set up Cayan for cheating. I could just steal his phone and not respond to Shaylee's texts like she's doing to me right now. However, any anger created would only be temporary. Unless ... I did it more than once. I could just imagine how that situation would unfold.

Cayan would yell back, "You crazy yo. Can't find my stupid phone," or something along those lines. This scenario would happen five or six times and then Shaylee would for sure realize this guy was a loser. I smile. Yes, that's it. That's the plan. Now just how will I get my hand into his pants to pull out his phone? Haven't worked that out yet, but I'm sure I'll think of something. *You always do, Addie.*

CHAPTER **28**

Speaking of hands in one's pants, Ava had her hands in mine. It all started when I arrived at school and I realized something. I may be a freak in a family of freaks, but at least I'm a freak that's famous. There was a giant picture of me hanging from the flagpole. That was the flagpole that the nameless masturbating kid, whose face and name I forgot, was hanging from. That I can forget but Pauline's purple G-string? Nope. I want to scrub my eyeholes and overwrite that image on my retina as a computer overwrites data.

Back to Ava's hands in my pants. It happened in art, where else? Helene was giving the most unsexy lecture on feminist artists from the '90s. Somehow to be an artist in the feminist movement, a woman has to turn her genitalia into a flower on a canvas. That, I definitely don't mind. Yet, these paintings are from women whose genitalia I don't want to acknowledge. Much like Pauline and her G-string.

As Helene flashes slides of unsexy (usually very hefty) and overly hairy bulldykes, I'm getting a happy ending. Seriously though, I wonder if this will have any effect on my psyche? Mess it up per se, even more so than it's current effed up state, as Shaylee calls it? If Ava continues to jerk me off to pictures of hairy armpit patchouli wearing obese women who own twenty cats, who knows, maybe that will be my new thing. I really hope not.

*　*　*

Well I'm having a great day and Cayan is a mancunt. I can't get to his phone. He's always holding it like he's on life support and it's his oxygen tank. His face is puffy. It looks like he's been crying but he insists it's just allergies. He even brought his dog today because he's sick. With his other arm, he clings to him and hugs him like he's some doll. Give me a break. It's just eczema. I look over and he's massaging some sort of cream on its snout. I need to distract that schwachkopf. I paint a stroke of black on the canvas but my mind is elsewhere.

"Cayan," I say, "do you know when Shaylee will be back?"

"Uh, think she went to Yvonne's funeral with Hector—"

"Well could you help me with something?"

"Uhhs …" Uh huh is not plural but whatever. He rises and walks over, reluctantly. "What?"

I gulp. Right. Have to ask him about something. "Uh … what do you think?"

He looks from me to the canvas, confused. "Of what?"

Right. I forgot, the canvas is empty except for one brushstroke. I'll wing it and channel Helene.

"Well yeah, that's the point," I add with my fake art snob voice. "It's deconstructionist." I think I heard Helene use that word once. I reach for Cayan's pants. He turns his hips away and I almost grab his cock. *Fucker.*

"Deconstructio … what is that shit?" Cayan asks.

"Wait. So you're telling me you don't learn that in school? Well what do you learn?" I ask in my snobby art voice.

"Hey man, we have good teachers. Better than your prissy old white dudes."

"Oh yeah?" I say. "So Shaylee says you're taking business?" I adjust my voice to sound as if I actually think he has potential. "You must learn a lot about economics and stuff."

He calms down. "Yeah, actually we do."

"You must learn real world theories to help you move mountains out there in the capitalist world of prissy old white dudes."

"Completely."

"If only at Reichfield we had business courses like you, maybe we could use a welfare grant toward starting a respectable crack trafficking biz."

A moment later, I'm on the floor rolling around with Cayan. This time my hand actually does brush against his cock that unsurprisingly is actually very much like a mancunt. Seriously, what does she see in him? We're having so much fun wrestling that I don't notice Shaylee standing over us.

"What the fuck?" She pulls Cayan off.

"You." She waves her finger at Cayan. "Don't hurt our star."

"That little shit started with me," Cayan yells with messed up hair.

She touches his cheek. "I don't care. I care that his delicate hands aren't broken so he can paint."

Cayan backs away and trips over a chair. "Fuck." He heads out. The door slams behind him.

I look up at Shaylee. "So I'm your star?" I say, smiling.

CHAPTER 29

When I'm walking home, I take out Cayan's phone that I managed to swipe while wrestling with him. He has some lame screensaver of some rapper dude decorated in bling galore. I'm relieved he doesn't have a passcode. His brain is a fish. Probably would forget it in two seconds anyway.

I open his phone. Curiosity overtakes me. I want to see his photos. What kind of guy is Shaylee into? Does he have any naked pics of her? I browse through his photos. Mostly they're of his pitbull who has a lot of different outfits and can drive a hummer. Must be hard living in the shadow of your pet. Nothing he can ever do in life can live up to the grandeur and fame of his pitbull. I put away his phone.

As I'm walking, I think more about the plan. Shaylee will receive my text "from Cayan". Then I'll wait for her to send me a text back and then I'll not respond for hours. If she's anything like Ava, that will drive her crazy. *Wait. No.* This won't work. Ava likes me more when I treat her like shit. I need to think of something else. *Scheisse.* Why are girls so complicated?

Suddenly, I feel a vibration in my pants. Maybe it's a message? From Shaylee? I reach for the phone and feel for a second what it must feel like to receive a message from a girl that you actually like. Every fiber in my being has come alive and my heart races. I turn on his phone and go to his messages. The message reads: "Where are you?" It's from an unknown number, not Shaylee. I close the message and accidently click on another one. A pic of a naked girl pops up. It's definitely not Shaylee.

A smile takes over my face. I feel elated. This is it. This is what I need. That sitzpinkler is cheating and his lover just messaged him to meet. This is too good. Wait. It's just a photo. What if it's not enough to break them up? I browse through the four other messages. I look at them. Nothing. He probably deleted the rest to cover his tracks. How can I get evidence? I need to catch them in the act and take a pic of them copulating. That would really sting. She'd for sure be able to leave that trash in the past way quicker with visual proof.

Wait. All the text says is, "Where are you?," and it doesn't give a location. I look back at the four previous messages and they are just as vague: "meet me," "I'm here," etc. There's no location. Where's "here"? I could return the phone to Cayan and then follow him, but it's way too late for that. Cayan is probably on his way there.

Wait. I pick up the phone and text back. "I'm on my way. Sorry. Are you at the same place?" A moment later, I get a text back: "Yes. I'm by the hummer." Hummer is that code? Then, I think ... hummer, hummer ... the pitbull. I flip through Cayan's photos. Then I find the one I want. The pitbull is driving a hummer in front of that broken-down ice cream parlor. The hummer must just be an art installation of some sort.

I run for ten minutes and I'm drenched in sweat, but this time I of course won't have ice cream. No need to go through that whole hypothermia incident a second time. Not that the parlor would be even open at this hour. Stealthily, I approach from the forest and yes, the hummer is there. Why they chose to have a hummer art installation beside an ice cream parlor is beyond me. Then I notice that the sides have pictures of ice cream painted on them. Oh, I get it. It must be a hummer ice cream truck. That makes sense, kind of. I see a hooded and slender, shadowy figure by the hummer, wearing a long, military style jacket. No doubt she's naked under that jacket like in a film noir. It would be great if the girl was even prettier than Shaylee. That would bring out her insecurity. I want to get closer to take a look but can't without drawing attention. From this proximity, any movement on my part would be highly audible through the quiet suburban air.

The metallic rattling noise from Cayan's car causes me to jump. Quickly, I duck behind a tree. He speeds in and stops next to the hummer, almost crashing into it. That fucker is either drunk or really arrogant. From the edge of the forest, shrouded in darkness, I watch as he gets out. He slams the door. He walks with such passion that I'm expecting him to grab this hooker and lay one on her seedy, slut mouth. I take out my phone and press record. Shaylee will love this. Bam. Instead of kissing the girl, he punches her. What?

My mouth drops open. Wait. What's going on? He punches her again. This time in the stomach. I suddenly feel the need to run out there and rescue her like any chivalrous man would do, but I stop myself. Her hood falls back. That's when I notice it's not a she but a he. Moonlight highlights the man's face and I realize … it's Thomas.

CHAPTER 30

Wait, Thomas? Perhaps he's a homosexual and I just never knew. Maybe that's why he was so mean to masturbating boy. Maybe he wanted to direct the attention away from himself so he wasn't the one hanging from the pole. That could be it. Wait. No. That can't be it. The looks. I see the way he looks at Ava.

"I didn't know." Thomas coughs after having the wind knocked out of him.

"You told me it was a different area," Cayan yells as he punches Thomas again.

"Get your hands off me," Thomas says with a stern authority. "It was an accident. It won't happen again."

"Accident? My friend died. You killed her. An accident, you're calling it an accident?" He punches Thomas again. "The levers. I pulled B15 like you told me. That was her neighborhood. I killed her," Cayan cries. He backs away. "'I'm out." I think he's going to see me. I duck behind the trees.

"You think there's an out?" Thomas laughs coldly.

Cayan stops.

"There's no out, Cayan. You know too much. Either you do it or someone else will. No more presents. No money for that expensive MBA. No more designer clothes for your little mutt. And what about your family?"

"You leave them out of it," Cayan yells, panic choking his voice.

"You know what I'm saying is true. Even if you did manage to get everyone out in time, what about your brother? Can he leave so freely? Will the guards just let him walk out of prison?"

Cayan turns around. "If this happens again." He waves his fingers.

"It won't," Thomas says calmly. "You. Your friends. Your family. Nothing will happen to them if you comply. But if you don't—"

"You, your friends, your family." *Scheisse. Turn off. Turn off.* My phone is playing their conversation.

"Did you hear that?" Thomas swings around.

He looks in the direction of the bushes. I freeze. He starts running toward me. I back away and I run. *Scheisse.*

I run through the wooded area. I make my way out of the trees. There's just an empty field with a broken fence, littered with trash. I start to run but then I remember there's no way I'll outrun Thomas. He's too fast. While I'm able to maneuver easily on the field due to my small size, Thomas has the speed. *Hide.* Where can I hide? There's nowhere to hide. For some reason the image pops into my head of a magician doing a magic trick at my fourth grade birthday party. If only I could make myself disappear. Wait. I don't need to disappear. I just need to distract. Footsteps. I hear them approaching. I look toward the fence. There's an empty milk carton. I run to it. I swing my leg back and kick it as hard as I can. It goes flying across the field.

"There. Over there," I hear Thomas yell. They run toward the sound. I slink back into the woods and run past the hummer in the opposite direction.

* * *

Skipping school the next day was surprisingly a lot easier than expected. I knew if I faked sick at home, I'd be confined to the house with Mother and we'd probably end up watching a German soap opera of sorts. So instead, I shoved my fingers down my throat and projectile vomited all over Helene's prized artwork. Payback.

Well, Helene was furious. Sorry Helene, guess you'll have to paint another abstract painting of your vagina or whatever the fuck that was. Anyway, figuring I had the flu, they sent me home. However, instead I'm standing by the fence of North Prep, watching the soccer players train.

Where's Shaylee? Where are those bouncy, perky, A-cups? *Come on.* Then, I see her. A stroke of sunlight catches the edge of her hair and she glows.

"Shaylee," I yell.

She doesn't look up from running.

"Shaylee," I yell again, louder.

She sees me and frowns. She comes over. "Are you stalking me?" she says with a hint of annoyance. "You left me a million messages telling me to call you? And that trying to kiss me on the bus, not cool."

"It's Cayan," I stammer.

"Cayan," she repeats, her voice dripping with skepticism.

"He's a traitor."

She smiles. "Wow."

"I'm serious. I caught him last night—"

"Addie, enough."

"Shaylee, you don't understand—"

"Understand? I understand perfectly well. You hate him because he's dating me."

"No. I hate him because he's a giant fuckbucket."

She turns away.

"But listen, I saw him with Thomas. I have a video. Watch." I take out Cayan's phone. Fortunately she doesn't recognize it or she'd give me a lecture on stealing.

Shaylee grows silent. I think I've gotten through to her. "Listen," she says, the previous certainty lost in her voice. "I'm dating him, okay? I like him—"

"He's an idiot and a traitor. I saw him. Just look at the video." I play the video for her.

"Addie. What is this? There's barely any sound and those people could be anybody in the dark."

"No sound?" I listen to it. The sound is momentarily muffled by the wind. "But they aren't anybody," I yell. "Listen." I put the phone to my ear. How come I didn't realize the wind was that strong for most of it?

"Addie, I have to go. I don't like you like that. I'm sorry if I did anything to make you think otherwise. We're just friends, okay?" She runs back to the track.

*   *   *

Just friends. I don't believe this. I contemplate Shaylee's statement while seated on the couch. Everyone's out at my abode. Good. I have so much time to think and think and think. "I love Landra" plays on the TV with the sound off. My mind goes in circles. She chose Cayan over me. Cayan. An idiot. Maybe she's an idiot and she deserves to be weeded out. Survival of the strongest. Survival of the smartest. Survival of people who will just say yes to sleeping with me.

Ava's head pops up right at the part Landra trips over a car. Okay, that wasn't Landra. Some other woman. Was a bit distracted. How did that happen? I know every episode. Am I developing dementia?

Clarity is important to me. I thought about sleeping with Ava, but then I thought that I wouldn't be able to multitask as well. This way I can be more efficient. Also, sleeping with her would actually require me wanting to touch her, which I don't. I just want to pretend she's someone else. If I squint my eyes, with the new hair, she even looks a lot like Shaylee.

Maybe it's a good thing Shaylee doesn't believe me. I don't know what we actually could do in the grand scheme of things. Thomas is a small part of the machine that created me. We barely even know who they are. My family. That dude in the book we found at the house. Thomas. I'm still mad at that. I opened up to that guy. I shared my feelings with him and all the while, I was probably just being psychoanalyzed or manipulated for their little experiment. All they view me as is an experiment. That makes me angry. Yet, at the same time I like that I have someone like Ava to take care of my needs. Maybe this situation isn't so bad. If Shaylee's never going to like me, maybe it really doesn't matter what happens to those lowlies after all.

Something's buzzing. Is it her? Ava reaches into my pocket and hands me my phone. I press the button and smile while looking at her. "Hel—" I look at the phone and realize it's not my phone. It's Cayan's. I fling it across the room. *Scheisse.* Cayan's phone scatters into a million pieces.

Ava tilts her head in confusion, like a dog.

"I just want to give you all my attention." *Good cover, Addie.*

"Awww. So sweet." She kisses me. She looks toward the smashed phone. "Strange … but sweet."

* * *

"No fucking fuckety fuck." Cayan stomps. He stares at his smashed phone on the floor, where I had planted it so that he would think that he was the one who had smashed it accidently. Pieces lie scattered about. "How did this happen? I just got this, Shay."

Shaylee looks up from texting. "I'll get you a new one."

"No way. I'm the guy here. You not buying me nothing."

"Anything," I say correcting him calmly as I add a brushstroke to my canvas.

Even from my peripheral vision, I can see him clench his fists.

With my proof destroyed, I'll need new proof. Then again, it wasn't that strong to begin with. Two shadowy figures in the dark. I'm not even sure you could even tell it was Cayan, but who cares? She should believe me. My stomach sinks. Werner. I could have got Werner to help improve the sound and make the video clearer. He builds electronics and stuff ... and rockets. Why didn't I think of that first? One time he even built me a bomb for my "birthday". He had bought that story all too easily.

"Your birthday? Of course," he replied with a smile. "I'll make it with a special black powder and use only the best squibs for you, Addie." Never know when you need a bomb. Doesn't hurt to be cautious. If he could make a bomb, no doubt he could fix the image and the sound. *Ugh.* Why didn't I think of that sooner.

I need new proof but I can't think. *Addie, think.* My brain's on overload. My thoughts are elsewhere. Shaylee comes over. "Addie, they didn't like the last one."

"Why ever not?" I look up from my canvas.

Shaylee brings the black portfolio carrying case over. She takes out the painting. She sets it down on the broken radiator.

"Well, perhaps they just don't understand genius," I say, my voice slightly raised.

"Ha." Shaylee lets out a slight laugh. "Addie, it's sloppy."

"Sloppy?" I feel a burst of rage coming on. I clench my fists. I want to punch something.

"And please do explain your inspiration, huh?"

I breathe in. I swallow my anger. I look at the canvas. Now, what was I thinking that day?

"I didn't see it at first as it's abstract, but this." Shaylee points to the canvas. "Looks like a woman giving a man a blowjob. Is this some joke?"

Oh right. I blush. Caught red-handed. Hey, an artist is supposed to draw from his life, right? Helene paints her vulva. I just thought I should paint something along those lines.

"I'll have you know," I respond in my snobby art voice, "paintings of one's private parts are very popular."

Shaylee's mouth raises in a half smile. "Well we're trying to sell these as Franz Marc's. Franz did not paint some woman abstractly giving him a blowjob, got it?" she yells. "And since when do you know anything about popular?"

* * *

I arrive at school and expect to see my face in the usual location, on a giant banner hanging from the flagpole. Instead, it's just the normal Reichfield flag. I walk inside. Instead of my poster plastered to the walls, the walls are now empty with exception to a few flyers. One of them reads, "Math Tutor Needed". Another reads, "Lost glove". The third is a poem in german called, "Erlking," by Goethe. It has an accompanying picture. It reads, "Now he's grabbing hold of me! Erlking has done me harm!" The glowing blood-red eyes of the Erlking shine bright. Instead of the evil spirit drawn as it usually is in black, the black is woven with the colors of North Prep: red, white and blue. Its claws reach out toward a boy wearing the Reichfield jersey and its spirit body of smoke surrounds him, coiled like a vaporous snake. The boy looks terrified.

It truly is a work of art. I wonder if Steinfeld did it. *Ha.* He probably did. It must kill him not to be able to take credit. I mean, he can't exactly take credit for anything nationalistic as he's been staunch against the soccer team from day one. For good reason, he's been playing the part of the so-called Jewish traitor of Reichfield. He's not even Jewish, I remind myself. Just an actor. Just an imposter. Much like … me. It suddenly occurs to me that no one will ever know that I painted what I painted. They'll just think it's Franz Marc. I slouch. I spot Ava by the lockers. She's with a group of girls. I walk in her direction. She glances at me, then turns away, casting her eyes down. I feel like an idiot. I turn away as well, feeling as if I hit a brick wall. Ava? Even Ava rejected me?

I bump into someone and I look up. It's Thomas. "Walk with me Addie," he insists, grabbing my shoulder. I follow him outside to the soccer field. I tell myself that there's no way he saw me that night. I'm safe. *Relax, Addie.*

"Addie, remember when they painted a dick on our new field?"

I nod.

"Well yesterday you made us look worse than that. What were you thinking?"

"I just had a bad day."

"Addie. Addie. Listen to me." Thomas shakes me. "It's survival out there. Survival of the fittest. We worked our way up to beat them, so many times. We can't fall back now."

It suddenly occurs to me that Thomas must want me to succeed so badly because his success is linked with mine. Since he's in on things and one of them, perhaps he's been given certain instructions to be a good soccer player but to never exceed me. I think of all the times Reichfield lost before this year. It always struck me as weird that Thomas, that musclehead, barely scored a goal. I think back to those times we would practice with each other in the street. Occasionally, he'd get one past me into the net but he rarely scored on the actual field. He brushed it off as just nerves. However, with his steroid-formed calf muscles and speed, there's no way with the odds of things that he wouldn't have scored at least one goal, alone. Yet, he only really scored goals when I scored as well. It must have been on purpose.

"Addie, are you even listening to me?" Thomas asks, frustrated.

"Sure," I say. "You're right, Thomas." I nod.

*　*　*

In the afternoon, I skip soccer practice just to piss Thomas off. I head to the house. Thomas has been texting me and I ignore his texts. My ghosting must drive him crazy. The fear he must feel. If I don't work on things and improve, he won't be able to utilize his skills at maximum strength. I hold him back. Suddenly, I'm happy. The only reason Thomas was ever my friend was because he thought I was someone I'm not. His friendship depends on circumstance. Whereas, Shaylee hates who I was designed to be but likes me as I am now. She believes in me. She sees my potential, I remind myself, even though my last painting literally sucked dick.

I know. I'll paint something for her. Thomas's theory of things is that you never let girls know how much you like them because that makes you vulnerable. He told me that one time. Although, it always struck me as strange as there was never any girl. It was just Thomas admiring himself in the reflection of a napkin box or Thomas talking to a poster of Lana Turner. "I know you think I'm swell," he'd say.

There was one girl who liked Thomas in the fourth grade but he complained that he didn't want to be friendzoned. As a result, she became friends with some other kid and in junior high, she dated that kid.

Well, I'm going to make Shaylee a painting in the style of Franz Marc and it's going to be an abstract painting of her. I think of what I like about her. I like the fact that she's strong, unpredictable and determined. On the field she doesn't let anything get in her way. I also like the fact that she's trustworthy. She's kept my secret and never lied to me, unlike well, everyone I know. She told me exactly who I was manufactured to be without ever hiding it from me, without ever manipulating me.

Suddenly, I'm inspired and it's not from anger this time. I paint and paint and paint, my heart light, my mind clear. I'm so absorbed that I barely notice when Shaylee arrives. I look up at her. She has a look on her face that I can't figure out. She looks almost sad. Why would she be sad? She won the game.

"Wow, that's amazing," she says, walking toward my art.

"You think?"

"Your best yet, Addie."

I look up at her and I can't get my words out. I want to tell her everything I feel, but I can't. Her expression fades to sadness once again. Perhaps she's still sad about Yvonne.

"Addie," she says. "It's over."

"What?"

"They've discovered they're fakes."

"What?"

"Yeah, Addie. Unfortunately, it's back to the same old."

"Same old?"

"Sorry."

I push the chair away. I stand up.

I head toward the door in silence. I don't want her to see the tears of frustration in my eyes.

"Addie," she yells after me.

CHAPTER 31

All of this was for nothing. I'm stuck in this shit town forever. I stomp home. No one will ever recognize my talent. I'll never get out of here. I'm stuck. Why did I believe that things could be different? That I could find happiness? *No.* There's no happiness for me. Nothing ever works out. I think something's going to work out and then surprise, everything falls apart. It's like those times I almost scored a goal and things looked so sure but then ... everything just turns to shit.

"Give me your wallet," a deep voice says.

I forgot I'm still in Lower Reichfield. I forgot to put my hood on. What was I thinking? I turn around to see a ruffian with bloodshot eyes.

"Give me your wallet," the verbrecher says again with conviction.

Scheisse! What am I going to do? If I look him in the eye, he might pounce like a wild animal and whip out his knife. I look down and that's when I see it. A rat scurrying about, next to the curb. I smile. *Vermin.*

"Sure," I say. "It's in my shoe."

I reach down and grab the rat by the tail.

"Hurry up," he yells, momentarily looking away. Quickly, I stand up. I take the rat and place it in his hand. The verbrecher screams. He drops the rat. It runs up his leg. He screams again, jumping about. I take off.

Running through Lower Reichfield, it's then that I realize that I have the strength. I look over my shoulder to see the ruffian verbrecher running haphazardly behind me. No doubt the rat bit him and he now has rabies. Good. I imagine him foaming at the mouth. Maybe he'll bite some of his other ruffian friends too and they'll be weeded out of humanity, as if they weren't already. I run faster.

My success at defeating such a lowly gives me new confidence. Shaylee, you're right. I can make it as an artist. They loved my paintings. We can both escape this town, somehow. There's a way out, I know it. If my paintings can get out, so can we. We'll leave. I'll become a successful artist and Shaylee, you'll be my manager. We can travel Europe and check out all the museums. Things might be hard at first having limited cash but the cash we make can be used toward gas money and food. Also, having the artist experience might make me an even better artist. Then I think of Cayan. An obstacle. An obstacle that perhaps I can finally get rid of. I could take him on.

I glance behind. Looks like I lost the verbrecher. I've reached the border of Lower Reichfield and Upper Reichfield. Go home? No. I should go back. I need to tell her. I turn around and take a different route. I get back to the house. I swing open the door. It's then that I see a face that I know too well, and my heart drops to my stomach. He looks up from his wheelchair. For a second, I think that maybe there's a chance he doesn't recognize me, but then his expression turns to one of anger, his eyes burning.

"Him. He ... was him. He did this," Kero Reyes slurs with a vehement look of hatred.

CHAPTER 32

I get some satisfaction at being able to outrun the former soccer champion, even if he is now in a wheelchair. When I get home, it hits me. Everything is ruined. I want to tear down all these walls. I pull a lamp out of the wall and knock it to the floor. It shatters. I want to rip off this cheap, green wallpaper. Anne is doing aerobics in front of the television on a mat. Mom comes out of her bedroom for the first time in a while.

"Everything okay?"

"No. It's not okay," I say with a huff.

"Oh Addie, everyone has their ups and downs." She walks toward me and hugs me. I let her hug me, reluctantly. I'm sweating from all the running. I'm surprised she doesn't comment. She probably thinks it's from practicing.

"It will be okay. Thomas told me what happened and you'll win the next game, for sure."

Anne looks up from her aerobics. "Ha."

"Something funny, Anne?"

"Why would he win, Mom?" Anne looks at us.

"Shut up. I won the last few games, I'll have you know."

"Really? You call that winning? Winning to me is when you actually beat them by a killing, not just a measly point."

"I'll have you know, I beat them by two."

"Wow." Anne smiles sarcastically.

"Anne," Mother exclaims.

"No, Mom." Anne turns off the TV and gets up from her mat. She walks over to us. "I see that Addie's having his little breakdown, but it's only because you spoil and baby him. Not to mention that Addie gets his picture hung everywhere for subpar athletics."

"Anne, enough," Mother yells.

Anne walks toward me. "No, Mom, why should he get a trophy for merely beating them by one point?" She glares at me. "Everyone here acts like he's a star but all he is is grandiose. All he is is average, at best."

*　*　*

"All he is is average," I hear over and over again in my head. I stand outside the fence surrounding the North Prep soccer field. I wasn't sure I'd have the guts to show up here after what Shaylee thinks I did. *Which I did do,* I remind myself. I keep on forgetting that. But that Addie was a different person. I've changed because of her. I know she's seen that. I can talk to her. It was mostly Mengela and Thomas anyway. I was just there for the ride. I'm here now. I spot Shaylee running out of the tunnel, chanting her school chant.

"Shaylee."

She spots me and runs faster.

"Shaylee," I yell.

She doesn't respond.

Maybe she didn't hear me. "Shaylee."

I climb over the fence, tearing my pants on the way down. My Aryan Galactic Warrior boxers show through but I don't care. I start to run. I run faster to catch up with her. Man she's fast. I'm so out of shape today because I barely slept. I can barely keep up with her and I'm panting. I'm like a grandma.

She runs around the track.

I hobble next to her. "Shaylee, it wasn't me."

"Save it," she says icily, not even looking at me.

"Okay it was, but it wasn't even my idea."

She clicks her tongue in disgust. She runs ahead of me. I'm not even in workout gear. I must stand out like a sore thumb.

"Listen, can we talk?"

"No." She sprints ahead.

I run faster to catch up to her. My hamstrings hurt. Their coach blows the whistle. The other players take a position on the field, each standing a few feet apart. Shaylee looks at me and runs to take her position. On the ground in front of each player, there's a soccer ball. Each ball is attached to a string. Okay, I've been playing soccer a long time and I have no idea what to do with that. She picks up the ball. Their coach blows the whistle and they start waving it back and forth like a gymnast baton. They face each other and kick it diagonally. It bounces back. They face in the other direction and jump on their feet two times like they are dancing a square dance. I watch from off to the side. Then they kick it again diagonally. *What the?*

The coach looks at me. I don't want to draw any more attention than I already am in my Aryan galactic boxers. If the other players recognize who I am, I'll for sure get a beating. No way I'd be able to fend them all off. I run to the center. Lucky for me there's one ball left. I pick it up and copy Shaylee, waving it back and forth. Now, all we need is their uncivilized fans to make this some mockery sports musical. I feel ridiculous. This is humiliating.

"Shaylee, I'm on your side."

Shaylee kicks the ball. It bounces back on the string. Then she twirls it in the air. She turns to the soccer player on the right and then back to face me. "Yeah right—"

"Just give me another chance," I say with desperation in my voice. I wish I could have sounded more strong. "I really like you," I add, my voice cracking. I feel like my throat is closing off. I've never said that to a girl. I want to kill myself now. For some reason, I expect her to say that she forgives me. Instead, she continues the routine in silence.

"I like you even more than just friends …"

Suddenly, I'm on the ground. Shaylee's on top of me. She hovers over me with a lifted fist, aimed at my head.

"You leave Cayan alone."

"Cayan?" I say, gasping for air. "He's bad, really Shaylee, you go to—"

"You're not going to harm him like Kero."

"Listen, Shaylee. He's bad. I told you. I saw him."

"Liar. Why would I believe anything you say? If you touch one hair on his head, I'll end you." With that she lifts her leg off of me and stands up.

CHAPTER 33

Maybe, it serves Shaylee right to be dating a monster. Cayan is the monster. Not me. I'm done with this. I've never been so humiliated. Things couldn't get any worse. Ava's not even returning my texts. *Ava.* The girl who couldn't get enough of me. Desperate beyond hell. I've been ditched by Ava. That stings. Shaylee won't return my texts either, even though I've apologized. Tried to explain that it wasn't me or rather that I was manipulated. Who knows what became of my painting? Did she trash it? Did she burn it? It was the best one yet. I don't care anymore about life. My life is nothing. I'm a failure at what they designed me to be and I'm a failure at what I want to be. Nothing is working out. I should just end things.

As I stand on the cliff overlooking the ruins of Oak Ridge, I step forward with one foot. Dirt falls off the edge. If only Shaylee knew Cayan was behind the attack and I wasn't lying. Maybe she would see that I've changed and that I'm on her side. Then again, she doesn't trust me. It's hopeless. Everything is ruined. I look over the edge at the ruins. It's a long drop. Suddenly, my knees feel weak. I'm such a coward. I can't do it. The thought of the fall and breaking one bone at a time and all the blood makes me nauseous. It has to be quicker. I was told Hitler just ended things with a handgun. We have a shotgun in our house. I could use that. But wait. There's no bullets. Think you have to be over eighteen to buy them. Hector might have a handgun hided somewhere to protect himself from the gangs. That might be easier. I step back.

*   *   *

It's the day of the game and I'm still here, for now. I know there's little chance of things getting better, but I'm going to give myself a little more time to think of a solution. From the dugout tunnel, I walk in silence next to Thomas. He's still pissed at me for the last game, I can see it. They were all counting on me and I let them down. For some reason I feel like the tunnel, barely lit with incandescent bulbs, is darker today than usual. Emerging onto the field, the bright light stings my eyes today more than usual. It's as if I lost something big. I lost the new life I was creating for myself outside of this shit. Now, there's only this. There's only the muck that I have to wade through. The light is false. The light is deceiving. The light is laughing at me because there is no light, only darkness.

We get onto the field and I glance in North Prep's direction. It's Shaylee. I spot her sitting on the bleachers holding Cayan's hand and swinging it back and forth. They are set to defeat us, to defeat me for what I did. I don't feel particularly bad at what I did to Kero. He was nothing to me but at the same time, I guess I understand that it was bad. I mean, would

I want someone to do that to me? At the time, I thought of him as a lowly, a nothing, something to walk over. I guess my viewpoint changed when I realized that Reichfield, Upper Reichfield, we're not so great after all. Why would I want to be associated with a set of pathetic losers? If it weren't for Thomas and me, we would never have won a game. They're all relying on me because they are weak while North Prep is strong.

Strong? Am I strong now? Shaylee's not bothered by the loss of our friendship. *I'm bothered. I'm weak.* She doesn't care if she ever sees me again. She'd be happy having Cayan in her life instead of me. She chose to see the good in him even though he's a giant flachwichser. She refused to believe me when I told her he was responsible for the leak. Even though she gave me a chance at first, seeing me for more than my DNA, for being more than this "Hitler," she refused to accept my apology. What's the point of changing when people don't see that you have? When no one sees that you have? When the friend you thought you had, doesn't see you as great? When she looks at you the way you looked at lowlies? I clench my jaw and tighten my fists, my stomach churning.

I look up at the mammoth crowd occupying the bleachers. Women, men, children. Upper Reichfield, are they all in on it? I imagine the look on their faces if I were to secure a win for Reichfield. I imagine them cheering. Cheering for me. Wanting me. They don't see me as a lowly. *No, Addie. No. Stop. You know what it would mean if you win this game, don't you?*

The game kicks off and we pass the ball first. I'm actually amazed that my fellow players seem more cool, more calm and more composed today than usual. North Prep chases us, trying to dispossess us of the ball but we prove to have the upper hand. North Prep gets the ball and I close in fast on a through ball sent by Karl. Our Reichfield onlookers rise expecting a goal. I can feel their tension.

I dribble past my marker with relative ease. As I near Cayan at the goal, I want to drive it right through his eye sockets and send him flying into the net. I fire a shot. *No.* It goes way past the crossbar. *Balls.* I know I can't win but at least I want to get a goal so they cheer for me and so I feel some love coming from somewhere other than Pauline.

Pauline, I spot on the giant screen they installed adjacent to the VIP area. I do my best to tune out her voice. "Here comes Addie," "Addie's looking stellar," "Addie has the ball," "Addie, Addie, Addie." You'd think the game was only about me. Normally I'd like this kind of attention but coming from her, I don't.

Bringing my focus back to the game, I play hard but I'm demoralized by that goal that should have been mine. It was so easy. Why did I fail? *Don't focus on the past Addie. Look to the future. Future success. Future goals.*

The game continues. Fifteen minutes after kick-off, we maintain dominance, having a higher ball possession. North Prep prepares to take a corner kick. I motion to the players to arrange our defense in order not to concede. *We have this.* As the spot kick is about to happen, Shaylee emerges.

A North Prep player sends a cross deep into the box eighteen. North Prep struggles to head the ball in while our defenders try to keep the ball out. However, we all miss the ball, fumbling. We watch as Shaylee rushes at the ball from outside the field of play, unmarked. She controls the ball easily, gracefully, so much so that it looks like it belongs to her, and takes a comfortable shot from the left angle with her strong right foot. Werner stands no chance. He watches helplessly as the ball flies past him into the net.

Thomas is the first to protest the referee along with the other players. Only for some reason, none of the referees saw what happened. Perhaps they had been distracted by North Prep's uncivilized fans who were doing that thing that Shaylee once referred to as "twerking."

The scoreboard changes: 1 to 0. North Prep's now leading by a lone goal. With five minutes to the end of the first half, Thomas gets a pass from Karl in center midfield. He sprints with the ball until he reaches the front of a North Prep defender whom he dribbles past by doing a leg over the ball trick. This splits the North Prep defense open and clears the way for me to make a run. Now's my chance.

Thomas finds me with a nice pass. This could be the equalizer for us. I can do this. I'm about to take a shot when I think about what happened last game, where we almost won. No. I can't risk it. I take a shot. This time, I purposely fire over the bar again for the second time. Thomas swears. I've never heard him swear. I glance behind. His face is red and his eyebrows are knitted together. I've never seen him this angry.

North Prep takes the goal kick and shoots the ball deep into the center of the field. Karl in midfield wins the ball and runs with it toward the right flank. He passes the ball to his friend who quickly finds Thomas on the far right corner. However, a North Prep defender intercepts and passes. He shoots the ball into the field to another player. That player twists and turns with the ball before he passes it to Shaylee. Shaylee, unmarked once more, receives the ball and dummies past the goalkeeper. She kicks the ball into an empty net to the delight of her team. The referee immediately blows for half time with North Prep leading by two goals.

Thomas is no longer silent. He explodes in the locker room. "What the hell is wrong with you?"

I sit there quietly with my face burning in my hands.

"Alright, if you don't want to talk. Fine. Just get your freaking act together, man."

I totally get Thomas's frustration. I even liked seeing him frustrated before, but for some reason, this time is different. Shaylee's not my friend anymore. Thomas is really the only friend I have even if I dislike him half the time. Maybe I should give him a chance. He after all has chosen me as a friend whereas Shaylee chose Cayan. Thomas at least has good taste.

The second half begins with North Prep displaying the confidence of a winner. They know they're in a comfortable lead. They can relax, whereas we look more desperate, especially with Thomas becoming more aggressive on the ball. I'm amazed. Our desperation actually pays off after ten minutes into the second half. Thomas is able to get a goal firing a shot just outside the 18-yard box.

Thomas shouts to the players, "Let's make them eat their testicles."

I hate him once again. That should be me. It would have been me, but I'm crippled. I can't act. I can't be myself. I can't win. I can't win as an artist and I can't win at this because my hands are tied. What can I win at?

Thomas hurries to get the ball from the net of the North Prep team. Reichfield begins to play with more confidence, but I maintain a poor form, repeatedly making silly mistakes. Something has changed. Now I'm sidelined by my teammates. They stop passing me the ball. Instead, they feed Thomas more passes.

Fifteen minutes left. A Reichfield left back takes a dangerous run. Now's my chance. I'm open and call for the ball. Why's he not passing to me? Then I remember, he thinks I suck. Instead he passes the ball to Karl in midfield who is tightly marked by a North Prep player. Karl manages to get away from his marker and finds Thomas with a through ball that goes right between two North Prep defenders. Thomas gets the ball. He lobs it over the goalkeeper who has left his goal line. The shout of "goal" reverberates and pulses across the stadium. The crowd is ecstatic.

"What a goal," Pauline screams.

Thomas is the hero. He brought Reichfield High level from two goals down. It's strange. This game he's not waiting for me to score goals. Perhaps I was wrong about that theory. I feel pride for my team but at the same time, I feel hatred. Thomas. Why him? Why not me? *It should be me.*

Pauline reads my thoughts kind of. "If only Addie could get it together this game. He's not his usual, strong, ripped, champion self. I have no doubt however that he can get his golden ratio proportioned body to number one."

"Golden ratio proportioned? Who the hell made her commentator?" I hear Thomas yell.

Eight minutes left. The game opens up with Thomas clinching the equalizing goal. This isn't right. I can't do this. I change form on purpose and improve. It shouldn't be his. It shouldn't be his glory. It's mine. *To hell with you, Shaylee. To hell with you, Cayan. Thomas, you will not steal my glory!*

Aggression rises within me, like hot air within my chest. I can feel Shaylee looking at me, wondering what I'm going to do. Good. Be scared, Shaylee. You deserve it for abandoning me. Thomas is my friend. You are not. Thomas passes me the ball. I run with it. Out of nowhere, a North Prep player brings me down illegally a few meters from the 18-yard box. The referee blows for a free kick.

"Addie. Addie. Addie. Addie." The crowd shouts my name. I breathe it in. This is what I should feel. Recognition. All adoring eyes on me.

The match has reached its final second. It is now or never. I brace up to take the free kick. Thomas looks at me with doubt as if he thinks I'm going to mess up again. Maybe I will. Maybe I won't. I don't know what I'll do. I think I know what the right thing to do is but do I care? Shaylee looks at me. That pang in my stomach. I hate her for making me feel this way.

I step back to take the kick. The stadium grows silent. Shaylee. Perhaps we could be friends again? Do I really want to throw my friendship away just for glory? I kick the ball. It flies over the North Prep defense wall to the far right corner of the goal post. Cayan stretches as much as he can but he can't stop it. The ball enters the net. The referee blows the whistle. *Yes!*

Shaylee, it's you who threw away our friendship, not me. I just chose to rise to destiny. The crowd goes wild. My teammates pick me up. Thomas is ecstatic. Shaylee looks at me, dejected. I smile. *This is on you.* If you had been my friend, this wouldn't have happened.

CHAPTER 34

A stripper? Apparently our afterparty has just become X-rated. Somehow Thomas, with his father's connections, organized this for us. We're standing by Thomas's pool. His father waves to us from the patio doors.

Karl rushes out. "You gotta see this. That bitch from the other team has lost her mind." He motions for us to join him inside.

We gather around the TV. In front of the run-down ice cream parlor, a blond Reichfield reporter holds her microphone. "... And now for some bizarre news, a local Lower Reichfield soccer star has apparently lost her mind after losing another game."

It's Shaylee. She stammers, "Y-you gotta listen to me." Her hands shake, and her eyes are wide and frenzied. She raises her hands to her head and back down. "The accidents are related to us winning or losing and we lost which means another town will be destroyed."

She sounds like a schizophrenic. Karl and Mengela laugh. I look away.

Thomas rushes out and puts a beer in my hand. "Drink up, Addie."

I shake my head.

"Aw come on, loosen up. We killed them."

Yes, we did. I look away. I think to myself of the repercussions, wondering when they'll carry out their attack. When Cayan will unleash the gas or fire or whatever he chooses to unleash on an unsuspecting community in Lower Reichfield. Perhaps it will be Shaylee's community. Suddenly, I feel sick. *No, Addie. You're not going to feel anything.* I grab the beer out of Thomas's hand. *You're not going to feel a thing.*

I spot Ava. She smiles at me. I walk toward her. I feel Thomas's eyes on the back of my head. For some reason, I sense anger, somewhat the way I sense anger on the field, the way prey sense a predator. I turn around and Thomas smiles at me. He toasts to us. No. I must be imagining it. Must be the alcohol.

CHAPTER 35

Footsteps sound on an empty Reichfield street outside of Reichfield Hyrdro & Gas. There's a park across the street. It's desolate. No one is in sight.

"Cayan?" Shaylee calls.

The party has ended and nobody knows where I am, not even my parents. I watch Shaylee across the street from behind a tree. They probably figure I'm with Thomas which has allowed me to move freely without a trace. Not to mention, I've defeated Lower Reichfield again so there's no way they would ever think that I've been turned.

I look at the tracking device that Werner gave me. This way I can follow Cayan without him knowing. I told Werner that I wanted to track an enemy's whereabouts which is true. I just didn't tell him who. It's hard for me to lie to Werner as I know he's a scientist. He's scientific also in the way he watches people and how he can detect a lie. He watches for cues.

During the game, when Cayan wasn't looking I snuck off and placed a tracker in his gym bag. I figured he'd come her, but I had to be sure.

When Cayan entered the building a few minutes ago, I thought of tackling him right there. Then, it occurred to me that I should wait to catch him in the act, in front of Shaylee. That way, she'd see it for her own eyes.

When I had access to Cayan's phone and could access that thing called "Internet," out of curiosity, I looked up the countries that Hitler had conquered. The first four were: Austria, Poland, Denmark and Norway. Shaylee was right. Each goal was linked to an invasion by the group she referred to as the Nazis, which was then linked to the destruction of an area in Lower Reichfield.

In 1938, the coat of arms of Austria was a double headed eagle. The fluke goal we had gotten many years ago represented Austria and the area that succumbed first was Eaglehammer. In continuation, the national tree of Poland is the oak, hence Oak Ridge was the second neighborhood to be wiped out. Red clover is the national flower of Denmark hence Red Cloverfield was the third neighborhood to go. The dipper is the national bird of Norway and the moose is the national animal, hence Dippermoose was the latest area to go.

By this logic, the next neighborhood on the list would be Belgium followed by The Netherlands. Belgium's national symbols include: The Common Kestrel (bird), colors (red, yellow and black) and the lion as their animal. On the map of Lower Reichfield, I found areas which might fit with one of these symbols: Kestrel Road, Lionfield, and three other areas that form a triangle on the map: Rouge Park (Rouge is red in French),

Geelfield (Geel is yellow in Dutch) and Schwarz Creek. Shwartz is black in German. It could be any one of these areas. But which one?

At this point, it doesn't really matter which area it is, what matters more is the time of the invasion. The time the Nazis invaded Belgium was at 5:30 a.m. I look at my watch. 4:30 a.m. Cayan's working the night shift. No doubt he'll be getting ready to carry out the next attack.

"Cayan?" Shaylee calls again. I'm amazed that Shaylee is even here, but then again she is a night owl. No doubt, actually possessing a conscience also probably makes sleep problematic, on a night like tonight. She also thinks she's meeting Cayan when in fact it was me who sent her the text to meet. Werner helped me by making it look like the text was from him. Werner was confused, but I just said I was doing some reconnaissance which sufficed. I watch Shaylee fiddle with her phone. Oh no, she's going to text him. What did I expect? That she was just going to catch him in the act? Why didn't I think ahead? I knew I shouldn't have drunk anything.

I rush out to her. "Shaylee," I yell in a hushed tone.

She looks up, her face paling with shock. She stops texting. Then, the shock transforms into hatred and disgust. "You."

"Shaylee, listen."

"Stay away from me, Addie," she yells.

She's going to attract attention. I jump toward her and cover her mouth and pull her around the side of the building where there's a parking lot that's mostly empty except for a few cars. We're now standing behind an SUV. She kicks and screams.

"Stop it. Listen, it's Cayan. We can save them." I let go of her.

She tries to scream, "Help."

I cover her mouth again and I don't know what I'm going to do. At that moment, out of the building exits Cayan, lugging a few canisters. Shaylee stops struggling, falling still. He pulls them to the back of a large van, off to the far right of us. He opens the back.

"What's he doing?" she whispers to me.

I grab her arm and pull her down so we're both ducking behind the SUV.

Shaylee peers around the side, confused. "He's supposed to work until six."

He gets into the van. Cayan reaches into his pocket. He sighs. He gets out of the van and hurries back into the building. I pull Shaylee's hand. She looks at me reluctantly but she yields. We run across the parking lot to Cayan's van. Perhaps now she realizes there is something to what I'm saying. We hop into the back of the van. Behind the canisters, there's a tarp covering something. I lift it up. Of course. Cayan's puppy mansion. A few power tools are scattered about on the floor. I lift up the tarp. Shaylee and I crawl inside the puppy mansion.

Cayan returns with his keys and starts the ignition. Shaylee looks at me. I must be allergic to something. Maybe this van was used for ragweed? I feel a sneeze coming on. Shaylee covers my mouth. I stifle it. Oh no. I sneeze into her hand, unleashing a big string of mucusy snot. Disgusted, she looks at me and wipes her hand on the side of my shirt. The van begins to move. Cayan puts on his horrible trance music, which repeats in an endless loop of musical hell. I cringe and plug my ears.

Fortunately, some time later, the van stops. We must be there. He unloads most of the canisters. However, just when he's about to unload the final three, I let out a sneeze. *No.* Shaylee looks at me. She moves forward. I pull her back. She looks at me intently. I let her go. She crawls out of the puppy mansion, leaving me hidden. She stands in front of Cayan.

"Shaylee?" Cayan's voice raises in surprise.

"Fess up. What are you doing here Cayan?"

"I ..."

"Is there someone else? Someone you're meeting, maybe?"

"What? No. Listen, you can't be here." Cayan looks around, anxiously. He runs his hand over his mouth.

I peer out from under the tarp.

"Shaylee, I'm sorry. You can't be here." Cayan walks toward her.

"What going on, Cayan?"

"I'm sorry."

All of a sudden, he grabs her and attempts to strangle her. I seize my moment and jump out from underneath the tarp. I push Cayan to the ground and punch him in the face five times. He fights back and tackles me. I'm pinned to the floor. I manage to wriggle free and punch him in the nuts. Then, Shaylee hits him over the head with a giant canister.

I catch my breath. I look around. The van is parked on a gravel road next to a metal fence. Off in the distance, across a large field is the highway. I get up and look from Shaylee to Cayan. We pull him into the van and cover him with the tarp.

"What now?" she asks, catching her breath, her chest heaving.

"We could drive it somewhere ... off a cliff," I suggest. I can't think of a more appropriate end to this sitzpinkler.

The sound of wheels on gravel distracts her. She jumps.

"Scheisse. He must be meeting Thomas," I say. I look around the van for a place to hide. We used the tarp to cover Cayan. Without the tarp, he'd for sure see us in the puppy mansion. I push the puppy mansion forward and pull Shaylee behind it. The wheels on the car come to a stop. Then we hear the car door opening, followed by footsteps walking toward us.

"Buddy." It's Thomas's voice. "Cayan?" He looks inside the van. Shaylee and I are silent, trying not to breathe. My heart beats fast. My muscles tense up. Thomas looks around. It's then that I notice a spot of blood on the floor. *Scheisse.* I take a breath and ball my fist, getting ready to pounce. Fortunately, a second later, Thomas closes the back of the van and we're now in darkness. We hear him walk away. Then, we hear what sounds like a rusty metal gate creaking open followed by the front van door swinging open. Then, the van rumbles and a vibration moves through the floor.

The van rocks about as it starts moving down what must be a dirt road. I glance at Shaylee, anxiously. We stop a moment later. Thomas gets out. We move carefully to the edge of the van. Shaylee opens the door a crack. We look out. We're at a farm.

I look to the side and I see a crop duster plane. Thomas has a notepad and looks to be doing some kind of security check. Of course. He's going to attack by air, the way Belgium was attacked by air. What's in the canisters is probably gas, some kind of chemical warfare or worse, a biological weapon. Yes, that makes more sense. Maybe it's targeted specifically for non-Aryan DNA. They cloned me so it's highly possible they'd also have that technology.

"Shaylee, it could be biological," I whisper. "We have to stop him."

"There's two of us." Shaylee looks at me, her eyes intense.

I step out of the van. "Thomas," I say.

He turns around and looks at me. I walk toward him.

"Addie?" He looks shocked. "What are you doing here?"

"Thomas, this is going too far and you know it."

"I don't know what you're talking about Addie," he says with a nervous smile, looking around for Cayan. I walk up to him.

"Give me the keys," I say to him, now two inches away. I stick out my hand.

"Addie." He smiles. "This is for your own good."

I see his punch coming. I block it with my arm. We fight. I roll around in the dirt with him.

I flip him around, holding him down. "Thomas, stop."

Thomas bites my wrist.

"Ow." I know if I look at the blood I'll feel nauseous so instead I concentrate on causing him damage.

We struggle some more. Thomas punches me. I punch him. He bites me again. *Sitzpinkler.* I punch him two or three times. Then a rooster crows. It distracts me. Thomas flips me over and punches me again and again and again.

Shaylee rushes to us. She tries to kick him in the head but he sees her kick coming. He grabs her leg, causing her to lose balance and crash to the ground. She hits her head and passes out. He has my head squeezed between his elbows. I struggle, my arms growing heavy, the world growing blurry, and then ... I lose consciousness.

I come to and I'm sitting in the back of the plane next to Shaylee. We're both tied up with rope, with a seat belt over top, to keep us in place. Shaylee looks at me desperately. What if we can't stop this? Cayan sits next to Shaylee. He babies a welt on his head. We taxi to the end of the runway. It's time for Thomas to take off. He pushes the stick forward.

Thomas looks at us and smiles. "Addie, you'll thank me later. These lowlies have infected you. You'll see."

The plane moves faster and faster and then ... it stops.

"What the?" Thomas looks around. "What's going on?" He looks back at us. He hits the steering wheel. He looks back at us again. Shaylee has a smirk on her face. "You," he bellows.

The plane door opens. Thomas pulls us out. Gas trails from behind the plane, down the runway. Shaylee must have punctured a hole in it when Thomas and I were rolling around on the ground. But how did she? Of course. Cayan's power tools. Thomas kicks the dirt in frustration. He balls his fists. Perhaps we only have moments left before he kills us.

CHAPTER 36

If I was Thomas, I'd be dead and so would Shaylee. Instead, we sit in soccer uniforms in Cayan's van. Instead of the usual red, black and white of Reichfield, I'm wearing Cayan's soccer uniform from North Prep; red, white and blue. It hangs loosely over my white t-shirt. Thomas stands over us, with his handgun pointed at me. I gulp. If he was going to shoot us in this van, he'd have shot us already. Still, it's quite disconcerting. I distract myself by thinking about how odd Cayan's shirt is. It's extremely baggy around the upper body, yet skinny around the waist. In addition, the giant v-neck is way too big for me. It's like the attention-grabbing shirts Ava wears to show off maximum cleavage however, instead I'm showing patches of chest hair. I never realized before just how fat Cayan's neck was. For a fit dude, his body like Thomas's physique, is extremely disproportionate. Helene opens the door, takes one look at us and smiles.

"Got your text," Helene says to Thomas. "Brought this." She holds out a black motorcycle helmet with hot pink trim. She jumps into the van and closes the door.

I find it somewhat amusing that Thomas, the one who tries to be so cool all the time is texting with Helene of all people. Thomas takes the helmet from Helene and plunks it down on my head. As Helene's head is thick, it's a bit loose.

"This will be amusing to say the least." Thomas grins.

Cayan sits across from us. He's tied up now as well but unlike us, he's gagged with one of Thomas's soccer socks. I'm surprised he's conscious. He must have a bad concussion but then again, being so thick, he probably has a thick skull. Cayan screams through the sock. *Shut up.* Have to hand it to Thomas, at least he thinks ahead. No doubt without that sock, Cayan would be talking Thomas's ear off. Cayan's so stupid. How could he have thought Thomas was his buddy?

Thomas waves his gun toward the door. "I know what you're thinking Addie, that you can escape, but here's the thing, you can't." He puts his handgun in the back of his jeans. He picks up a machine gun from an open bag at his feet.

"Do you know what this is, Addie?" He asks.

I don't answer him.

"Well, it's a sniper machine gun, developed by our top engineers, capable of functioning as a sniper and a machine gun at the same time. If you're interested in the history, Addie, it's a highly evolved German version of the M2 Browning from the first world war. My father gave this to me as a present." Thomas smiles. "Okay, no he didn't. I took it without him knowing but if he could see how you've fallen, Addie, I'm sure he'd approve. And that's not all, Addie, guess what? It has the capability of automatic precision shooting, meaning even if you're running, it will lock onto your movement. Basically, what I'm saying is, it doesn't miss." He hands it to Helene.

She examines it. "Now this is a work of art." She points it at us and takes aim. "Should I splatter his blood like paint?"

"Admit it, my art is great. You know you liked it. You were lying to make me think I was a crap artist."

Helene grins. "Thomas. Just tell me when."

Thomas pushes Helene's arm down. "No. Listen. You only shoot them if they don't comply, got it?"

Helene whines, "Oh come on. Just let me pull the trigger. I want to try this baby out. The others will execute him anyway when they find out. Can't I just pull the trig—"

"Helene, listen to me. If you shoot Addie the others will be mad and you'll be in trouble. No doubt they'll want to harvest his DNA and examine him, likely with brain scans before they put him down. If they don't understand what went wrong, then how will they know how to fix it?"

Helene pouts, with her finger hovering over the trigger.

"Helene I have seniority here, do I need to remind you? If Addie doesn't behave you don't shoot him, you shoot her." Thomas lifts Helene's gun up to point at Shaylee. "Got it?"

Helene sulks. "Fine." She opens the door of the van and jumps out. She slams the door shut.

Thomas looks at us. "So here's the thing guys, you kind of messed up my plans for Belgium, I mean, Lionfield."

"I knew it," I say with satisfaction.

Thomas continues. "So here's the other thing, the Nazis actually carried out three attacks on May 10, 1940."

"Thomas, don't do this," I yell, struggling in my restraints.

Thomas's nose wrinkles in disgust. "This works perfectly. Oh, Addie, I see how you're not happy, but you should be. Hitler, a man light years better than you, attacked Belgium, Holland and Luxembourg on May 10 and that's what we're going to do. Thanks Addie, for allowing me to be more historically accurate."

Thomas kneels down next to me. "Just to be entirely sure you get what I mean, as your brain is no doubt damaged by just breathing the same air as these lowlies, Addie, so here's how it's going to go, you and Shaylee are going to let us win by two goals and if you don't there will be consequences."

"You're forgetting something?"

"Oh, what's that?"

"I'm Hitler. If you win these games, it won't be me winning, it will be you. That's not exactly historically accurate."

Thomas smiles. "And that's why I have this." He pulls a full coverage wrestling helmet out of his bag. He puts it on. Then, he unbuttons his jacket to reveal my soccer jersey with my number on it. I'm surprised it fits him. Aside from it rising up around his waist, It looks tight but no tighter than some of the jerseys worn by a few of the players from North Prep. I'm stunned.

"It's too much for me to hope that the others will change their minds overnight and see me as their true leader. So, in the meantime, I'll be the one winning the games for you. I'll win all the games and then Addie, tragically like Hitler, you'll kill yourself. Yet, instead of it being because of the enemy closing in, it will be the pressure of success being too much for a teenage boy like yourself. That pressure, unfortunately, leading to your untimely death. Then fortunately, I'll be there to take over as the rightful leader."

"You'll never be me," I yell.

"Maybe … but I want you to suffer, Addie. To watch. I want you to watch me be triumphant in your place. I must teach you Addie how a true Aryan wins a war." Thomas shoots his arm straight up in the air. "For Reichfield." The under pit of his jersey rips.

"You're crazy. No one is going to buy you're me, with your build."

"Oh Addie, most of the men already know that you're Hitler. You're a legend. A god, in their eyes. They won't doubt for a second that you were able to rise to the occasion and bulk up overnight."

Maybe he's right, I think. If they do worship this man, Hitler, no doubt, they'd believe such a miracle could occur.

Thomas smiles. "After these games, you'll return home and for assurance, I'll have her in my possession. That way you'll comply for future games."

"Don't harm her," I yell.

"Oh I won't, if you obey. FYI, Helene will have eyes on you at all times. She won't take her eyes off you. I've heard from her all female, skeet shooting retreats, she takes a mean shot." Thomas takes two steps toward the door.

Cayan glares at me with hatred.

Thomas returns. "Oh, one more thing. Just so you know I'm serious." Thomas reaches into the back of his jeans for his handgun. He aims it at Cayan. Cayan screams through his sock. Thomas shoots him through the head. Blood spatters close to me. I feel nauseous. Shaylee breathes in heavily, almost hyperventilating.

"Don't worry, Ava will be in here shortly to untie you." Thomas turns away.

"Thomas." I struggle in my restraints. "You're weak."

"Excuse me?" Thomas turns back around. He walks to me and kicks me in the head. Helene's helmet crashes against my face. My jaw flings backward. I feel my lip. The taste of salty blood. No doubt he busted it.

"You're weak, you heard me. You know we'd beat you under normal conditions which is why you want us to lose on purpose," I stammer.

Thomas laughs. "You, Addie. Win?" He laughs some more. "Those times when you won, Addie, they were flukes and let me remind you, I was the one who scored a few goals. Without me, you would have merely tied."

"Oh yeah, if you're so confident in your ability, why not allow us the possibility of winning? After all with your Aryan blood, you can't lose."

Thomas turns away. He grows silent.

"If you force us to lose, basically what you're saying is that you're the one who is weak," Shaylee adds.

"Okay. Huh. You actually think you can win? Forget the purposely losing thing, you'll lose anyway. I'll one up you. You can play like you normally do. If you win, I'll let her go. But if I win ... if I win ..." He points the gun at Shaylee. "You kill her."

"Deal."

Thomas smiles. "Okay."

Shaylee glares at him.

He looks at her with an amused grin. "Your death is on him. Cheers."

"Go fuck yourself, Nazi." Shaylee sneers.

Thomas jumps out of the van and closes the door behind him. We sit in darkness.

"He'd kill us anyway, you know? At least now, you'll have a chance."

I feel the darkness on my shoulders. Shaylee squeezes my hand.

"Did you ever like me?" I ask, feeling tension in my chest.

"Addie."

I feel her turn away.

"You almost kissed me. Was that just a game to you? Was I just an experiment?"

"Addie."

"We're probably going to die, I want to know."

"Fine, I'm attracted to you Addie. I am ... it's just—"

"What?" I yell.

"It's just there's something inside of me, I know myself. I just knew ... it wouldn't work ... that's all."

"Oh." I sit back. "Okay."

Shaylee lifts her hands up. I hear the sound of biting. I'm guessing she's biting at the restraints around her wrist. Thoughts race through my head.

"Do you think there's a God?" I look at her silhouette in the darkness, trying to make out her face.

"You want to have this conversation now?"

I'm now deep in thought. "Is the one who cloned me, God?"

Shaylee lets out a nervous laugh. "If he was, wouldn't it be you out there on the field being the Nazi, instead of Thomas?"

Shaylee fidgets, trying to loosen her restraints.

I smile. "Yeah. Guess, even if I die, I'll have that, right?"

My eyes become accustomed to the darkness and I look toward Cayan, lying off to the side, limp and lifeless. I watch as Shaylee looks around the van, probably for something she can use to untie herself. However, the van is empty. There is nothing. Thomas removed the power tools and threw Cayan's puppy mansion out on the highway.

"We're getting out of here." Shaylee squiggles toward the door. She shoots her hips out, followed by her legs, then her shoulders and then repeats the cycle. When she arrives at the door, she tries to kick it open with her feet.

"I'd like to think there's a God but I'm not sure," she says.

"Yeah. Sometimes I think there is. I mean, you look at a leaf and it's so simple but then you look closer and you realize that it has all these veins and it's so complex."

My feet tied as well, I copy Shaylee and squiggle my way to the door of the van. I join in and kick it. "I mean, even a worm, it's so simple, right? Maybe one of the easiest things to paint. I can paint it for sure and copy it, right? But can I create it from nothing? Sure, I can create a copy like me but it's just a copy, right?"

Shaylee kicks the door. "You're a bad copy."

"Thanks." I frown, not knowing if she got past what I did.

Shaylee laughs. "It's great you're a bad copy. I mean, you're a good bad copy. Thank God you're not like him." Shaylee kicks again and the door swings open, sending Ava flying backward.

"Well, that wasn't nice." Ava brushes herself off and stands up.

My eyes move to the gun lying next to her on the parking lot asphalt. She rushes to pick it up. She points it at us.

CHAPTER 37

With our hands still tied, we walk in front of Ava, to the field. She points the gun at us from under her red and black, spandex shirt. Her neck, red and irritated, matches her outfit. When Ava had went to untie Shaylee's feet, Shaylee had tried to use her legs to strangle her. However, Ava was able to do some sort of back flip which broke the hold. Like Thomas, I had to talk her down, into not harming Shaylee. I think I was only able to because I'm a clone of that dude, Hitler and Ava may still harbor hope that I'll come around to his way of thinking.

My leg hurts and I notice that my knee is scraped. I must have hurt it in the fight with Thomas. I'll have to ignore the pain if I'm going to do my best. Shaylee has dirt on the side of her face and her cheek looks swollen.

We arrive at the field. It looks a brighter shade of green today, against the dark gray sky. Thick clouds gather in the distance. I glance around. We are the first ones here except for a few Reichfield spectators. Normally, I'm on the Reichfield side but today I stand on the opposite side. Since the building of the VIP area, the area of the bleachers for North Prep is now just a sliver. It can house ten people max.

More spectators pour in and the VIP section is now at maximum capacity. From the looks of it, most of Reichfield is here. Hector waves at us from the other side of the field. The North Prep soccer players are just now trickling onto the field, one by one. Thomas comes over.

"I took care of your coach."

Shaylee glares at him.

"I made this fair. As I'm coach, now you or Addie can decide who's coach of your team." Thomas looks to the roof of Reichfield where Helene must be. "I think this position will suit Helene much better, don't you think Addie?" He smiles at me, expecting me to smile back as I once did. I don't. Helene must be lying down on her stomach. Sunlight reflects off something metallic. The gun she has pointed at us.

"This is hardly fair," I say to Thomas, moving around trying to loosen my restraints.

He spots Hector looking at us from afar. He looks at us and then at Ava. "Why are they still tied up?" he says in a hushed tone to Ava. "People might notice."

Ava sighs and slips the gun to Thomas, who points it at us through his jacket. Ava goes to untie Shaylee's hands. "I still can't believe this is my competition." Ava says to me with a look of disgust. She loosens the rope around Shaylee's wrist. It falls to the floor. Shaylee punches her in the jaw, causing Ava to fall backward. I smile.

"Thomas, enough of this. Shoot her," Ava yells, with a busted lip.

Thomas reaches for Ava's hand and pulls her up. He grabs her waist. "After the game, babe, Addie will shoot her, wouldn't you like that more?"

"I want her dead, now."

"She's not going to shoot me, bitch. If she shoots me, Addie won't comply." Shaylee smirks.

Thomas wipes the blood away from Ava's lip with his thumb.

"Thanks," she says looking into Thomas's eyes. They look to be sharing a moment. Then, Ava blinks. "Wow, I never noticed before but in this light you're kind of a gingie."

Thomas steps back. He lets out a long breath and heads to the other side of the field. Ava follows him.

I glance around for a chance to escape. I look toward the top of the school. Helene sits up momentarily and then lies back down, holding her gun. There's no escape. Shaylee and I walk toward Hector and the North Prep team. I pull down my helmet.

* * *

Shaylee and I stand on chairs. North Prep stands in front, looking up at us. "Listen up guys, we must stick to the game plan no matter what. We have to make sure that we maintain possession of the midfield. Then, Ad-Angelo and I will finish off Reichfield."

"Angelo?" I whisper to Shaylee with confusion. "Angelo?"

"What? I gave you a name that blends in."

"Who the fuck is Angelo?" I hear a player say. "And why is he wearing a ladies motorcycle helmet?"

"Where's Cayan?" a player asks.

"He needed a vacay. Who wants to fill in for that fu-fun guy?"

A burly player raises his hand.

"Great, you."

"Where's Coach?" another players asks. "Wasn't he on the bus?" another player says in confusion.

"He had to be somewhere. An emergency," Shaylee says. "He asked us to fill in. This is Coach's cousin, Angelo."

I wave.

CHAPTER 38

The referee blows the whistle and the game begins. Reichfield kicks the game off in style, confidently passing the ball around. The right midfielder sends a long ball in. Thomas takes a run deep with the ball. Then Mengela takes the ball to the flanks and dashes with it. He sends a dangerous cross into the 18-yard box. North Prep's defense is in disarray. Thomas jumps high above the defender to nod the ball into the net.

"It is a goal," screams Pauline.

The crowd erupts into a large cheer, their excitement almost palpable in the air.

This is bad. Reichfield has scored within minutes of the start of the game. If it continues like this, we'll lose for sure. I was right, they were holding back in order to let me shine. This game, Thomas must have told them they have orders from above to unleash their full strength.

Shaylee motions to the defenders of North Prep. They storm up to the referees to protest the goal. We all saw it. Thomas had put the ball into the net with his hand and not his head. I look at Pauline on the screen. The side of her mouth raises. I can tell when she's nervous or lying. She obviously spotted the infringement. The referee disregards the protest and sides in favor of Reichfield.

I look at Shaylee who's furious. Thomas laughs.

"If they're going to play dirty, so should we," I say to Shaylee. She agrees.

The game continues. Instead of Shaylee using her upper body to control the ball, she uses her hand. The referee blows the whistle. Shaylee throws a fit. She comes back to me.

"This game is rigged. Of course we can't win. I'm dead." Shaylee panics.

"Listen, if we prevent them from scoring goals and if we in turn score obvious goals, goals they can't contest, there's no way they can deny it. If they do, all these players will walk off the field and they won't have a game to win. Remember you've won before."

Shaylee breathes in and out. "It's my nerves." She takes a deep breath in, trying to calm herself down. "How do we even know he doesn't have both referees in his pocket?" Shaylee asks me, nervously. We look at one of the referees, standing beside the mascot. Thomas could have definitely paid him off, just like he did Cayan.

Shaylee perks up. "Got an idea." She pulls me close. "Listen. I'll create a distraction. You take care of him."

Shaylee struts in the direction of the Reichfield players. She heads right up to Karl and pushes him in the shoulder. Reichfield players gather around. All of the crowd's attention is now on the potential fight. As a result, I'm able to sneak away. I pull Hector aside and quickly fill him in on the situation. He doesn't believe me at first. I'm losing patience. Fortunately, Helene moves and I'm able to point to her on the roof. She points the gun straight at Hector's head. Well, it's pointed at my head but Hector's in the way. He glances up at Helene and turns back, startled. Hector follows me, now fully on board.

Hector stands in front of me, blocking vision from Helene. The rat mascot has his head turned. I punch him in the side of the head, knocking him over. I'm still amazed at how easily he collapses for a giant. Then, I stand in front of Hector, blocking vision from Helene while Hector takes care of the referee. No doubt, Helene's focused on me, rather than on the spectacle occurring behind me. In seconds, we are able to strip down the giant rat and switch their costumes.

"What's going on man?" the former rat mascot asks in groggy confusion as Hector and I take turns putting the referee uniform on him. He looks at me more closely. "Hey, don't I know you?"

"You're the new referee, got it?" Hector pats him on the shoulders.

"Ok-ay." He looks from Hector to me, confused.

Hector glares back.

The former mascot looks down at his uniform. "Okay, Great. I deserve a promotion."

Good. At least now we have one referee on our side. As I walk back, I glance behind at the real referee slouching in the rat mascot costume, on the bleachers. His hands and feet are tied with the mascot's socks. Someone might notice … Then again, who ever notices the mascot anyway?

Shaylee spots me coming back. She stops fighting with Karl. Normally, she would be forced to sit on the sidelines. However, Thomas lets it go, probably because he wants to prove that he really can beat us.

The game continues. I cringe hearing Pauline's squeaky voice over the speaker. "And Reichfield still leads by one goal. The goalkeeper will now place the ball on the spot for a goal kick."

The game moves forward. Our midfielders struggle for the ball and Karl steals it. He tries to pass to the winger. The pass is intercepted by a North Prep left-back who sends a long ball in trying to find me.

"Here, here," I yell.

I gain control of the ball skillfully and do a flick to deceive my marker. It works. I'm able to send a through ball to a North Prep winger on the run. Yes. A goal might be just around the corner. The winger sprints with the ball on the right flank and sends a cross into the 18-yard box. I attempt to nod the ball. I miss.

Fortunately, Shaylee's there. She's up for it. She does a backflip and sends the ball right into the net. Now that's why I like her. So what if she sees me just as a friend? She's not just my friend. She's my ally. We celebrate with the rest of the team.

"It worked," Shaylee shouts. I smile at our teamwork. Purposely missing the ball allowed their defense to be open so that Shaylee could score as we planned. And score we did, minutes before the end of the first half, nonetheless. The referees argue but in the end, we get the goal.

Thomas looks furious. I smile. Thomas whistles to his team. His team gather around him. We watch as they take their position on the field once more. Thomas looks at me and smiles from cheek to cheek. What's he up to?

Moments into the game, we discover the reason for Thomas's malicious smile. One of Reichfield players gives our center-back a jab. Then on a corner kick, another Reichfield player decides to give one of our players another jab. Both players suffer injuries and are carried off the field.

"What now? We're down two strong players?" Shaylee panics.

"Don't worry," I say. "The midget is in action."

"The midget?"

"Just trust me."

She gives me a confused look, but says nothing.

When the referees were arguing, I had remembered about the remaining Rohypnol that I couldn't reach in my locker. I sent the midget to retrieve it. I chose him because he moves fast and could get past people undetected. Hopefully he found a chair and could reach to the back. It was hard even for me. If this works, we could actually get out of this possibly alive. I see the midget crawling back along the North Prep seating area of the bleachers. I smile. Shaylee looks around, extremely worried.

"We have to put our players in defense now," she says.

The midget walks up to me. I lean down.

He whispers, "It's done."

"You put it in the black and red one?"

He nods.

I watch as Thomas takes a big sip from his black and red bottle.

The game restarts but our defense has been hit badly. We watch as Thomas scores a goal a few minutes into injury time. The referee blows for half time. We are now trailing by a goal, exactly what Thomas wants.

On the sidelines, I come up with another idea. "Obviously everything is working against us. We have one referee who hates us and our best defenders are out." I look down, deep in thought.

What to do. Think, Addie. Think.

Then it hits me. I look up. "Let's go on an all-out offensive."

Shaylee nods. She turns to the team. "Listen up, we're going on the offense."

I continue, "We'll leave only the goalkeeper to guard the net. In that way, we'll overwhelm their defense."

We return to the field and implement our new strategy. Yes, it's working. Reichfield is overwhelmed by the continuous wave of attack. They are dropping like flies around us. The pressure is too much for them. Now's my chance. I fire from outside the 18-yard box, straight into the net. *Victory.* The game is now tied 2-2. Thomas sneers at me.

Only ten minutes to the end of the game and we are still tied. We manage to contain most of Reichfield's dirty tricks. Then another one of Reichfield pushes one of our midfielders to the ground. Looks like he's twisted his ankle. Paramedics attend to him but we're down another player.

I see Thomas on the side. He's been drinking from his water bottle and the Rohypnol hasn't kicked in. What gives? Then I see Karl stumble onto the field and collapse. *Scheisse.* Karl must have bought a similar black and red bottle without me noticing. Either that or the midget is color blind. Well, at least we've knocked out one of Reichfield's stronger players making us somewhat even. They, after all, knocked out three of ours.

Shaylee pulls me aside. "What we're doing is working but, not for long. We need to change tactics." Shaylee has read my mind. She summons the players to the side.

I clear my throat and speak loudly so everyone can hear. "We're playing well but it would be a mistake to be too confident. We might have scored a goal or two but it doesn't matter unless we win. And that is why we have to change things up. We need to adapt, like in chess."

Shaylee adds, "We need to think five moves ahead of Reichfield, if we want to win."

I look around, suddenly paranoid. Perhaps Thomas has ears on us. I motion for the men to come in closer. I whisper to them our strategy.

We get to the field and take the free kick. I get the ball and pass it to the winger. Heinrich intercepts the pass. The North Prep midget makes the ball disappear by shifting focus like a magician. Simultaneously, another one of our players trips drawing attention elsewhere. We now have control of the ball. Then, Shaylee and I do a one-two pass, sending the defense of Reichfield in disarray.

I kick the ball toward the net. Then, I feel a pull on my jersey collar, sending me backward. Thomas. No. He's not going to do this. I lift my hands in the air and lower my body and shoot it backward, nearly losing balance. My jersey flies upward. For a moment, my shirt obstructs my vision but then I hear a rip as it tears on my helmet. I propel myself forward, kicking the ball. Thomas falls backward, holding on to the remnants of my ripped jersey. I'm free. In my t-shirt, I race toward the net with the ball. I'm now one on one with Werner. I look him straight in the eye, daring him. I kick the ball with my eyes closed and I hear a cheer. I'm not sure if it's from North Prep or Reichfield. I open my eyes, slowly. I look toward the net and then toward our team. North Prep celebrates. Shaylee smiles at me and my heart lifts.

The Reichfield players slouch on the sidelines, looking defeated and demoralized. Thomas swears loudly and kicks the ground. I celebrate our victory with the rest of the team. Suddenly, I look over and see Thomas talking to the referee. I don't like this. The referee and Thomas rush up to Pauline in the booth. Most of the crowd focuses on the North Prep players who sing their celebratory cheer but I don't take my eyes off Thomas.

"You," I say to our referee. "Follow them."

"But I'm not a real referee," the mascot dressed as a referee, protests.

"Just disagree with whatever they say," I add, reassuring him.

He follows them up into the booth. I look up. There seems to be arguing amongst the referees. Then there's a loud bang. Blood spatters on the glass windows of the booth. The former rat mascot slides down the glass. Thomas holds a gun over him, looking out the window. The microphone screeches with feedback, piercing our ears.

Pauline's voice sounds shaky. "For a one time occurrence, Reichfield will be given three free kicks to reward them for their bravery against uncivilized hooligans."

"What?" Shaylee yells, looking up.

"This isn't fair," I yell. "We agreed."

Thomas takes the field and kicks the ball into the net once, twice and three times. The score changes on the board to Reichfield leading by two goals. Shaylee looks at me in horror.

"How can they do this?" Shaylee panics.

"Don't worry," I say.

"Don't worry?" she says to me. "Don't worry? This was your idea. We trusted a Nazi. Why did we trust a Nazi?"

The Reichfield spectators in the glass area cheer. I look up at Helene who has aim on both of us. We could run in opposite directions to escape. No. What am I thinking? We can't. It's a machine gun. There's no outrunning a machine gun, let alone a sniper machine gun.

Thomas walks toward me with his gun, holding it out to me. The crowd's eyes must be on the celebrating Reichfield players. Thomas knows he can get away with this. He smiles with a triumphant smile.

Shaylee looks around, panicking. There's nowhere to run. We're far from the bleachers. I doubt we'd make it there, even if we tried. Thomas is now a few feet from us. I look him in the eye. He has a pompous smile on his face as if he won the game by his own might.

He holds out the gun. "If you shoot me, Helene will shower both of you with bullets." He looks me in the eye. "Likely you first. You're best to comply."

My head spins. I look around. I hear cheering. If I take the gun and shoot Thomas, Helene will shoot both of us. If I don't take the gun,

Thomas will shoot Shaylee. If I shoot Shaylee and thank Thomas, then I might have a chance of convincing him to drop this. I feel sick. I take the gun.

Suddenly, there's a high-pitched scream. Helene falls off the edge of the building. She lands in a contorted position, like a squashed bug. We look up at Kero Reyes who looks down at us from his wheelchair. Hector gives me the thumbs up.

Shaylee looks towards Hector and then to the remaining audience members on the bleachers. "Take them to safety," she yells.

Hector yells at the North Prep players and the North Prep audience, "Go, go, go." He runs off with them. They flee from the field.

Reichfield. Ah Reichfield. Reichfield spectators try to open their VIP unbreakable glass room, only they can't. Hector took care of locking them in. Then, gas comes out of the hole that Hector punctured in the air conditioner. He did this inconspicuously as I had instructed. I had told him to do it at a the perfect time, when they stood up and cheered. I knew that vat that I asked Karl and Karl's twin to hide would come in handy.

Thomas glares at us. I jump on him, knocking him to the ground. I roll around with Thomas on the grass. The gun lays beside us. I can't reach it. He punches me repeatedly in the stomach. I'm lucky I'm still wearing my helmet or he would have punched me in the face.

Suddenly, there's a loud explosion. Body parts rain onto the field. I had instructed Hector to plant the bomb that Werner had custom made for me as well. Smoke now rises out of the spot where the Reichfield team had been standing. At the same time, in the glass VIP area, the Reichfield spectators grab their necks and fall, choking and gasping for air.

"No," Thomas yells. "No."

I use the distraction to roll on top of him and punch him repeatedly in the face, but Thomas is too strong. He flings me back around and sits on top of me. I look up and see an injured Karl with a bloodied face, limping out of the wreckage.

"Draugar," I yell, pointing at Karl.

This distracts Thomas. He looks up at Karl, his eyes wide with fear. I get the upper hand once more. I punch him and punch him, but he flings me around once more. He's on top once again. His punches are strong. He reaches for the gun and points it at me with his finger on the trigger, but I knock it away. The gun fires. I hear a giant yelp. Karl's been hit. He's down.

I use this distraction to hit Thomas with an elbow. He hunches forward. With the other hand, I twist his wrist back with a sudden jerk and get ahold of the gun. I grab the gun and smack him on the head with it. He falls back.

I take off my helmet.

"Addie?" I hear over the speaker.

I look up at Pauline in the booth. She looks upset.

"Addie?" I hear confusion in her voice.

"Addie," she yells with panic. On the screen I can see her looking at me with a pained expression. I look away and then I hear another scream as Pauline jumps out of the window of the booth and plummets onto the field.

Ava rushes to Thomas who is on the ground, barely moving.

Shaylee comes to my side and pulls me up. I hand her the gun.

"You did this." Ava looks up at me. "Why didn't you love me? Why? Why?" Her expression turns to rage. She turns to Shaylee. "Her." she says as she glares at her.

Before Shaylee can react, Ava rushes at her and tackles her. The gun lies next to them. Ava reaches for it and picks it up. They struggle.

"Bitch," Shaylee yells. The gun goes off. It's Thomas. He had just stood up and now he's been shot in the foot. There's a hole in his shoe and it looks like his big toe has been blown right off.

He lets out a giant, "Fuck." What a non-German thing to do, to swear so lowly-like, even in such an occurrence.

Shaylee rolls around with Ava some more. Shaylee tries to take the gun from Ava and loosen her grip. Ava struggles to point the gun at Shaylee but then Shaylee twists Ava's hand. The gun goes off again.

It's Ava, she's been shot. She rolls over on her back with her hand to her wound.

"No," Thomas screams. He limps to Ava and kneels down. He puts his hand underneath her neck. "No. Ava, don't. It will be okay."

He tries to kiss her. Blood spurts out of her mouth on to him.

"Ava," he sobs.

She lets out her last breath. Her eyes go glassy. She stares up at the sky. Thomas screams, "No."

He stands up and stomps towards me, his face contorted with rage and pain and hatred. He pushes me. I fall on the grass. He brings his hand up to hit me.

"Don't," Shaylee says with the gun pointed at him. "What you're going to do is leave town and never bother us again."

Thomas lets out a little laugh.

"Shaylee, he'll never give up," I say to her.

"Well, friend, you know me too well," Thomas says.

Shaylee holds the gun on him. She pulls the trigger. It's out of bullets. She pulls it again.

"Ha." Thomas smiles.

I rush to Thomas and I tackle him. We roll around on the ground. I dig my fingers into his open wound. He lets out a scream but doesn't let up. Thomas punches me. He manages to get his hands around my neck and squeeze. Shaylee tries to pull him off. I twist and twist but his steroid-built hands are too strong. I feel myself losing consciousness. Then, a bullet pierces Thomas's shoulder. He puts his hand over his wound. He looks up.

"Dad?" Thomas looks at his father who stands there with Helene's gun. "Dad, why?"

Thomas's dad walks toward his son. He looks down at Thomas. "Thomas, why on earth are you wearing Addie's jersey?"

"Dad. He—"

"Thomas. Only Addie can be Addie."

Thomas puts his hand to his wound and looks at his blood. "You shot me?"

"You were trying to hurt Addie and I can't let that happen. Don't worry, it will heal."

Thomas's dad looks down. "What happened to your toe?"

Thomas looks at Shaylee. "That whore shot me."

"She's not a whore," I yell.

Thomas's dad glances around. "Where is it?"

"Where's what?" Thomas looks up at his father, confused.

"Your toe?"

"I don't know. Gone. Completely blown off. That monster."

"This is serious, Thomas."

"I know, Dad. Shoot her. Get it over with."

Thomas's dad glances around the field, probably for Thomas's toe. "You don't understand son. I'd take you to a hospital but there's nothing to attach. Even with modern prosthetics, you'll, you'll never be able to play soccer again. You'll be … gosh, how do I say this … a cripple."

Tears stream down Thomas's face. "Shoot her already. What are you waiting for?"

Thomas's dad turns towards Shaylee. I get up and run in front of her. I expect him to push past me. Instead he swings the gun around and points it at Thomas.

"This is hard for me, but I'm sorry, son. You know what we must do to cripples."

"Dad, No!" Thomas yells.

Thomas's dad fires the gun. A bullet shatters right through Thomas's temple splattering his brains all over the green field. Thomas collapses.

Shaylee and I look at Thomas's dad, in shock.

"Hello, son," he says looking at me. He's smiling, but his eyes are blocks of ice.

CHAPTER 39

We sit in Thomas's dad's jeep, tied up again. Only this time, I ride shotgun. With one hand, Thomas's dad points a handgun at me and with the other he steers. Helene's gun sits in front of me, on the dashboard. It's inches from me but I can't reach it as my hands are handcuffed behind my back with pink leopard print handcuffs. In addition, the seatbelt restrains me. Thomas's dad fiddles with the music. He puts on some classical.

"I really did want to spend more time with you as a kid," he says. "Maybe if I did, you wouldn't have turned out this way."

I fidget in my handcuffs. In the back, Shaylee's tied up with barbed wire. She's blindfolded. My blindfold has slipped off. I'm amazed that he just happened to have handcuffs and a blindfold in his car. I look around and there's other stuff too; a leather suit, some sort of cage, a black mask, chains and what looks like a mini whip.

"The father who raised you was hard on you, wasn't he? He was supposed to be, but then he had a change of heart. Due to that, we had to terminate him much earlier than Hitler's father. Sorry for that. Maybe if he had been more stern with you as I had instructed, you would have turned out differently, but alas."

He fiddles with the music again. "You'll like this, Addie. Flight of the Valkyries."

"Actually, I prefer hip hop," I say with a cocky smile.

He flinches. For some reason I expected him to be shocked and lose control of the wheel and then I'd be able to ... well, I don't know what I would have done with my hands tied. Maybe head butt him and then go flying through the windshield? But then again, anything's better than this.

"Can you at least put on something else?" I kick the glove compartment.

"I see. We'll just have to fix you now, won't we? There's a scientist in Germany. An old friend. He left the fold long ago but I'm sure he can be convinced with enough incentive to return. He's a pioneer of the latest research in neuroplasticity. If anything, he'll be able to rewire those little neurons of yours." He puts his finger close to my head. I move away.

"Otto was very useful to me before our fall out."

A flash. I remember a doctor's face.

"Otto, listen to me," Thomas's dad pleads in my vision. I recognize the ceiling of the house, with it's familiar off-white ceiling tiles that I occasionally glance up at when contemplating an artistic idea to paint. I must be on some sort of stretcher. The boy who looks like me lays on the couch. For a second, I think he's asleep, but it's then that I notice the bullet hole in his head. He's dead.

"What you did is wrong and you know it," a man in a white lab coat yells. "You didn't have to kill him."

"Well it's not like we don't have more, don't we Otto?" Thomas's dad pokes the doctor. They both look toward me.

"He was backup. Only to be awoken if something went wrong—"

"Which it did," Thomas's dad adds.

"You call not being able to control your desires, something going wrong?"

"I don't know what you're referring to," Thomas's dad stammers. "He fell from the couch. He had an accident. Hit his head too hard. I had to shoot him because he wouldn't be the same."

"Liar," Otto yells.

Thomas's dad pushes Otto with his finger. "Need I remind you that I pay your salary. I'm the one who supports your lavish lifestyle."

"Fick dich ins Knie." Otto storms out, slamming the door.

Thomas's dad glances at me in the passenger seat. "We had a bit of a falling out." He speeds up. I'm pretty sure we're going double the speed limit by now.

"The sooner we fix you, the sooner you'll be your old self," he says with a cheerful smile.

"I'm not him." I kick the glove compartment. "I'm not." I kick it again.

Then an idea occurs to me. I recognize a sign to the left. I know this area. Better to be in an area I know. I swing my legs up onto the dashboard and kick Thomas's dad in the face. The car spirals out of control and crashes into a ditch. I fidget in my restraints.

Thomas dad tries to drive in reverse. The car won't back up. "You didn't have to do that," Thomas's dad yells. Small shards of glass stick out of his head. "Oh well, change of plans." He grabs my collar.

He pulls me out, leading me up to the road. Then he kicks me in the back. I fall to my knees on the dirt road. He opens the back door and pulls Shaylee out. The side of her head is bleeding from the crash. He holds her by the shirt and with his other hand, he holds the gun.

I kick at his leg. He bends over.

I look into Shaylee's eyes. "Run," I yell.

She takes off down the road. I hear a shot. She falls.

"Shaylee." I rush to her, falling beside her. I fidget in the handcuffs, trying to break free.

"Don't worry Addie. I didn't kill her," Thomas's dad says as limps toward us across the dirt road. He puts his hand on my shoulder. "No, I'm leaving that for you. I'm giving you the opportunity to prove we can move forward in our relationship."

Blood comes out of the gunshot wound in Shaylee's leg. I want to cover it but my hands are tied.

CHAPTER 40

We stand on the cliff overlooking Lower Reichfield, five feet or so from the edge. Thomas's dad holds the gun to Shaylee's head. Shaylee can barely stand on her feet. Thomas's dad knows I won't do anything as long as he has the gun on her.

"So Addie, perhaps it's good we're here. Monumental, even. Things do happen for a reason. You know this was where it all started? We were originally supposed to live there, nestled in the valley." He points to Lower Reichfield. "But then I decided it would be best to be able to see the sunrise first. Therefore, the lowlies would inhabit the lower region as fitting."

"Shaylee, Addie tells me you're good at math."

Shaylee glares at me, thinking I betrayed her.

I shake my head. "Thomas. It was Thomas."

"Yes, Thomas. Thomas told us you had things under control but perhaps ... you still needed a little more guidance, to know what's right."

"You just couldn't handle that they were beating us at soccer."

"Watch your mouth Addie. I instructed Thomas to let them win until you had the strength to rise up and take command."

"I took command."

"Yes you did. Of the wrong team. We really should have had full eyes on you but it was our belief that giving you independence would make you a man. You let us down, Addie. You let Reichfield down." Thomas's dad looks out at the destroyed neighborhoods. "Beautiful isn't it?" Thomas dad smiles. "Well Shaylee, if you're so good at math, what do you think the odds are of surviving a gunshot to the head vs. the odds of surviving a fall off a cliff?"

Shaylee is silent, her eyes cold and aloof. I can sense her anger but she shows no fear.

Thomas's dad looks at her. "No comment?" He looks toward me. "Addie, push her."

"You'll have to take these off for that," I say, motioning to my handcuffs.

"Nice try, Addie. You can use your legs, as you used on me, or body even."

"No," I say.

"Push her off or I shoot her and she dies anyway."

"I'll push her if you untie her."

He lets out a laugh.

"There are greater odds of her surviving if you do," I add.

"Fine." Thomas's dad flips Shaylee around. Her back is to him. He unties the wire with one hand, while holding the gun to the back of her head with his other. He keeps his eyes on me the whole time.

"You're not really good with math, are you? Don't worry, Hitler wasn't either but it was only because of a bad teacher. If he had had a great teacher, he would have been great."

"I'm not Hitler."

"Addie, with math, the chances of her surviving this fall even with her hands untied are near zero. She'll hit rock after rock after rock. If she's lucky she'll break her neck first."

I flinch.

"It's okay," he adds. "We can't all be geniuses in everything."

He drops the wire on the ground. Shaylee's hands are now free. There are red marks where the wire dug into her wrist. Thomas's dad senses she's going to try something. He pushes his pistol into the back of her head. "Don't."

He looks at me. "Addie, I did as you asked. Now, push her."

What am I going to do? I can't lunge at him. He has the gun too close to her head. If I push her, she will probably not live either. *Probably.*

I gulp, my mouth dry.

Okay.

There's only one solution.

I run to the edge.

"No," Thomas's dad yells.

I jump. At the same time, Shaylee pushes all her body weight into him like a football player. She lets out a grunt. There's a scream as he flies to the edge and tumbles off the cliff, after me.

"Addie," she yells.

CHAPTER 41

Something's creaking. And my hands. I can't feel them. My arms I can't feel them either. Nor can I feel my body. Then, I hear, "Addie." Someone is yelling my name. Who is yelling me name? And then I remember. Shaylee. Shaylee? I look around. It's like I'm in a plane. I have an aerial view of Lower Reichfield. The sun is coming out from beyond the clouds. I'm dead.

"Addie," I hear and sobbing. "Addie!"

She's crying for me. I feel some satisfaction, as Shaylee's crying. For me. I smile. And then I feel it. The pain intensifies at ninety-nine miles an hour. Dead people don't feel pain. Wait, I'm not dead? What just happened? Where am I? Where's my body? Where am I in space? I'm in some sort of limbo. I look down. I'm on a motorcycle. I've lost my mind. I've gone completely mad.

Then I hear the creaking again. I feel something tilting, my body tilting. Wait. The motorcycle. The sign. The motorcycle coming out of the sign that reads "Lower Reichfield." *Shit.*

The motorcycle tilts downward. My body is thrust forward. My hands. Move. Move, I tell them. Not that they'd do much, they're behind my back, in handcuffs. Right. My body is in shock, it's not responding. I feel an intense pain in my groin. Everything feels heavy. Dead weight. I concentrate. Then I remember, my legs. I squeeze with my legs.

And then, one last creak. Oh no. The cheap glue or dollar store chains that had affixed the motorcycle to the cliff give way. It breaks free from the cliff.

"Scheisse," I yell.

I'm falling, falling again. And then I land. I land on something. Dirt. Right. The cliff isn't a steep drop all the way, only at the top. Dust blows all around me.

Ha. I laugh, the wind blowing through my hair and dust, lots of dust. And then the motorcycle hits a rock, and I go flying. Thud. I land in the dirt. I cough. The adrenaline must have kicked in for the pain that I felt all over has dissipated. I look back up a the "Lower Reichfield," sign.

Shit.

EPILOGUE

I guess you could say, I'm finally free, but at the same time one can never be too cautious. Nonetheless, if I hadn't been, "stubborn as fuck," as Shaylee would say, I never would have gotten out of that shit town.

Anne and Mother fled when they heard what happened. Using a burner phone, I learned this from Hans who never took a day off work. Mother must have had connections on the outside that helped her get out. We got out a whole other way and even helped Lower Reichfield citizens to escape as well. The thing about working in the customs office is that you have access to mail trucks. You can also see where drivers leave their keys when on a break.

On the journey to America, Hector had one of his doctors repair my groin. My extremities had been damaged from landing groin first on that scheisse motorcycle. This doctor looked like no doctor I had ever seen. Doctor Death Row as I called him, had numeros face tattoos. With the dirty equipment Doctor Death Row pulled out of his knapsack, thought I'd have everything cut off later due to tetanus. What a relief that didn't happen. Although, I'll never have kids, everything works down there and looks even better than before. Although I had been very well endowed, I now have another few inches added which will of course make me even more popular with the ladies. It's also a relief that although I can't have kids, everything still functions. As if that's a loss, can clones even have kids?

When we arrived in California and I breathed in the true air of American soil, I headed east as I wanted to get as far away from Reichfield as possible. I also feared that Mom or Anne or someone from Reichfield who had survived the massacre would find me. I travelled endlessly, never staying in one place for too long. Shaylee stayed in Cali and became some big hotshot soccer star. We've actually kept in touch. Something about facing near death makes for strong bonds. We're like comrades.

When I finally returned to visit her, she introduced me to Pyper, a kinetic artist. We clicked so much that I even ended up relocating. Finally, I stopped moving and I settled into the life of being in one place. The fear that someone from Reichfield would find me, subsided. I was relieved to be in a place that never heard of Reichfield and didn't know me, as was the case for all the places I visited. However, I would soon discover that I wasn't as unknown here as I thought.

Outside of the Modern Art Museum of Innovation hangs a sign that reads, "Forgeries and Fakes." I stand in front of a painting, a painting I know by heart, as I gave it my heart.

A woman with shoulder length brown hair and glasses looks up at my artwork. "Exquisite, isn't it?" The woman sports a fitted floral blazer and denim jeans and gives off a sophisticated air. I'm pleased she likes my work so much. She steps closer to examine the brushwork.

"Yes, it is," I reply.

"I'd even go as far to say, it's even better than Franz Marc. Whoever made this forgery should be an artist in his own right."

"You think?" I say.

"Of course."

"Uh you see. You see ... I ... it was me," I add, somewhat awkwardly.

"Excuse me?" she says with an eyebrow raised. I can see from her expression that she doesn't believe me.

"I can prove it to you," I say. I fumble through my bag. "Where is it?" *Scheisse. Did I leave it at home?*

Doubt flashes across her face. She shakes her head. She doesn't believe me. She turns around.

"Wait." I sigh. I found it. I pull out my phone.

I rush in front of her, holding out a picture that Shaylee had sent to me. In it, I'm applying the finishing touches on this very painting.

She grabs my phone. She holds it and looks closer. There's a moment of silence. It reminds me of Helene before she trashes me.

"Remarkable." She finally beams. I sigh. Then she looks up. "You know, you could get in trouble for this."

I freeze.

"However ..." She hands me back my phone. "It can stay between us, that is, if you paint more."

"Paint more?" I say, suddenly confused. Is she hiring me like Hector?

She reads my mind. "No. Not fakes, of course. I'm the museum curator and I can commission you to paint something original for us."

"Are you serious?" I'm in shock. I always thought this moment could happen. However, for some reason everything feels surreal.

"Listen, I'm late for a meeting." She backs away. "Be here Monday morning. Tell the receptionist you have an appointment with Director Gallagher." With that, she struts toward the exit.

I start to smile, giddiness bubbling in my chest. I can't believe this. Is this really happening? Am I not only a clone but am I also in some alternate universe?

"Oh." She turns around. "I didn't even get your name."

"Ad-die," I stutter. "Addie."

"Addie what?"

I think to myself. "Just Addie," I say, "I've left my past behind."

"Alright, 'Just Addie'. You have a bright future ahead of you." She smiles. I watch her exit into a corridor filled with sunlight. The sunlight shines brighter and illuminates the area that I'm standing in. I hold my hand up to the sunlight, its warmth embracing my skin. These hands painted that painting in front of me. These cloned hands painted something original. Suddenly, I feel at peace with the world. At peace with myself because I know even though I was formed in a lab, my creators did not create me.

CPSIA information can be obtained
at www.ICGtesting.com
Printed in the USA
BVHW03*2247121018
530059BV00003B/6/P